HORROR EXPRESS VOLUME ONE

Edited by Marc Shemmans

HORROR EXPRESS PUBLICATIONS

Printed in the United Kingdom

Thank you for shopping at Amazon.co.uk!

081314 A2

Invoice for
Your order of 18 September, 2012
Order ID 202-5577221-7899507
Invoice number D8rqJP04N
Invoice date 3 October, 2012

Billing Address
Mrs A C Bretney
34, Western Avenue
Woodley
Reading, Berkshire RG5 3BH
United Kingdom

Shipping Address
Mrs A C Bretney
34, Western Avenue
Woodley
Reading, Berkshire RG5 3BH
United Kingdom

Qty.	Item	Our Price (excl. VAT)	VAT Rate	Total Price
1	**Horror Express Volume One: 1** Paperback. Hutson, Shaun. 147013019X (** P-1-E88B22 **)	£6.50	0%	£6.50
	Shipping charges	£0.00		£0.00
	Subtotal (excl. VAT) 0%			£6.50
	Total VAT			£0.00
	Total			£6.50

Conversion rate - £1.00 : EUR 1,26

This shipment completes your order.

You can always check the status of your orders or change your account details from the "Your Account" link at the top of each page on our site.

Thinking of returning an item? PLEASE USE OUR ON-LINE RETURNS SUPPORT CENTRE.

Our Returns Support Centre (www.amazon.co.uk/returns-support) will guide you through our Returns Policy and provide you with a printable personalised return label. Please have your order number ready (you can find it next to your order summary, above). Our Returns Policy does not affect your statutory rights.

Amazon EU S.a.r.L, 5 Rue Plaetis, L-2338, Luxembourg
VAT number : GB727255821

Please note - this is not a returns address - for returns - please see above for details of our online returns centre

0/D5rVJq04N/-1 of 1-//RMSD13/exp-uk-timed/9081314/1004-18:00/1004-08:35 Pack Type : A2

Horror Express Publications
PO BOX 11600
Birmingham
B30 2QW
United Kingdom

10 9 8 7 6 5 4 3 2 1

First Edition

ISBN-13: 978-1470130190
ISBN-10: 147013019X

CONTENTS

Shaun Hutson

VOICES

The hospital corridor seemed to stretch away into forever as Kate Openshaw and her dad walked slowly along it, their footsteps echoing around them. They had made this walk more times than Kate cared to remember in the three *months* since her mum had been taken mysteriously ill.

Outside, the rain was pelting against the large windows that overlooked the hospital grounds. Kate shivered.

'Dad,' she said, unable to bear the silence any longer. 'How many more tests will they have to do on Mum?'

'I don't know, Kate,' her dad replied quietly. 'They'll just keep on until they find out what's wrong.'

'But they've been doing tests for months now,' Kate protested. 'And they still haven't found anything. Not even when they did that big operation on her throat last week.'

'I know.' Kate's dad slipped a comforting arm around her shoulder. 'But we've got to trust the doctors. They're doing their best.'

There was a large set of double doors ahead. Kate pushed them hard in frustration. They swung back on their hinges and she and her dad passed through into the next stretch of corridor. To Kate, it felt as if the pale walls were somehow closing in, growing more and more narrow. 'I hate this place,' she said as they continued their endless trek.

'No one likes hospitals, Kate,' her dad said gently. 'But you know we've got no choice about coming here. Maybe when the doctors have finished the latest set of tests they'll have a better idea of what to do.'

Kate wasn't sure whether he was trying to reassure her or himself. Probably a bit of both.

The rain was falling even more heavily, whipped by an increasingly strong wind that caused some of the bushes close to the windows to slap their leaves and branches loudly against the glass.

Another set of doors loomed ahead, WARD 6 displayed above them. Kate swallowed hard. Her mum's ward.

She followed her dad through the doors. A few nurses and patients waved to them. Kate waved back. Everyone on the ward was so friendly, and had been ever since her mum had first arrived there.

Kate knew she shouldn't be afraid of coming here but she couldn't help herself. She glanced at some curtains that were drawn around one of the beds to her right and wondered what was going on behind them. Then she decided she would rather not know.

'You OK?' her dad asked, as they approached the two beds at the end of the ward.

Kate nodded.

One of the beds was empty.

The other one was occupied by Kate's mum.

There were two doctors and a nurse standing around the bed. Kate saw that they were all looking very serious.

The older doctor, who Kate knew was called Dr Venner and was in charge of looking after her mum, looked up. Seeing Kate and her dad, he walked over to meet them.

'Has there been a change in my wife's condition, doctor?' Kate's dad asked anxiously.

'I'm very sorry to say that your wife's condition has worsened, Mr Openshaw,' Dr Venner replied quietly.

Kate felt a shiver run through her when she heard the words.

'In all my years as a doctor I've never seen a case like Mrs Openshaw's before,' Dr Venner went on. 'We've tried everything.' He put a sympathetic hand on Kate's shoulder. 'We'll keep trying, but I can't promise anything, I'm afraid,' he said gently.

Kate felt tears welling up in her eyes.

'We'll leave you alone to have some time with her,' Dr Venner finished. He beckoned to the other doctor and the nurse, and the three of them walked slowly away, heads bowed, deep in discussion.

Kate waved at her mum and smiled as bravely as she could. Then she walked over, leaned forward and kissed her cheek. 'How are you feeling, Mum?' she asked, looking at the thick dressing that still covered her mum's throat.

Kate saw her mum's lips move and leaned in closely, as she'd been forced to do since the illness had reduced her mum's voice to a whisper.

'I'm fine, darling,' her mum croaked.

But Kate could see that wasn't true. It wasn't true at all.

Kate's dad sat down at the other side of the bed looking anxious.

Her mum reached up and squeezed his hand before turning her attention back to Kate. 'How are you, darling?' she asked. 'How's school? What have you been doing today?' She gasped, as if the effort of speaking was now even more painful.

'Just the usual stuff, Mum,' Kate replied, holding her mum's hand tightly.

Just then, another doctor came over. Kate could see the man's name badge on his long white coat. Dr Gregory Solomon.

Dr Solomon gazed over the chart hanging at the bottom of the bed, occasionally making a mark with the pen he'd taken from his pocket. Looking even more serious, he asked Kate's dad to go and chat with him in his office.

Kate watched as her dad disappeared through a door halfway down the ward. Then she felt her mum's hand take her own to get her attention. She leaned in closer so that her mum could whisper in her ear.

'Darling, will you do something for me?' her mum said, again having to force the words out in a gasp.

'Of course, Mum,' Kate replied. 'Anything!'

Her mum smiled. It was a sad smile. She lifted her head from the pillow to give Kate a kiss, her lips catching Kate's ear. Then she gave a long sigh. 'It would have been Gran's birthday tomorrow,' she said. 'Could you get some flowers and put them on her grave for me?'

'Sure, Mum.'

'Take the money from my purse in the locker by my bed,' her mum said. 'Get a bouquet of irises if you can. Your gran loved those.'

'OK, Mum,' Kate agreed. 'I can get them from the florist's in the hospital on our way home and take them to the graveyard on my way to school in the morning.'

'Good idea,' her mum gasped. 'I'd rather you did that than go to the graveyard after school. The evenings draw in pretty quick now and I don't want you wandering about in the dark on your own.'

As she moved back slightly, Kate saw that her mum's eyes held an urgent expression. 'Don't worry, Mum, I usually walk home with Susie,' Kate reassured her.

Then she looked up to see her dad returning from Dr Solomon's office. He looked pale and defeated.

'I love you, Mum,' Kate said, fighting back the tears.

'I love you too,' her mum said, squeezing her hand. 'That's why I'm determined to get better. I don't want to leave you and your dad.'

'Come on, Kate,' her dad said. 'We'd better go, let Mum get some rest.'

Kate kissed her mum and walked back down the ward. She turned and waved, and her mum smiled weakly back.

As she'd promised, Kate visited the hospital florist near the main entrance of the hospital and bought a bunch of irises, and then she and her dad hurried through the rain to the car.

Kate glanced over her shoulder at the hospital as they drove away, the rain still hammering against the windscreen.

Somewhere in the distance there was a low rumble of thunder.

By the following morning, the rain had stopped. Despite a sharp chill in the air, the sun shone brightly, reflecting on the puddles that Kate skirted as she walked along the road that led to the church. The air smelled beautifully fresh and crisp. Early morning dew sparkled on spider webs like diamonds on thin silver chains.

The streets were still relatively quiet; Kate had left earlier than usual, so that she could visit Gran's grave before school. She looked down at the bouquet of irises she'd bought the night before.

Ahead of her, the church spire thrust upwards towards the clear blue morning sky. Her footsteps crunched on the gravel path as she made her way through the churchyard entrance and along one of the pathways to the area of the graveyard where her gran was buried.

Many of the gravestones near the church were extremely old and Kate slowed down to glance at the wording on them. Some of them were hard to read, the letters worn away by the passage of time. A couple of the oldest-looking stones were so blackened by mildew and mould, they looked like rotting teeth sticking up from the ground.

Kate moved closer to wipe some of the mould away, so that she could read the lettering. As she did so, a fat black slug slid into view on top of the gravestone. Kate wrinkled her nose and quickly drew her hand away. She watched the slug glide slowly down the stonework on its sparkling silver slime trail until it disappeared into the wet grass at the base of the stone.

'You won't find any names on those two headstones.'

The voice startled her and she spun round quickly, standing up.

It was the vicar – Reverend Dodds, who had performed Gran's funeral a few months ago. His priest's collar stood out with brilliant whiteness against the blackness of his robes.

'Sorry if I startled you,' he said, gently.

'It's OK,' Kate replied.

The vicar narrowed his eyes slightly then smiled at her. 'It's Kate Openshaw, isn't it?' he said. 'We met at your gran's funeral.'

Kate smiled and nodded. 'That's why I'm here,' she told him. 'It would have been Gran's birthday today. My mum asked me to put these on her grave.' Kate held up the bouquet of irises.

'What a lovely thought,' said Reverend Dodds. 'I won't keep you, then.'

Kate was about to continue on her way, but then paused and looked back at the two cracked and mouldy headstones she'd been inspecting before Reverend Dodds appeared. 'You said I wouldn't find any names on these two gravestones,' she said. 'Why not? I know they're very old but ...'

'It wasn't the weather or the time that caused the damage to the stones. It was other people,' replied Reverend Dodds.

Kate looked up at him, puzzled.

Reverend Dodds grinned. 'You'll have to forgive me, Kate, but I can be quite a bore on this subject. I've been studying the history of this church since I arrived here a few years ago. Those two graves are over three hundred years old. They belong to a mother and daughter who were believed by some parishioners to be witches. The vicar of the time dismissed these claims and allowed the women to be buried here on church ground. But the parishioners who disagreed with him scratched the women's names from their headstones.'

Kate shivered. 'Those poor women. I'm on the vicar's side. I don't believe in witches.'

'Not even the broomstick-riding kind?' Reverend Dodds asked, smiling.

Kate grinned back and shook her head.

'Many of those accused of witchcraft were executed in those days, you know,' Reverend Dodds went on. 'It was often because they seemed able to foresee the future. Those who executed them said they'd been given the power by the Devil, so must be witches.'

'It doesn't seem to be such a bad thing to be able to tell the future,' Kate remarked. 'You'd know about things before they happened. Like which numbers would win the lottery!'

Reverend Dodds smiled. 'Well, in times gone by, that kind of ability would have got you burned at the stake as a witch.' He looked down at the two ancient, weathered gravestones, his tone darkening a little. 'Anyone who lived alone, who wasn't liked by others or who was a little unusual, they were all likely to be accused of being a witch. No one was safe.'

Kate nodded.

'Anyway, I'll leave you to get on with what you were doing,' Reverend Dodds said, and he turned to walk back towards the church.

Kate watched him disappear inside, then walked briskly along the gravel path to her gran's grave.

'Hello, Gran,' she said softly, kneeling beside the headstone. 'Happy birthday.' She wiped some fallen leaves from the base of the marble headstone and laid the bouquet of irises there. 'I brought these for you, from me and Mum. I know they were your favourites.' Somehow, it seemed natural, to be speaking to Gran like this. 'Mum can't come herself as she's still really ill in hospital, Gran,' Kate went on. 'The doctors still can't find what's wrong with her. I hope that you're watching her, keeping her safe. Wherever you are, Gran, I hope you're listening and that you're OK.'

'I'm fine thanks, love.'

Kate spun round, looking for the voice that had whispered into her ear – so close she could have sworn she felt the breath.

The graveyard was still empty apart from herself.

She looked back down at her gran's gravestone and swallowed hard. 'Gran?' she said uncertainly. 'Gran, is that you?'

A slight breeze ruffled the hair around the back of her neck. It felt like the soft touch of a hand.

Kate looked round again, but there was no one to be seen. The skin on her arms rose into goose bumps. The cellophane that the bouquet of irises was wrapped in crackled in the wind.

She rose to her feet and then backed away, almost stumbling on to the path.

'Oh, I wish I'd been able to be there! Describe it to me.'

'Well, as Aunt Augustine requested, everyone was wearing purple and white. And you should have seen the way they'd made those flowers spell out her name. It was beautiful. They'd really done her proud.'

Again Kate looked around. No one could be seen. Where were these voices coming from? Her heart was thudding against her ribs now.

Kate hurriedly made her way towards the church gate. As she passed the church, the voices seemed to grow louder.

'It was absolutely beautiful. It really was the most beautiful funeral I've ever been to. Just what Aunt Augustine would have wanted ...'

Kate sighed to herself in relief. A funeral service must have started inside. The church was old. Its ceiling was high. The sound of voices in there would carry.

Kate nodded to herself. That must be it. Mystery solved.

She headed on towards the gate.

'I'm sure Aunt Augustine would have been watching. She'd have been looking down on it all and smiling.'

'Especially when she heard her favourite hymn being played at the end. She always loved 'The Old Rugged Cross' ...'

The voices were growing fainter again.

Kate left the churchyard and hurried on down the road towards school, a cold breeze whipping her hair around her face.

That day at school passed the same as every other: a few laughs with Susie and her other friends, a couple of arguments with some of the boys in her class. Talk of what they'd watched on TV the night before. What they were going to do at the weekend.

The only downside had been Daisy Barton, as usual – who had told Susie she had a spare WestZone CD that Susie could buy for half-price. WestZone was everyone's favourite band at the moment, and this was the only WestZone CD that Susie didn't have.

'She never told me it had a dirty great scratch across it,' Susie complained, as the two girls sat at the back of the class. 'I didn't realize until after I'd paid her for it and tried to play it at home last night. And she wouldn't take it back. She's always doing things like that to people.'

'Daisy only cares about herself,' Kate replied. 'And she's probably jealous that you managed to get a ticket for the WestZone concert and she didn't because she was too lazy to get to the box-office and queue for hours like we did.'

Susie smiled. 'You're probably right,' she said, looking more cheerful.

'I've got to nip down the shops on the way home,' Susie told Kate when the final bell went. 'Do you want to come?'

'I'd better get home,' Kate replied. 'I usually get Dad's tea ready before we go and see Mum in hospital.'

'OK, give your mum my love, Kate,' Susie said, and she rushed off in the opposite direction.

Kate stood alone for a moment then set off in the direction of home. It was getting dark already as she passed the church.

'Tell him I want those photos by Friday or I'm not paying.'

Kate slowed her pace, the voice loud in her ear.

'I've told him, but he says there's nothing he can do about it.'

The tone of the argument was growing more heated. Kate found herself wandering closer to the open church door.

'I'm not going to tell you again, I want them Friday, or I'm not paying.'

She poked her head around to see what was going on.

The church was empty.

'Do what you like. I've spoken to him and that's all I can do.'

Confused, Kate couldn't work out where the words were coming from. She took a couple of steps inside the building, glancing at the beautifully coloured stained-glass windows.

'Hello, Kate.'

She spun round, startled – but this time it was a familiar voice.

Reverend Dodds was standing close behind the door, pinning something to the notice-board there. 'Sorry if I made you jump,' he said, cheerfully. 'Can I help you?'

'I heard someone talking,' Kate said, falteringly. 'In here.'

'Not unless you heard me talking to myself,' he smiled. 'And I hope you didn't, they say that's the first sign of madness, don't they?'

Kate nodded, looking around the church again, the other voices still echoing inside her head. She was sure that the argument had come from inside the church. 'Sorry to have disturbed you,' she said. Then she turned and quickly left.

Kate sat beside her mum's bed. She couldn't stop smiling. Her mum was sitting up, looking better than Kate had seen her for months.

Dr Venner glanced at the chart he held and shook his head, a smile playing on his lips. 'I must say, your mum is a constant puzzle to us, Kate,' he began. 'First she comes into the hospital and we can't find out what's wrong with her, and then she suddenly begins to recover and we don't know why. I must say, the improvement is remarkable.'

'Does that mean she can come home?' Kate asked.

'Hopefully,' Dr Venner said. 'But let's just see what happens, shall we? You want your mum back to her old self, don't you? And we certainly don't want her leaving here until she is.'

He replaced the chart, smiled at them all and turned in the direction of another patient further down the ward.

'Happier now?' Kate's dad asked her.

Kate nodded and smiled. 'Do you really feel better, Mum?' she asked.

'Much better,' her mum said quietly, reaching out to squeeze Kate's hand.

'It's weird that they didn't know what was wrong with you and now they don't even know what's made you better, but I don't care – all that matters is that you'll be coming home soon,' Kate beamed. 'I can't wait.'

'Your mum's still got to take it easy,' her dad told her. 'If she became ill without warning then it might happen again.'

'No, it won't,' Kate's mum said softly.

'But if you don't know what put you in here, love,' said Kate's dad, 'how can you be so sure?'

'I just know,' Kate's mum replied. 'Anyway, you two will keep your eyes on me, won't you?'

'I'll do whatever you want, Mum,' Kate said.

'Even your homework?' her mum said with a smile.

Kate nodded and laughed.

'I got better because of you, Kate,' her mum told her, touching her cheek. 'You always cheer me up when you visit me. You and your dad.' She leaned forward and kissed Kate. 'Thank you.'

Kate hugged her mum.

'I'm sorry,' her mum whispered, looking a little upset.

'What for?' Kate asked, surprised.

'For all the trouble I've caused. All the worry ...' her mum replied.

'But everything's going to be fine now, Mum, isn't it?' Kate said.

Her mum smiled but didn't answer.

'What are you thinking about, Kate?' Susie asked at school the following day. 'You've hardly said a word all lunch-time,' she added, pushing another crisp into her mouth. 'Is it your mum?'

Kate shook her head. Staring out across the playground, she bit into her sandwich and chewed thoughtfully. 'I know this is going to sound stupid,' she said, 'but have you ever heard voices?'

'What kind of voices?' Susie asked.

'You know, *voices* – when there doesn't seem to be anyone there.'

Susie looked thoughtful. 'Well, I read in one of my brother's science magazines that alien waves could be picked up by fillings in teeth,' she told Kate.

'Alien waves? What are they?' Kate asked.

'Well, the sounds from flying saucers I suppose, from spaceships. Not sure I believe it myself,' Susie replied, shrugging. 'Seems a bit far-fetched that aliens can contact people by using their fillings. But it's supposed to be something to do with the metal fillings being a conductor or something – like a radio,' she finished. Then her eyes widened. 'Why? Have *you* been hearing voices, then?'

'Yes ... well, I don't know. I'm probably imagining it. But I'm sure it wasn't aliens,' Kate said, smiling. 'These were proper voices. People having conversations.'

'It *could* have been aliens,' Susie insisted. 'I mean, they might look just like us, mightn't they? *You* might be one for all I know.'

Kate grinned. 'If people can pick up alien waves with their fillings,' she said, 'do you think your brother could pick up a radio station on his brace?'

Both of them collapsed with laughter.

As she neared the church on her way home, Kate felt tense, wondering whether she'd hear voices again. Or was she really just imagining all this?

'I'll see you about six, then, after you've dropped the kids off.'

'That's right. Twelve red roses, to be delivered to Ms B. Burkeman. Thank you.'

'Don't forget to pick up some dog food on your way home.'

Kate closed her eyes. It had started again. All different voices – seemingly unrelated.

'What time does the film start? We don't want to be late.'

'Tell her I'll wear that black dress. I don't want to turn up in the same outfit as Kelly.'

The voices were raining in on her like missiles.

Feeling panicked now, Kate opened her eyes again, wanting to run, escape from the noise. And then she saw it. A shiny-looking plaque, attached to the church wall near the entrance.

ROOF OF ST BARTOL'S CHURCH

RESTORED BY NATIONAL TELECOM

She looked up. Perched high on the steeple of the church, like a metallic beacon, was a mobile phone antenna.

'Yes, it's lovely, isn't it, the new roof?'

At first Kate thought it was another of the voices in her head. And then she felt a touch on her arm.

'Are you all right, dear?' came the voice.

Kate turned to see a kind-faced old lady staring at her, looking concerned. Kate nodded dumbly, unable to explain what was happening to her.

The old lady smiled and pointed to the roof. 'They paid for it,' she went on. 'They did it in exchange for Reverend Dodds allowing them to put the mobile phone mast-thingy up there, you see.' She studied Kate's features for a moment and shook her head. 'Are you sure you're all right, dear? You look awfully pale.'

Kate nodded again, and then hurried away, her mind reeling. As she did so, the voices began to lessen.

She stepped back towards the church again.

'I'm telling you, they should have had at least two more goals before half-time ...'

'You have reached the voice mail of National Telecom mobile phone number ...'

'Oh ... hello ... This mobile phone I bought. I'd like to change it.'

That was the answer. It had to be.

Kate wasn't going mad. The voices she'd heard, the snippets of conversation, they were being relayed backwards and forwards on mobile phones.

And somehow, Kate was picking up conversations from the phone mast.

'Mum, you look so much better,' Kate said happily, looking at her mum who was sitting up in bed. She had a couple of pillows propping her up and much of the healthy colour she used to have had returned to her cheeks.

'I *feel* much better, Kate,' her mum told her, sipping at a cup of tea. 'But how do *you* feel, darling?' she asked Kate.

'I'm fine,' Kate shrugged. For a moment, she wondered whether to mention the voices, but it seemed selfish. Her mum needed all her strength to get better. The last thing she wanted was to be worrying about Kate.

'Are you sure?' her mum persisted. 'Everything all right at school? Susie all right?'

'Mum, I told you. Everything is fine. Why do you keep asking?'

'I'm concerned. You've had a lot of responsibility since I came into hospital. It hasn't been easy for you. I know that. I'm sorry.'

'You keep saying sorry, Mum. It's not your fault you got ill,' Kate said.

Her mum shook her head slowly. 'You know I love you, don't you, Kate?' she said.

'Mu-um,' Kate said, blushing.

'Just remember, I'll always be there for you,' her mum said, quietly.

'A taxi at eleven thirty – yes, I've got that.'

'Get out of here and don't come back.'

Kate opened her eyes and turned over in bed so fast that she nearly fell out. *Not again! Not in my house! How is this happening?* she thought desperately. She put her hands to her ears in frustration, wanting the voices to stop. Somehow, she was now picking up mobile phone conversations even when she wasn't close to an antenna.

She stared at the ceiling but it was a long time before she drifted off into an exhausted sleep.

She awoke with a start the following morning. Sitting up in bed, Kate cautiously touched her ears. She yawned – and could hear herself clearly. No mad collection of voices drowned out the sound.

Kate felt a little more at ease as she washed and dressed.

'Sorry, darling – I'm going to be late – traffic's awful!'

Kate swallowed hard. *Please don't let it be starting again!* she thought.

'Oh, let's go to the Italian – I really fancy spaghetti tonight ...'

Kate waited awhile, listening to the snippets of conversation passing through. The babbling inside her head seemed to have settled to a manageable level now. How it got there was another matter, though.

Her dad was finishing his breakfast hurriedly when she wandered into the kitchen, the voices still buzzing inside her head.

Kate wondered about confiding in him.

'I've got to go, sweetheart,' he said, rushing past her. 'Or I'll be late for work.' He stopped, turned back and kissed the top of her head, then disappeared out of the front door. 'Love you!'

'Love you too, Dad,' Kate sighed, listening to the sound of his car starting outside.

She quickly ate a bowl of cornflakes and then set off for school.

Kate approached the church nervously. But now that the phone conversations were reaching her just as easily away from the antenna, nothing much changed as she drew near.

There were several cars parked outside. A funeral was taking place.

Kate could now hear church music mixing with the voices – the congregation was singing 'The Old Rugged Cross'. She remembered overhearing someone in the church mention that hymn. They'd been talking about the funeral of a lady with an unusual name. What was it again? Augustine something or other. And she'd wanted everyone to wear purple and white.

Kate paused, looking up at the telephone antenna on the church roof, wondering what she should do about the snippets of conversation that still mingled with the mournful hymn inside her head.

The hymn came to an end and Kate saw six men dressed in black emerge from the church carrying a coffin on their shoulders. Each of them wore tall top hats, with purple ribbons wound around them. They fluttered in the breeze like flags of mourning. The congregation followed – all dressed in purple and white.

As the coffin was turned, she saw that the purple and white flowers adorning the coffin lid formed a name.

AUGUSTINE

Kate didn't wait to see any more. She turned and walked hurriedly down the road. She wanted to cry out. To scream at the voices to get out of her head. She wanted to ignore the even more scary thing that had just become obvious to her: some of the conversations she was hearing hadn't even happened yet! She'd heard Augustine's funeral *days* ago. But it had taken place this morning.

What did Reverend Dodds call it? Kate thought. *Witchcraft? But I'm not a witch!*

The dustmen were making their rounds, emptying bins into the back of their slowly moving dustcart. The noise of the cart's crusher as it chewed up the rubbish was deafening. Louder even than the voices inside Kate's head.

'Kate.'

She kept walking.

'Kate.'

The voice grew louder than the others and Kate realized it was coming not from within her skull but from just behind her.

She turned to see Susie scurrying across the street towards her.

'I thought you were ignoring me,' Susie said, catching her breath.

'I didn't hear you,' Kate told her friend.

'I'm not surprised with the racket the dustmen are making,' Susie replied. 'But I'll tell you someone else who'll be making a racket today: Mrs Lawson.'

'Why?' Kate asked.

'Hello! Because hardly anyone will have got that maths homework she set right. I mean, I know she's a bit of a slave-driver but even *she's* never set us anything that hard before. Please don't tell me you thought it was easy.'

'Oh, Susie. I haven't even looked at it,' Kate said.

'Oops ...' Susie said. 'Any other teacher would probably let you off, what with your mum being in hospital and that – but not Mrs Lawson.'

Kate sucked in a deep breath. 'What am I going to do?' she murmured.

'Er ... leave the country? Have plastic surgery so she doesn't recognize you?' Susie suggested. 'Sorry, there's no point copying mine – I know it's wrong, so she's bound to guess one of us has copied if we both have all the same wrong answers.'

'I'll do the homework after registration,' Kate decided.

'It took me two hours to do one little part of it,' said Susie. 'And there's two whole pages of questions to work through. You'll never do that after registration.'

As they entered the playground, Susie went on and on, worrying about the maths homework. 'I mean,' she continued, 'how can she expect us to do all that in two nights? I bet she never got homework like that when she was at school.'

'I'm so sorry, Mr Johns. I really do feel quite unwell ...'

The voice belonged to Mrs Lawson.

'So as I won't be in class today, I'd appreciate it if you'd tell the class that they can have an extra day to complete the work.'

Kate turned to Susie. 'Maybe Mrs Lawson won't be in today,' she said as the bell went.

'Of course she will,' Susie protested. 'She's never off. She never gets ill. She's like some kind of alien, she never even gets colds.'

Kate looked at Susie and, for a second, considered telling her friend that she'd just picked up Mrs Lawson's telephone call in her head. Then she thought better of it.

She walked over to Daisy Barton. 'Daisy,' she said.

Daisy Barton turned. 'What do you want?' she asked.

'You've done the maths homework, haven't you?' Kate asked.

'Of course I have,' Daisy replied sniffily. 'Why? Haven't you?'

Kate shook her head. 'But listen, I'll do a deal with you. If Mrs Lawson is off sick then Susie and I get to copy your answers, right? If she's not, then you can have my WestZone concert ticket.'

Daisy looked at her in shock, and then a smile crept across her face. 'Deal,' she said. 'You must be really scared of Mrs Lawson, that's all I can say!'

'Kate – what are you doing?' Susie whispered. 'You'd better be right.'

'I will be,' Kate said, confidently.

'And if you're wrong?' Susie whispered worriedly.

'I don't think I will be,' Kate whispered back.

'Well, we'll soon know if you're right,' Susie said. 'Maths is the first lesson.'

After registration and assembly, the class all waited anxiously for Mrs Lawson to arrive.

But the door opened to let in Mr Johns the head teacher, instead. He nodded a greeting. 'I'm sorry to tell you that Mrs Lawson isn't feeling very well today,' he informed them. 'She's just called me on her mobile phone to say she started the journey here, but has now turned around to go back home and won't be coming in.'

Someone at the back of the class cheered.

Daisy's jaw dropped, her lips opening and closing like a goldfish.

Kate let out a sigh that was a mixture of relief and delight and glanced sideways at Susie who shrugged and mouthed silently at her, 'How did you know?'

'Mrs Lawson told me that she set you all some homework,' Mr Johns continued. 'And she asked me to tell you that you can have this lesson and until she returns to complete it.'

There was another cheer.

Kate looked at Susie again and smiled.

Susie leaned close to her. 'You must be a witch,' she whispered, grinning broadly.

At first Kate thought that she was dreaming.

Then she realized that the words and hysterical voices whirling around inside her head were all too real.

She sucked in a deep breath and tried to focus on what the voices were saying. It was almost like trying to tune in a radio.

'Leaving the band ... can't believe it ...'

The words continued to spin through her head.

'... millions of records ... sell-out tour ... WestZone won't be the same without him ...'

Kate closed her eyes tightly again for a moment and one single sentence seemed to glow inside her mind like torchlight in the dark.

'Nooo! How can Richie do this to us?'

Kate shook her head slightly. Richie – leaving WestZone? That was *worse* than a nightmare. He was her favourite singer in the world.

She looked across to her bedside table where her ticket for WestZone's sell-out show was lying there like a trophy.

Swinging herself out of bed, Kate crossed the landing quietly, wincing when one of the floorboards creaked. She waited to see if she'd woken her dad but then, deciding she hadn't, she continued on down the stairs and into the living-room and flicked on the light.

The daily paper was lying on the sofa. Kate flicked through it quickly.

No mention of Richie leaving the band in there – and surely, Kate reasoned, one of her friends would have mentioned it, would have heard about it by now. Especially Susie. She was mad on WestZone – though her favourite band member was Karl. You couldn't see her wallpaper for posters of him.

Kate waited a moment then switched on the TV, hurriedly turning down the volume.

The news came and went with no mention of Richie leaving. She tried Teletext and Ceefax.

Nothing.

She turned off the TV and curled up on the sofa, her heart beating fast. It was clear that Richie hadn't left the band. Not yet.

She thought about the telephone conversation she'd heard taking place at a funeral – when it hadn't even happened yet. And how she'd heard Mrs Lawson's call to Mr Johns before that had happened too.

If the voices in her head were correct again, then Richie leaving WestZone was still to come.

Kate sat still for a long time before heading back to bed. But it was ages before she could sleep. And not just because of the voices buzzing inside her brain.

When the alarm woke Kate the next morning she still felt a little groggy from lack of sleep, but as she looked across at her WestZone ticket, an idea began to form in her mind.

She put the ticket into the side pocket of her schoolbag then hurried downstairs.

Kate ate her breakfast quickly that morning and she was out of the door before her dad, who just about managed to say goodbye to her before she hurried off down the road.

'Why have you got your WestZone ticket with you?' Susie wanted to know when Kate took it out of her bag at school. 'You'd better hide it from Daisy Barton, she'll only start moaning again because she was too late to buy one herself.'

'Well, she can buy this one if she wants to,' Kate told her.

'What?' said Susie, open-mouthed. 'I thought you were desperate to see Richie live. I read that WestZone won't be touring again for at least a year.'

'Well, if Daisy wants this one she can buy it,' Kate replied. 'I've gone off WestZone a bit, and now I'd rather buy my mum a nice present for when she comes out of hospital.'

'Ah, that's really kind – but I can't wait to see Karl in the flesh!' Susie smiled. 'I wouldn't sell for a million pounds!'

Kate grinned.

'Well, all right then ... maybe for a million pounds,' chuckled Susie.

They saw Daisy Barton walking across the playground with her mates.

Kate strode straight across to her, the ticket proudly displayed. 'You wanted a ticket for the WestZone gig, didn't you, Daisy?' she asked.

Daisy's eyes widened as she saw the ticket. 'Is this a joke?' she asked suspiciously. 'Trying to make me jealous?'

Kate shook her head. 'If you want it you can buy it off me,' she told her. 'I've not as keen on WestZone as I was.'

'All right,' Daisy said. 'I'll go home at lunch-time and get the money.'

'Sounds good to me,' Kate smiled.

Daisy grabbed her arm. 'You'd better not change your mind.'

'I won't – I promise,' Kate said.

'Cool,' Daisy grinned. She and her friends walked off.

'That was easy, wasn't it?' Kate said, looking down at her ticket.

Susie stared at Kate and shook her head. 'I still don't know how you could have done it though, Kate. There's no way I'm selling mine. I'd go mad if I had to miss WestZone.'

'I think I'll survive,' Kate replied as they walked to their classroom. The voices in her head had stilled to a low buzz. A little like flies around a light. It was annoying but she could put up with it. And by the time she'd collected her money from Daisy that afternoon, her head was pretty clear.

'You could get three or four CDs with that,' Susie said enviously. 'Or a couple of new tops.'

Kate pushed the money into her purse. 'I told you, I want to get something for my mum as a coming home present,' she said, looking out of the window.

'Do you know when she might be leaving the hospital?' Susie asked.

'Not yet, but soon I hope,' Kate replied. 'It'll be great to have her home again.'

When Kate arrived home from school, she made herself a sandwich and then wandered into the living-room and put the TV on. She switched to one of her favourite music shows.

Kate immediately noticed that there were photos of WestZone behind the presenter. She reached for the remote and turned up the sound.

'So, the unthinkable has happened ...' the presenter said. 'In the last hour, Richie has announced he has left WestZone! Hard to believe, I know. He is due to appear shortly at a press conference to talk of his future plans ...'

Kate chewed thoughtfully on her sandwich as she watched.

'WestZone has sold over twenty million albums worldwide, with Richie as lead singer,' the presenter continued. 'The band has said that the forthcoming tour will go ahead – but unfortunately for those Richie fans out there, without him.'

The phone rang.

Kate got to her feet and picked it up. 'Hello,' she said, one eye still on the TV screen.

She recognized the voice at the other end of the line immediately. It was Daisy Barton.

'Kate, I've just heard about Richie leaving WestZone,' Daisy told her.

'I know, I just saw it on the TV,' Kate replied.

'Well, the only reason I wanted to see them was because I like Richie!' Daisy yelled down the phone. 'I don't want to go any more – I want my money back!'

'Sorry, Daisy,' Kate said firmly. 'It's nothing to do with me that you don't want to go to the concert anymore.'

Kate hung up and then walked back to the sofa and sat down, gazing at the TV screen. The presenter was still going on about WestZone.

Kate took another bite of her sandwich and wondered how Daisy Barton was feeling.

'Listen, I'm not going to put up with much more of this. My heating's been off for two days now and no one's come to fix it.'

A man's voice. He was angry.

'Did you see the state of her in that dress the other night? I told Zena that I wouldn't be caught dead in something like that.'

A woman's voice this time.

Kate heard the snippets of conversation moving around inside her head. She felt tired and the low buzzing of the voices was making her feel even more sleepy. She hadn't slept well for the last two nights and now, seated close to the soothing warmth of the radiator in the classroom, she was having trouble staying awake.

'I know it's sad about her dog dying. She'd had it for ten years. It was like a member of the family, I suppose.'

Another woman's voice.

'So, in the Greek myths, most of the characters were either punished or rewarded by the gods. A bit like Kate is likely to be punished by me for not listening in class.'

Immediately, Kate jerked her head up from her desk, to see the face of the teacher staring at her.

'Sorry, Mr Currell,' Kate said.

'Is the story of Cassandra boring you, Kate?' Mr Currell asked.

Several of her classmates were laughing now. Kate felt herself blushing. 'No, Mr Currell,' she said.

'So, Cassandra was given the gift of prophecy by Zeus, king of the gods,' Mr Currell continued. 'She was able to see into the future, but the problem was, no one would believe her prophecies, and more tragically, she was powerless to change what was going to happen.'

Kate looked apologetically at Mr Currell and tried to concentrate on the words she heard coming from the front of the class.

'Matt really fancies her. I asked him.'

Kate shook her head, trying to ignore the new voice.

'He fancies Kate. I'm telling you the truth. I spoke to him after he played football yesterday.'

Suddenly Kate didn't want the voice to go away. Matt fancies Kate? It could only be Matt Albert. Not only was he the best footballer in the school, he was also the fittest boy by a mile.

Matt fancies Kate.

'Wow,' Kate said loudly.

'Something interesting, Kate?' Mr Currell asked her pointedly. 'Have you found a part of Cassandra's story that's finally grabbed your attention?'

'Sorry, Mr Currell,' Kate replied, her cheeks turning red.

She dropped her head towards the textbook opened on her desk, as much to mask her delight as anything else. So Matt Albert fancied her, did he? Well, perhaps it was about time she told him that she felt the same. Wow – she might have her first boyfriend!

Kate glanced at the clock and saw that it was almost lunch-time. She decided she'd go and speak to Matt then. He was always to be found in the same place: kicking a ball around with his mates on the school field – usually with three or four girls watching him as they pretended to talk about something else.

The time passed slowly for Kate, but when the bell finally sounded she was the first one out of the classroom.

Kate ate her lunch hurriedly, impatient to get over to the playing-field and wait for an opportunity to talk to Matt.

As she got up to leave, Susie got up too. 'Where are you rushing off to?' she asked curiously.

'I need to do something,' Kate told her. 'I'll tell you all about it later – won't be long.' Then she hurried away, leaving Susie looking puzzled.

Kate forced her way down the crowded school corridor until she reached the exit into the playground. She could see that there was already a group of boys from the next year up, kicking a ball about. As she drew closer, she picked out Matt Albert among them.

Matt fancies Kate. She felt a tingle run up her spine.

But the thought of marching across the field in front of all his friends and saying that she fancied him too, was way too embarrassing. Kate decided she'd watch him and his mates playing football, and then try to get to talk to him on his own, afterwards.

Two of the boys kicking the ball around had already noticed Kate standing there. She smiled at them. Maybe they already knew that their mate Matt fancied her.

'Who did you say Matt fancied?'

Kate winced, the boy's voice in her ear was so loud. There was a crackling sound like static.

'Kate. But I don't think she knows yet.'

Kate recognized the same whispered voice in her head she'd heard in class. She smiled to herself.

'Kate's in the year above him, though. I suppose he likes the fact that she's so sporty. And she does look great in her netball outfit.'

For a second, Kate was confused. And then she remembered tall, slim, sporty, netball-playing, blonde Kate Kirby in the year above them.

Was *that* who Matt fancied? Not her? Kate went all hot and cold in embarrassment.

'Fancy a game, Kate?' one of the boys called, kicking the ball towards her.

Matt Albert ran past her after the ball. He didn't even look at her.

Kate felt her face burning red. 'I was looking for Susie, I thought I saw her come this way,' she lied. And she turned and headed back towards the playground.

'If you want to play, just come back and tell us,' one of the other boys shouted.

She heard laughter echoing behind her. But the laughter was nothing compared to the embarrassment she would have felt if she'd gone through with talking to Matt. What a narrow escape! Kate felt almost sick at the thought of how close she had come to making an absolute fool of herself.

The voices had their uses, but it seemed that they could get her into trouble too, if she wasn't careful!

'That noise is enough to drive anyone mad,' said Susie as she and Kate approached school the following day.

There was a lorry parked in the road outside the tower block that loomed over the school. Part of the street had been dug up; the eardrum-shattering sound of a road drill filled the air.

Kate didn't answer. The loud and abrasive sound of nearby construction meant that she was spared the more intrusive sounds of voices inside her head for a while. She saw two men unloading a large black metal object from the back of the lorry.

She realized with horror that it was a mobile phone mast, identical to the one on top of the church spire. 'They're putting that on top of the flats?' she gasped in alarm.

'Yes, didn't you hear about it on the local news?' Susie asked. 'They're putting them up all over town. Some of the residents are really angry about it.'

Kate winced. She'd had a headache from all the snippets of phone conversations coming into her head since she'd woken up that morning. Over the last few days there had been more and more of them. And no wonder, if mobile phone masts were being put up all over town. But now there was going to be one next to school too. It would be intolerable!

'Are you all right, Kate?' Susie asked.

Kate shrugged vaguely, her gaze fixed on the top of the tower block. 'I've got a bad headache, that's all ...' she said. As they watched, Kate saw the mast being raised – a black arrow-head against the clouds.

During the history lesson that morning, the hum of voices coming into Kate's head suddenly escalated to a roar, rushing in at her from all directions. The new mast must have started to work. It felt to Kate as if her brain was a roundabout in the centre of a busy junction, words driving at it from everywhere at once. She put a hand to the back of her neck.

'You should see the school nurse if you don't feel any better,' Susie whispered.

Kate tried to nod but the pain was too intense. She feared she would either pass out or simply go crazy right there on the spot.

'You'll have to go to the nurse,' Susie insisted.

'You're right,' Kate agreed. She didn't really want to go to see Nurse Williams. The rather sour-faced school nurse was never very sympathetic. But Kate had to do *something*.

She put her hand up to ask their teacher's permission.

Slowly, trying to keep her head as still as possible, Kate approached Nurse Williams's office. She knocked on the outer door and then walked in.

From the small waiting area, Kate could see Nurse Williams at her desk in the office beyond. She was on the phone. She signalled for Kate to take a seat.

Kate slumped on to the chair and put her hands to her head again. The pain was increasing.

'Hang on a minute,' Nurse Williams said. 'I've got someone waiting. I'll just see what they want.' She put the phone to one side and came out to Kate, eyeing her somewhat suspiciously. 'Yes, dear?' she said.

'I've got a really bad headache,' Kate told her. 'I was wondering if there was something you could give me for it.'

The nurse looked at her again then nodded. 'Wait there,' she said, and then disappeared back into her office.

Kate saw her pick the phone up again.

'Another one with a headache,' Nurse Williams said into the mouthpiece. 'Backache. Stomach ache. Headache. They use any excuse to get out of lessons, some of them.'

Kate felt like calling over that she *wasn't* using the pain as an excuse. She would have given anything to make it stop. Just as she would have given anything to silence the ever-chattering voices inside her head.

'Always complaining,' Nurse Williams continued to her unseen friend. 'I'm fed up with it. They're all the same. Anything to get off school for a couple of hours.'

She returned with two white tablets and a glass of water. 'Take these,' she said, sharply. 'And then you can return straight back to class.'

'But I think it might be a migraine,' Kate replied, accepting the tablets. 'I feel a bit sick and dizzy too.'

Nurse Williams rolled her eyes. 'So you want to go home, do you?'

'Yes, please,' Kate said faintly. 'I don't think I could go through the rest of the afternoon like this.'

Nurse Williams sighed and called Kate's dad.

He arrived within half an hour.

Kate climbed gratefully into his waiting car and lay back in the passenger seat.

'You look awful, Kate,' her dad said worriedly, reaching out to touch her forehead. 'Let's get you home. It's a bit of luck I'm on the late shift at the factory tonight, otherwise I wouldn't have been there when the nurse rang.'

'I just need to lie down, Dad, and try to get rid of this headache,' Kate told him.

'I hope you can sleep with all the noise,' her dad said.

'What noise?' Kate asked.

'Outside the house. National Telecom are putting up one of those mobile phone antennae right across the street.'

Kate almost burst into tears. *Not another one*, she thought.

As her dad swung the car into their street she saw the National Telecom van parked across the road and the men busily erecting the antenna.

Kate practically fell from the car and her dad hurried around to the passenger side to help her.

'Come on, let's get you inside,' he said comfortingly.

Kate's vision swam, and she thought her legs were going to buckle. Her dad supported her as they made their way into the house. The sound from outside dimmed but the roaring inside Kate's head continued.

Her dad helped her into the living-room and she sat down on the sofa.

He knelt beside her, stroking her forehead. 'Trust you to feel bad today of all days,' he said, smiling, still gently brushing her hair from her face. 'I wanted to give you the good news when you got home.'

'What good news?' she asked groggily.

'I spoke to the doctor at the hospital today and he said that your mum can come home in a couple of days. Whatever was wrong with her has now almost completely cleared up. She still needs time to get back to normal but she's improving all the time.'

Kate gave a weak smile. 'Mum starts getting better and I start to feel bad,' she joked.

'I spoke to your mum myself on the phone,' her dad continued. 'It was great to hear her sounding more like her old self. She said she couldn't wait to speak to you. There's something she wants to tell you.' He got up. 'I'll go and make us a cup of tea, eh? You just lie here and try and get some rest. We'll go and see your mum tonight before I go to work.'

Suddenly Kate felt she just couldn't wait any longer to see her mum again. 'No, Dad, I want to see her now,' she said, sitting up. She winced at the pain inside her head.

'But you're not well enough, Kate,' her dad said, looking concerned.

'I want to see her, Dad. Please ...' Kate pleaded. 'I really miss her when I'm not feeling well.' She hesitated. 'Dad, I haven't been feeling well for a while now,' she confessed. 'But I haven't wanted to worry Mum, her being ill herself. Now though ... Well, I just want to talk to her about it all ...'

Her dad looked at her then reached out gently and touched her forehead with his hand.

'I understand, Kate, and it's good of you to consider your mum.'

'So can we go and see her now, Dad?'

'Come on, then,' he smiled. 'I'll get my coat.'

Kate's mum was sitting up, the bandages removed from her throat, her hair done, and her make-up on. She looked like her old self. Healthy and beaming. 'Hello, darling,' she said to Kate in a clear, if somewhat husky, voice.

Kate rushed over to her mum and hugged her.

'I didn't expect you at this time of the day,' said her mum. 'You should be at school.'

'I had to go home,' Kate told her. 'I had a terrible headache. I've been getting them for days now. Headaches and—'

Kate's mum placed a hand on one of Kate's. 'I bet you haven't been drinking enough, darling,' she said, interrupting. She looked at Kate's dad. 'Would you mind going and getting a couple of drinks from the machine, Harry?' she asked.

'Of course,' Kate's dad replied with a smile. 'Won't be long.'

When he had gone, Kate's mum turned and gazed at Kate intently. 'And what else has been happening to you, Kate?' she asked quietly.

'Phone conversations. Coming into my head. I can hear people talking, Mum,' Kate told her. 'On mobile phones. All the time. And sometimes, the stuff I hear hasn't even happened yet. It's like I hear what's going to happen before it actually does. Like I can hear the future. But I know that's stupid. What's happening to me, Mum? Am I going crazy?'

'No, Kate, you're not ...' Her mum lowered her gaze slightly and squeezed Kate's hand. 'Kate ...' she continued hesitantly, 'I knew this time would come for you and now that it has, you need to know what's happening.'

Kate looked warily at her mum.

'You have a gift, Kate,' her mum told her. 'At least that's what we call it. Some people might call it a curse but it can be used for good so we've always looked on it as a good thing.'

'Mum, I don't understand,' Kate said, feeling a little scared now.

Kate's mum sighed. 'It started with your great great-grandmother, Elizabeth,' she began. 'Elizabeth was celebrating her twelfth birthday. The house where her family lived was right next to a telegraph pole. There was a terrible storm raging, but Elizabeth insisted on trying out her new umbrella. She went out into the garden, and in a freak accident, lightning hit the pole and then forked into Elizabeth.' Kate's mum paused for a moment, as if waiting to be sure that Kate was taking the information in.

'At first, everyone thought Elizabeth was dead,' she continued. 'But somehow, she had survived. And she had also contracted the gift.'

'What *is* the gift, Mum?' Kate asked her impatiently.

'As Elizabeth got older she developed the ability to overhear telephone conversations – just like you can now,' Kate's mum explained. 'And when her own daughter turned twelve, it was passed on to her too. It's been passed on from generation to generation ever since – always from mother to daughter, when the daughter turned twelve. And from the time you were born I knew that you'd have to inherit it one day.'

Then she sighed. 'But by the time you turned twelve, three months ago, the world had become so filled with telephones, the voices had become almost unbearable. I decided not to inflict the gift on you. I resisted and resisted the urge ...'

Her eyes filled with tears. 'Kate, I think that if I hadn't given in and passed the gift on to you when I did, I would have died ...'

Kate's eyes widened. '*That* is what made you ill?' she asked incredulously.

Her mum nodded. 'But I couldn't tell anyone. Elizabeth confided in two people and they both collapsed and died.'

Kate shook her head, finding it hard to take all this in. 'So that's why you began to get better again? Because you passed the gift on to me?' she asked.

Her mum nodded again. 'When I kissed your ear ...' She wiped away a tear that ran down her cheek. 'Do you remember? Just before I asked you to buy flowers for Gran's grave.'

Kate nodded, and then hugged her mum. 'It's not your fault, Mum.'

Kate's mum gave her a watery smile. 'Thanks, darling – I was worried that you'd hate me ...' She blew her nose. 'But you must learn how to control it. You have to master the gift, not let it take over your mind. I can help you do that. Gran knew how dangerous it could be if it was used wrongly. She warned me about it just like I'm warning you now. She was frightened of it towards the end. She heard of her own death ...'

'What do you mean?' Kate asked, startled.

Kate's mum squeezed her hand again. 'She heard her doctor talking on his phone with the hospital. She knew what was going to happen but she couldn't stop it ... That's why your gran and I moved home so many times. We had to.'

'I don't understand,' Kate said.

'People are always scared by what they don't understand, darling,' Kate's mum said sadly. 'Sometimes your gran tried to warn someone of something that was about to happen – but it would scare them. Gran was once even called a witch, and they threatened to burn our house down if we didn't leave.'

'And I first heard voices in a churchyard where people had been victimized for being thought witches too,' Kate said flatly, as she remembered the scratched-out gravestones Reverend Dodds had talked to her about.

'As I said, Kate, people are afraid of things they don't understand. I want you to understand. I want you to let me help you cope with the gift – and use it to help others, even if we must guard against letting them know what we are doing, to protect ourselves.'

Kate sat still on the edge of her mum's bed, her head bowed, and voices whirling around inside her brain. '*Am* I a witch?' she asked quietly.

Her mum pulled her close and hugged her. 'No. You're not a witch,' she smiled. 'You're not a freak and you're not a monster. You're just ... special.'

'But what if I don't want to be?' Kate asked, her irritation rising. She felt tears stinging her own eyes now.

'Don't be angry, Kate,' her mum pleaded. 'It won't do any good.'

'Tea for everyone,' Kate's dad said, walking in balancing three plastic beakers of tea.

'I just want to go home,' Kate said. 'Take me home, Dad, please.'

Her dad looked surprised. He looked at Kate then at her mum. 'I thought we were going to have a drink,' he said.

'I'd like to go now, please,' Kate insisted. She looked at her mum. 'Unless there's anything else Mum wants to tell me.' Then she turned and walked away.

'We'll talk more when I get home, Kate,' her mum called. 'Everything'll be fine.'

Kate wished she could believe that.

It was after midnight. Kate knew that. But how late she had no idea. She didn't bother looking at her watch. All she knew was that she couldn't sleep. The voices were still inside her head but so too was the news her mum had given her earlier that evening: the knowledge of why the voices were there and the fact that, as far as Kate knew, they would be there for the rest of her life.

She turned over in an effort to get to sleep but it was useless.

Her mum's words, the words of other conversations from inside her brain, they all mingled together to form one mass of confusion.

Then suddenly a conversation came into her head with such crystal clarity it was as if it was being spoken directly into her ear.

'You'd better be right about this job. I'm not getting caught again. Ten months in prison was enough for me. If anyone gets in the way this time, they'll be sorry.'

This voice was low and menacing. Little more than a growl. Kate felt a shiver run down her spine.

'It'll be fine. Trust me. The owners are away for the weekend, the whole family. There's no burglar alarm. We'll be able to break in really easily. He keeps his collection of gold coins in a cupboard in the dining-room. It'll be a piece of cake.'

This voice was quiet and nervous.

Kate sat up. Susie's dad had a collection of gold coins. And she and her family were away for the weekend. Then she shook her head. It must be a coincidence, surely.

The low, menacing voice cut in again: *'Just remember: this job is too big to mess up. If there is anyone inside the house when we go in, then we finish them – nice and clean. Tell me the address again.'*

'Twenty-two Acacia Avenue ...'

There was a deafening hiss of static in Kate's ear and she winced. Her heart was thumping. That was Susie's house! It was going to be robbed!

She waited, hoping to hear more of the conversation, but there was nothing. Instead she picked up two people talking about a movie they'd just watched. She let out a breath of frustration.

What should she do now? Alone in the darkness, Kate realized that she might be able to stop the robbery. Was this what her mum had meant about the gift being used for good?

She would have to go to the police. She would warn them. They'd be waiting for the criminals; they'd catch them in the act.

Kate nodded to herself. She even managed a smile.

She switched on her bedside light and fumbled for a paper and pencil, writing down as much of the conversation as she could remember.

She'd ring the police and tell them what she knew. Tell them she'd heard a robbery being planned. She didn't have to tell them how she knew. She didn't even have to give them her name. For the first time in what seemed like ages, Kate felt in control.

She crept downstairs and dialled the number of the local police station.

'Hello, police,' a voice said. 'Can I help you?'

'I want to report a robbery,' Kate said.

'Where?' the policeman asked.

'At number 22 Acacia Avenue.'

'And when did it happen?'

Kate swallowed hard. 'Well, it hasn't happened yet. But it is *going* to be robbed.'

'Oh, really, when?' the policeman asked.

'Well ... I don't actually know,' Kate replied. 'But I've just heard two men talking about it.'

'And where did you hear them talking about it?' the policeman asked.

'I was in my bedroom,' Kate told him.

There was a pause.

'In your bedroom?' the policeman asked. 'The men were in your bedroom?'

'No,' Kate replied impatiently. 'I heard their telephone conversation – in my head.'

Kate heard a sound somewhere between a cough and a groan at the other end of the line.

'Inside your head?' the policeman said, slowly. 'And where are these men coming from to rob the house at 22 Acacia Avenue? Mars? Saturn? Jupiter?'

'I did hear them, honestly!' Kate insisted. 'They're going to steal a collection of gold coins!'

The policeman sighed. 'So they're going to rob this house, are they? You heard them say so inside your head. You just don't know when they're going to do it?'

'No, I'm sorry, I don't. It could be any time,' Kate agreed. 'And they said if anyone got in their way they would kill them!'

'What is your name, miss?' the policeman asked, sounding more serious now.

Kate hesitated. 'I don't want to give my name,' she said. 'But you've got to believe me.'

'You don't want to give your name because you know you'd be in trouble for making this sort of a call,' the policeman said. 'Now what is your name?'

'This is going to happen, honestly,' Kate said. 'You have to believe me!'

'Well, when it does, you come and let me know. Until then – stop wasting police time.'

Kate slammed down the phone in frustration.

She considered calling Susie on her mobile to tell her about the conversation she'd overheard, but thought better of it. Susie wouldn't be any more likely to believe the story than the policeman, and Kate wouldn't have blamed her.

Kate hurried back upstairs to her bedroom and got dressed. Then she searched out her camera. She checked to see if the camera had a film in it then stuffed it into the pocket of her jacket.

If she could get some photos of the robbers then she could at least show those to the police. They'd have to believe her then.

She went back downstairs and then stepped outside into the cold night and set off in the direction of Susie's house.

It took Kate less than twenty minutes to reach Susie's road. She looked up at the high bushes that formed a natural barrier and shielded the house from prying eyes.

Susie's family home was large with a big front garden and a driveway that ran for about fifty metres from the road to the front of the double garage beside the house.

There were a number of trees around the front of the house and Kate thought that one of those might give her the best vantage point to watch from.

She climbed up into the lower branches of one near to the front door, then took the camera from her pocket and peered through the viewfinder. She had a good shot of the driveway and the front door and windows.

Now, all she had to do was wait.

Inside her head, the voices babbled away without stopping.

'Why won't you just shut up?' Kate muttered, banging her forehead with one hand.

Suddenly she heard two unpleasantly familiar voices inside her head.

'Have you found the girl?'

It was the rasping, gravelly-voiced burglar.

'Yes. Got her.'

The other burglar sounded more edgy and nervous than ever.

'Good. Now finish her – nice and clean.'

Kate swayed in shock, her heart beating madly against her ribs. Were they talking about Susie? Had Susie and her family returned home early? Was Susie going to disturb the robbers? Kate had to stop it happening somehow! But she knew there was no point in calling the police again. If they hadn't believed her the first time they wouldn't believe her now either.

'Do as I say.'

And then something amazing happened. It was as if a switch had been thrown inside Kate's brain. For the first time since the voices had started in the churchyard, there was complete and utter silence inside her mind. Beautiful, undisturbed peace. Like it used to be.

She waited a moment, expecting the voices to begin again, but they didn't.

For a moment she forgot everything except the blissful silence inside her head. Perhaps, as her mum had said, she was at last beginning to gain control of her power.

It was getting colder, and Kate's breath clouded in the air every time she exhaled. She was shivering, despite her thick coat and jumper.

She was about to look at her watch when she heard footsteps coming up the driveway.

It was two men, keeping to the shadows as they drew nearer to the house.

Kate could see that one of them was carrying something in his hand that looked heavy. She thought it might be a metal bar.

She reached into her pocket and pulled out the camera, preparing herself.

The men made straight for a side door. They were inside the house within seconds.

Kate slid from her perch, landing on the ground, and ran across to hide behind some bushes near the side door.

From that position, she could get a clear shot of the men as they came out carrying their stolen goods.

She waited.

And waited.

It seemed as if hours passed but no one came back out of the house. Kate felt her heart thumping harder. What if they'd gone out another way and she'd missed them? She'd have no evidence of the robbery to show the police.

Kate decided to go in.

Just inside the doorway was an open trapdoor. Kate looked down the steep flight of stone steps that led to the cellar.

Perhaps it wasn't such a good idea going down there. But she overcame her fear and edged slowly downwards, step by step.

After all – if her best friend was in trouble, she might be the only person who could save her. Mercifully, the voices were still silent in Kate's head, making it easier to listen for any movement.

Even though she knew the dangers of her situation, Kate couldn't help taking a moment to stare in amazement at the contents of Susie's dad's cellar. It was a gigantic room that ran the length of the entire house, disappearing into black shadows in all directions. There were packing-cases everywhere, some of them open. But there was no sign of the men. Kate went back up the stairs and out into the cold night once more. *The men must have left through the front of the house*, she thought.

And then she spotted the two men making their way back down the driveway.

Kate ducked back behind some bushes and raised her camera, preparing to take some pictures – but she lost her balance and the camera dropped to the ground.

The noise shot through the air like a bullet.

The men turned round and saw Kate.

'Catch her!' the gravelly-voiced robber roared.

Kate had no choice. She knew her only hope was to run back down into the cellar. If she could find somewhere to hide down there then she might escape them. She scrambled into the first open packing-case, pulled the lid shut and lay still, heart pounding, among some wood shavings and polystyrene packaging.

The sound of footsteps came thumping down the steps into the cellar.

She heard the footsteps coming closer. They paused right next to where she was. She heard the dialling of numbers, and the breath of the man as he answered the phone.

Kate could just make out the words coming through the phone. 'You found her yet?' said the voice.

'No,' the man replied, leaning slightly against the case that Kate was hiding in. She squeezed her eyes closed in terror, and hugged her knees. 'Anyone around up there?' he said down the phone.

'Not a soul,' the tinny voice replied. 'Take your time, but make sure you find her.'

It was at that moment that Kate realized with horror that the wood shavings used as packaging inside the case were tickling her nose.

She was going to sneeze.

Kate pinched her nostrils together, desperate to avoid the sneeze that would give her away. She sucked in her breath, and held it, until she could feel pressure behind her eyes and in her head. With a feeling of incredible relief, she felt the sensation pass. Then heard the footsteps move away slightly.

But the footsteps came back.

The lid of the packing-case was lifted.

Kate could hear the voice, tinny and distant from the man's mobile phone.

'Have you found the girl?'

A shadowed face stared down at Kate, the green LCD screen illuminating a rough and stubbly cheek. 'Yes. Got her,' said the other robber.

'Good. Now finish her – nice and clean,' he said.

The other man hesitated.

'Do as I say.'

And then, as when Kate had heard this conversation before, the voices stopped.

Everything went quiet.

Joanne Shemmans

SANCTUARY

1

It started with the storm.

A sudden roar swept over the valley and through the woods; a gale tore up trees and dragged cars off the road; a sheet of rain beat down upon the roof of the house like a hail of bullets. Ruth said it wasn't uncommon for this part of the world, in this place where the trees watched from all sides like voiceless sentries, yet the wail of the wind stirred unpleasant thoughts in Anna's head, like the eye of frog and tail of newt swirling the black cauldron of a fairy tale witch.

It was almost midnight when the thunder giants they had been told about as children stopped hurling boulders at each other, and the storm retreated, although the rain continued steadily. The hush which resulted seemed a little unnatural, but the two sisters barely noticed, filling it with the sounds of laughter and conversation as they sat at the kitchen table, flicking through old photograph albums and reminiscing childhood memories of the life they had shared with their parents in the city.

A sudden hammering noise which echoed through the house made Ruth start, and the coffee cup she was holding shook visibly, allowing a few drops of liquid the opportunity to escape onto the beige fabric of her pleated skirt, producing a dark stain.

'What on earth . . ?' Ruth began.

'Sounds like somebody at the front door.' Anna offered, tucking a stray tress of hair behind her ear and setting her cup down on the rough kitchen table.

'At this time of night, out here, in the middle of a storm?' The older plumper woman caught her breath and rubbed nervously at the coffee stain. 'After the rain we've had tonight, the bridge is probably sunk, and there's no other way into town.'

Thud-thud-thud.

The hollow sound came again, and placed against the steady drip of rain from the roof falling onto the porch, made an icy shudder of uncertainty trickle down into Anna's belly. She did not know why it made her feel edgy, but she had only been here for a week and the isolated location of the house was far more remote than she had anticipated, accustomed as she was to the constant buzz and whirr of city life. She supposed being this far from humanity made her uncharacteristically nervous.

There was an uneasy silence, broken only by a fat droplet of water escaping from the faucet over the sink, until the hammering started again.

'Well, are you going to answer it?'

Ruth's eyes widened. 'Who, me?'

'Well, it is your house. I doubt if anybody would be here to see me.'

'But nobody comes here.' Anna's sister clasped her broad hands together in earnest. 'I don't know anybody.'

Thud-thud-thud; slow but persistent.

'Ruth, you can't just leave them out on the doorstep.'

'Will you go, Anna? Please.'

At forty-one years old, Ruth still behaved like an awkward teenager at times. Never married, she had moved out here when their mother had died ten years ago to take up a position as the village midwife, whilst Anna, five years younger, had stayed on as a music teacher at a school in the city. As far as Anna knew, delivering babies was the closest her sister had ever come to the act of copulation.

But perhaps Ruth's sheltered existence had its benefits, Anna considered. If you never fell in love, you could never be hurt. If you never had love, you never knew the crushing pain of losing it. . .

Anna carefully ordered these thoughts and placed them away in order to deal with the current situation. She must learn to accept the past if she intended to survive in the future.

'I'll go.' she resolved. 'Before they knock the door down.'

She took off and folded her reading glasses, straightened her sweater and padded through the house into the front reception room. It occurred to her that despite the bravado she had exhibited for her sister's benefit, it might be wise to peek through the window at the visitor before unlocking the door, just as a precaution. However, as she lifted the net curtain away from the front window she realised that being unfamiliar with the layout of the house she had forgotten that the construction of the porch made it impossible to see from this angle.

Regardless, Anna went out into the unlit hall, noticing a sudden chill which made her skin prickle, colder than she might have expected for the beginning of June. She made a mental note to suggest to her nervous sister that she ought to at least install a peephole in the front door for her safety. Her fingers worked to draw back two stiff bolts, but then hesitated, leaving a barrier of solid oak standing between her and the stranger.

Why the hell had she paused? She had never been like this in the city, despite the soaring rate of street crime and the sparse police presence. Upon reflection, perhaps she should have.

Anna opened the door.

A man stood on the porch, staring back at her intently. His hair was dark and cropped short, and water was dripping down his face and off his nose, although he seemed barely aware of the rain. He had no coat, and his plain white shirt was plastered to his skin.

'Can I help you?'

He responded with silence, and for an instant, it seemed as if the world around them had frozen, and she was left standing there, alone upon the face of the earth with this man whose cold blue eyes bored down into her soul.

She severed the connection and looked him up and down.

The front of his shirt was stained bloody red.

'Oh my God!' Anna said aloud.

The stranger swayed and collapsed against her. Her reflex acted just in time to catch him; he was not powerfully built but fairly tall, and she could barely hold him.

'Ruth!' she yelled. 'Ruth, for God's sake get out here, now!'

The flap of her sister's moccasins echoed through the house as Anna tried to keep the stranger on his feet, wrapping his arm around her neck.

'Oh my Lord!' cried Ruth as she arrived in the porch, her hands flying to her face in dismay.

'Don't just stand there! Help me get him inside, will you?' Anna ordered, frustrated by her sister's panic.

'But we don't know who he. . .'

'Just do it!'

Ruth slipped the man's other arm over her shoulder, in a mirror of her sister's action, and the two women hauled him inside and laid him down on the couch. His eyes were barely open now, having lost the intensity with which they had regarded Anna on the doorstep. Looking down at her blouse, she discovered that it was covered in his blood.

Too much blood.

A sickly flashback screamed in front of her eyes, an image of her husband Michael, stabbed to death in a side street for his Rolex watch six weeks ago. She had come here to forget, and now it seemed as if fate was cruelly rubbing her nose in the memory by bringing this injured man here.

'What shall we do?' Ruth wailed, fingering the tiny gold crucifix around her neck anxiously, her plump cheeks flushed pink with exasperation.

'Call an ambulance!'

'But they won't get through, the bridge. . .'

'I don't know; they'll airlift him or something. Just call, now!'

Ruth hurried into the kitchen where the telephone was situated. Anna lifted the stranger's shirt. His stomach and chest was lacerated with punctures, ugly zigzag cracks which oozed blood onto his rust stained flesh.

Michael. This must have been how. . .

But Michael had died alone.

On closer inspection, the wounds did not appear as deep as Anna had first anticipated. The man was badly injured, but none of the wounds were bleeding heavily.

'Don't worry. Help will come, soon.' she promised him, as if by reassuring this stranger she was somehow giving comfort to the lover she had lost.

'The lines are down.' said a voice behind her.

She turned to look back at her sister. 'What?'

'The phone's out. It happens all the time in bad weather.'

'Oh God!' Anna exclaimed, suddenly feeling more trapped in the middle of this vast landscape than she ever had in the sprawling metropolis she had left behind.

The injured man's eyes were drifting, clouding over, as if he was vacating his body at intervals.

'No!' Anna said firmly, tapping his stubbled cheek harshly with the back of her hand. 'Stay awake, stay with me.' She turned back to Ruth. 'He could be going into shock. Stay with him while I see if I can get through on my phone.'

'What?' Ruth echoed.

'Ruth for heaven's sake, you're a qualified midwife; you deliver babies kicking and screaming into the world, you cut umbilical cords for a living. How can you be so nervous?'

'But who is he?'

'Well if you don't know and you live here, what chance do I have?'

Anna dashed out into the hall and pulled her Mobile from her coat pocket; a jingle of metal joined forces with the sound of the rain as her keys fell out with it. She stared at the display. No reception. Frustrated, she ran upstairs and stood on the landing in the hope that this high-tech contraption might actually prove useful when she really needed it.

Still no signal.

'Damn it!'

She jogged back downstairs, noticing again how cold the house had become, and opened the front door. Standing outside, the rain-soaked woods observed her as she paced up and down the porch hoping to get a signal. Defeated by the contraptions inability to prove useful at a time when she needed it the most, she trudged back inside.

Surprisingly, Ruth had finally emerged from her hysterical coma and had brought out the First Aid kit.

'There's no reception on this thing either.' Anna told her.

Ruth was undoing the stranger's shirt, and so Anna reached over and helped her peel it off whilst her sister started to clean his wounds. He flinched slightly when the damp wadding found the broken flesh, but his eyes focused upon Anna again, and seemed unable to leave her.

'I'm Anna. This is Ruth, my sister. We're going to get you to a doctor.' She reassured him 'Can you tell me what happened?'

He didn't respond, simply stared at her blankly.

'Can we drive into town with him?'

'We could, but I can't see the roads being open, let alone the bridge. I don't think it's a good idea to try and move him without proper medical attention. These wounds aren't as bad as they look but he does seem to be in shock.' Ruth unrolled a sterile bandage, appearing to have made the transformation from timid spinster into resourceful nurse seamlessly.

Anna paced back and forward for a few moments, listening to the laboured breathing of the invalid, which was punctuated by the occasional sharp inhalation as a result of Ruth's intervention. Ruth had said the wounds were not that deep, but he was still badly injured. Anna felt obliged to help him. This wasn't fate's way of turning a knife in her heart, so recently fractured. It was a second chance, a way of easing her pain by giving her the opportunity to help this man in the way she was unable to help Michael.

She turned back to him and put her hand against his cheek, looking directly into his eyes. 'Who are you? What happened to you? How did you get here?'

He didn't answer, continued to observe her as if transfixed.

'Like I said, in shock.' Ruth repeated grimly.

'Do you understand me? Can you tell me what happened to you?' Anna persisted. 'We are going to help you; we are going to make sure that you get help. You need to tell us what happened to you.'

Silence.

He turned away finally and regarded Ruth as she applied another dressing, wincing as a sterile pad connected with shredded flesh.

'It's not uncommon after a trauma like this.' Ruth remarked. 'Probably can't even remember his name.'

'Surely he could say something.'

'He might be suffering from amnesia. He could be deaf and dumb for all we know.'

Anna sighed and checked her Mobile once more, although her effort went unrewarded. The rain had gained momentum and was hammering down against the house once more.

'I wonder how he got here.' she said aloud, resigned to the fact that the stranger was unlikely to answer.

A sudden thought occurred to her, and she crossed to the window, pulled back the lace and studied the drive through the wet glass. The only vehicle in sight was Ruth's battered Land Rover. 'I don't know why I bothered looking. No-one could drive in his condition even if the roads are open, and anyway he's soaked through. He must have walked her, but how could he, in that condition? He couldn't have come from the village, it's at least ten miles away, isn't it?'

'Twenty.' Ruth corrected. 'God only knows what happened to him. These look like knife wounds.'

Anna winced against the unpleasant coincidence. She was certain it had already occurred to her sister too, but Ruth had tactfully decided not to mention it.

'So what do you think we should do?' Ruth asked her.

'What can we do?' Anna shrugged. 'You said he can't be moved properly without an ambulance or some sort of medical attention, and it's likely the route into town is flooded anyway. We'll just have to wait, until the lines are back up or he seems strong enough to attempt the journey by car. We should be able to take care of him until morning, and by then the storm will hopefully have passed. Perhaps by then he'll have recovered enough to tell us who he is and what he's doing here.'

2

The house remained silent for a few moments.

'I know what we should do. It's always the best way to find the answer at a time like this.' Ruth appeared suddenly jubilant. 'Why don't we say a prayer for him together?'

Anna sighed. 'How do you know he's a Christian?'

'Well, even if he isn't, that makes no different. Jesus loves every single one of us, no matter if we know it or not, nor matter if we want him to or not.'

'I'm still not sure it's the right thing to do at the moment.'

Defeated, Ruth offered an alternative. 'Well, I could make us all a nice cup of tea. A warm drink always helps after a nasty shock.'

Anna smiled, listening to the combination of rain and wind which had started to attack the outside of the house with renewed intensity. 'You do that, Ruth.' she said softly, feeling more than a little guilty for becoming frustrated with her sister's anxious behaviour.

The sound of moccasins flopping against the floor accompanied Ruth's departure. Alone with the stranger, Anna knelt down heel to haunch on the floor beside him, momentarily repulsed by the sight of flecks of blood on her jeans.

'Can you hear me?' she asked him.

The man stopped staring at the ceiling and regarded her instead. His observation was interrogative, intrusive, and yet she did not feel threatened by it.

'Can you understand anything? Even if you can't speak, just nod, just give me some sign.'

He blinked slowly, but gave no outward indication that he comprehended a word she had said. The clock ticked softly, the storm raged outside, stirring the foundations of the house and making the treetops hiss like cobras coiled and ready to strike, but the stranger remained silent. At least he seemed more alert; she had expected him to lapse into unconsciousness when they had first brought him inside. She noticed that his jeans were dirty and worn, that his boots were caked with mud, and that there were black wells beneath his eyes.

'Wait a minute! I know what we need! Why didn't I think of it before?'

She leapt to her feet and hurried over to a nearby bureau, where her sister kept correspondence and writing materials. It had been in the family for three generations, shaped from rich mahogany and one of the things Ruth had asked to keep when their mother had died and all of her possessions had been divided. Anna slammed open the drawer and shuffled through the contents, stopping only when she laid her hands upon the objects she needed, and took them over to the stranger. Carefully, she pressed the pen into his hand, noticing how mud had caked his nails and worn into the creases of his fingers, and held the pad out for him to write on.

'Can you write down what happened?'

The tall man stared at her for a while. He did not immediately clasp the object, and he observed the tablet of white ruled paper as if he had no idea what it could be for.

Then, when Anna was about to abandon the idea, as if a long forgotten memory had just surfaced, he gripped the pen between his thumb and forefinger, and began to write slowly and carefully, as if the shape of each letter must be made perfectly if it was to be understood.

'What is it?' Ruth was back again, hovering behind her sister anxiously. 'Has he said something?'

'No, but I thought maybe he could write something down instead.' Anna held the pad firmly, a knot of anticipation forming at her solar plexus. 'It appears to be working.'

The stranger worked diligently for what seemed like an eternity, but could only have been a few minutes, while the two women waited in the quiet room, where the scratch of the pen against the pad and the softly ticking clock were the only noises that separated them from the banshee wailing outside. Finally, he allowed the pen to slip between his fingers and fall upon the floor and relaxed against the cushions, his eyes still fixed upon Anna.

She turned the pad over hesitantly.

'What in heaven's name can it mean?' Ruth said aloud, peering over Anna's shoulder.

Anna stared despondently at a series of straight vertical lines, arranged in groups across the page in a manner not dissimilar to a tally chart. Each mark was made perfectly, of equal height to the one before it, and sitting neatly on the line. The spaces between the lines were also even, imprinted in a way which gave her the impression that the writer considered their exact representation to be of great significance.

'What is it?' she asked him.

He exhaled deeply in response, as if exhausted by her interrogation.

'Nothing is what it is.' Ruth concluded in answer to her sister's question. 'I've seen this kind of thing before, usually done by people with learning difficulties or mental conditions. This is probably the closest he ever got to being able to write. I've seen children like that draw shapes, squares and triangles, as if they were trying to make letters, but couldn't grasp the concept. That probably explains why he can't say anything.'

Her sister was momentarily crushed, the breakthrough which had seemed within their grasp disappearing down a dark tunnel again.

'Is there anywhere near here he might have come from, a hospital, a residential home?'

'No. Who would build a place like that out here in the middle of nowhere? Maybe he came out here with somebody, his family or his carer, and got separated from them. He could have been wandering for days.'

'But how did he get so badly cut up?'

'Lord knows there are some sick people out there in the world.' Ruth said, wearing a face which suggested she saw herself as separate from the rest of humanity. 'Could even have been his family who did this to him, dumped him out here and left him for dead rather than take responsibility for him. It wouldn't surprise me.'

Ruth's explanation, coupled with the man's inability to speak or even write legibly, made a lot of sense, yet somehow it did not sit comfortably with Anna. His eyes were intelligent; they told her there were many things he wanted to say but couldn't, although she had no idea upon what basis she had formed this opinion, or what evidence she had to support it, other than gut instinct.

'Here.' Ruth leaned over and held the cup in front of him. 'Do you want me to help you?'

The stranger sat up and took the cup from her clumsily, spilling a little, then starting to gulp it down as thirstily as if he hadn't drunk in days.

'Good job I made it weak.' Ruth remarked. 'I gave him two sugars. Of course, I don't know how many he takes, or even if he knows what sugar is, but almost everybody has two, don't they?'

'Judging by his response, I don't suppose right now he's particular.'

'He needs some dry clothes. There are some I kept of Dad's upstairs, they're the only thing that might fit. Shall I go and get them?'

'It wouldn't do any harm.' Anna responded, aware that keeping busy was a good way of helping Ruth remain calm in situations which made her nervous.

Anna took the pad away and placed the pen inside the spiral which held it together. She watched the stranger whilst her sister disappeared, and took the cup away when he had finished drinking from it. Despite his condition, it was apparent now that he wasn't at the point of death. This wasn't like Michael, she reminded herself, it was different and she had to stop constantly comparing the two situations if she was to keep a level head. She rubbed her arms to combat the chill as her sister reappeared armed with a sweater and a pair of worn corded trousers.

'Can I have a word with you?' Ruth nodded towards the kitchen to indicate a private meeting place.

'Should we leave him alone?'

'He doesn't seem in any immediate danger. I should think it would be safe to leave him for a minute.'

Anna followed Ruth into the back of the house and closed the door.

'What is it?'

'Well, him.' Ruth answered in a hushed voice. 'I mean, how did he get here? I just don't see how he could have wandered here in his condition. We don't know anything about him. He could be dangerous; an escaped convict, or worse.'

'So what do you suggest we do? Give him a change of clothes and send him back out into the storm. That's hardly a charitable Christian attitude, Ruth. '

This was a cheap shot, but it hit home. 'I'm not suggesting we throw him out.' Ruth twisted her hands upon her skirt in the manner she always did when extremely nervous. 'He just makes me feel uneasy, that's all, the way he stares all the time, especially at you.'

'Me?'

You must have noticed he's barely taken his eyes off you since the minute we brought him in.'

'Ruth, the poor man's suffered some terrible ordeal, God knows what. I doubt if he knows what time of day it is, as you so rightly pointed out, and if he does have some disability he must be terrified. I hardly think he's noticed much about either of us.'

'Anna.' Ruth made an unpleasant face, as if she were about to spit out something which tasted well past it's sell by date. 'I wasn't going to bring this up, but don't think I haven't noticed the similarities, between this and. . .'

'Ruth, there no need!' Anna interjected.

'I know it must be terrible for you, for something like this to happen now, but you can't let it influence your judgement.'

'I know.'

'You say you know but. . .'

'Ruth!' Only saying her sister's namely loudly and firmly seemed to give Anna an opportunity to make her point. 'I know he's not Michael. I'm still grieving, I can't pretend that having him here like this isn't like turning a knife in the wound, but that doesn't make me stupid. I'm well aware that we know nothing about this man, and yes, I suppose he could be dangerous, but right now, what alternative do we have but to keep him here and look after him until the storm blows over and we can get help?.'

Her heart leapt up into her throat suddenly as the door handle turned and the stranger walked into the room. He still looked unsteady on his feet, but made it as far as the table and sank into one of the chairs. Once seated, he placed his head in his hands and froze, as motionless as a statue.

Anna frowned, and shot her sister a glance.

'Perhaps he's hungry.'

'I'll make some soup.' Ruth suggested, all too eager to busy herself again.

Pulling out a chair, which screeched loudly across the floor and set her teeth on edge, Anna sat down opposite the man. He looked up out of his elbows at her. She put the pad she was still holding in front of him, ready at a fresh page, and handed him the pen. It seemed pointless to keep pestering him, but a part of her still clung to the idea that even if his ability to compose anything intelligent was limited, as he seemed to have some grasp of the concept of writing he might eventually make some markings which could tell them something about him.

He sighed and picked up the pen. She watched in silence as he produced another series of perfectly straight and evenly spaced markings, almost identical to the first. The sound of soup boiling on the stove filled the room. The intensity of his eyes as he worked, and the earnest expression on his face which suggested that the committal of these lines to paper had relevance, made a lasting impression upon her.

As he gave the pad back to her, their fingers made contact and she noticed the roughness of his hands.

'I don't understand. I wish I did.'

His head returned to hide in his arms, as if her lack of comprehension brought deep disappointment.

When the soup was ready, the women watched him devour it hungrily, along with three fresh rolls Ruth had given him.

'Looks as if he hasn't eaten for days either.' she remarked. 'Soon as he's finished he needs to get out of those wet clothes. He might need some help.'

'I'll give him a hand.' Anna volunteered, aware that her embarrassed sister would be mortified at the idea of helping a fully grown man undress, despite having helped so many of them arrive naked into the world as part of her job

As expected, Ruth made no argument, but slurped tea whilst leaning her behind against the worktop. 'He seems much stronger now. We could try and take him in the car. We could see if the bridge is open.'

'Not in this weather. He can spend the night on the couch- I don't fancy trying to help him upstairs and I don't think he'd make it by himself.'

Ruth's expression told Anna that she was far from contented with the prospect of allowing the stranger to stay with them overnight, but had resigned herself to it.

Her plump hand took the empty bowl away from him at the split second he finished and rinsed it out thoroughly. The gurgling of running water sounded loud in the quiet room.

'Tomorrow the storm should be over.' Anna told the man in front of her, although she was fully aware that he was unlikely to understand. 'If the lines are still down, we can drive into town in Ruth's car. You can see the doctor there. You'll be alright, I promise.'

If only she could have promised Michael the same thing.

Wind was howling around the house as the stranger lay down on the couch. Anna settled the spare quilt over him, thinking how odd he looked in her father's clothes, particularly as she still remembered their original owner wearing the sweater and trousers he had climbed into wearily. Another loss which his arrival had caused to surface; it was as if he was unwittingly holding the knife which kept turning in her heart. Both she and Ruth had kept items belonging to their parents, for sentimental reasons, but items as personal as clothes were not the kind you wanted to be faced with every day, and this was the first time in years she had seen anything which had belonged to her father.

The stranger had changed his clothes in the kitchen whilst Ruth had gone to find the spare quilt and pillows. Anna had attempted to help him, but he had pushed her away gently, so she had left him alone. On her departure she had noticed for the first time a series of scars running down his back- old wounds shaped into puckered flesh.

Straight lines.

'Get some sleep.' she said to him quietly. 'We'll get help tomorrow.'

After some debate the women had agreed to sleep downstairs and take turns at watching him. Anna wondered if Ruth's growing distrust of him was apparent- if it was he didn't show it and had no means of expressing it anyway. Regardless of her observation as she took the first watch, he closed his eyes and slept almost immediately. She watched his intense, morose expression disappear and his lips part slightly as his muscles relaxed, until he looked as innocent as child.

Before Ruth settled down to sleep, she knelt down and said a prayer, murmuring voicelessly with eyes closed and holding her gold crucifix aloft. Their parents had held firm Christian beliefs, but had not been obsessive and not inflicted it sternly upon their child. Anna had grown up a committed atheist, yet her sister, by contrast, considered her faith to be the centre of her Universe. Coming here to see Ruth for the first time in years, as Anna had observed the many images of the naked man suffering upon the cross which decorated the walls of her sister's bedroom, she had caught herself wondering if Christ was Ruth's substitute for sex. It was a harsh judgement to make, but Ruth had never shown any interest in physical love, and had moved away here to a place where she was unlikely to find any other husband but God.

When the prayer was over and Ruth had put her feet up on the sofa, Anna took the armchair and tried to read. The sound of the man's deep breathing filled the room against the noises of the storm. The soft tick of the hand on the mantel clock as it counted the seconds, and each of his exhalations seemed louder now as the room became quiet. Glancing at Ruth after reading only a couple of pages, Anna was surprised to find her sister asleep so quickly, slumped with a blanket across her knees.

She shivered.

Was she the only one who had noticed the cold?

In order to make the time pass more quickly, she attempted to find interest in the pages of the book, but the irregularity of the situation caused her to jolt back into reality every few minutes, preventing the plot from holding her attention. Seconds ebbed away, and despite her intention to stay awake she was suddenly slipping into a foggy dreamscape, populated by dark faceless figures. Her father was there, coming towards her out of the fog, but when they were almost close enough to touch, his face shifted into the shape of Michael's, and then melted again, until the eyes became those of the man she had found standing out on Ruth's porch. As soon as she saw him, she found herself backing away, and they lost each other again in the fog. . .

'What on earth is that?'

Ruth's voice, raised in alarm, caused Anna's eyes to flick open, wide and alert, although her senses were still disorientated for some minutes, having been torn too harshly from sleep.

The stranger was still sleeping soundly, his face devoid of expression.

'What?'

'Listen.' Ruth hissed, sitting bolt upright on the couch.

Anna strained her ears to try and locate a sound hidden under that of wind and rain. For a time she could find nothing, until it came, loud and vibrant, crashing like cymbals through her head.

It was a loud dragging noise, echoing down through the house from somewhere on the floor above, like the vibration of a heavy piece of furniture being dragged across a bare wooden floor.

'It sounds as if it's coming from your room.'

'I know.' Ruth conceded, words escaping from a face which had lost all colour.

The scraping noise set Anna's teeth on edge.

'Why doesn't he hear it?' her sister wanted to know.

There was a silence. Anna stared up at the white painted ceiling, waiting for the reverberation, but it didn't come.

'He's probably so exhausted an earthquake wouldn't wake him. So would you be in his shoes.'

The noise returned, and with a force that seemed to set the whole house shuddering as if in a fit of epilepsy.

'What is it?' Ruth's voice was shaking too.

The stranger shifted, and groaned uncomfortably.

Anna glanced at him, leaving her eyes upon him until she was content he had returned to sleep. 'Is there anything upstairs that it could be?'

'What? What could be up there that would make that kind of sound?' Ruth's breath was coming out in gasps which bore the mark of hyperventilation as she gripped her crucifix again. 'Oh my God, Anna! What is it? What is it?'

Anna crossed the room and held her sister's hands firmly, looking straight into her tense brown eyes. The older, Ruth, would be assumed to be the wiser and stronger of the two, but in fact it had always been like this. Ruth had always been nervous, and Anna had always had the task of calming her down, even when they were children and despite the six year gap between them. Not for the first time today Anna caught herself wondering how Ruth ever managed to reassure women in the throes of labour, when she herself was so apprehensive of anything outside of her limited experience.

'It's okay, Ruth. There's bound to be a logical explanation for it. Perhaps the roof has been damaged in the storm and there are some loose slates clattering.'

'Someone's up there. What if it's because of him? What if he's in some trouble, what if somebody's after him?'

'Ruth. . .'

'Anna, we have to get him out of here!'

Tears of panic were beginning to well behind Ruth's brown eyes; she resembled a deer caught in headlights. In this kind of situation only a firm response could prevent her condition for accelerating from anxiety into full-blown hysteria.

'Ruth, be quiet! For heaven's sake, if there is anybody upstairs the best thing to do is keep your voice down, instead of carrying on fit to wake the dead, let alone the living. Now stop!'

Shocked, Ruth's lips parted momentarily.

'I'm going upstairs.'

'Anna, don't leave me here.'

'Someone has to stay and keep an eye on him.' In truth, Anna was less worried about the stranger and more worried about how much of a handicap her sister would prove to be if they went upstairs together.

The house trembled again as the noise thundered upstairs.

'You can't leave me with him.'

'To be fair, if he meant us any harm I think we'd know about it by now.'

As if to question this assumption, she heard the quilt rustle behind her. The stranger was sitting up, and his eyes were focused upon the ceiling, watching, waiting for the noise to return.

'He's heard it now. I have to go up there. Stay here. He's not going to hurt you; look at him, he's far too weak.'

'Take something with you, to protect yourself.'

'If it makes you feel better.' Anna picked up a heavy earthenware vase from the dresser. 'Wait here.'

The sound had not occurred again for at least a minute, but the empty feeling which had spread through Anna's stomach would not disappear until she had checked the house. Despite the suggestion she had used to try and reassure her sister, the racket which had come down through the house towards them sounded nothing like a couple of loose slates being harassed by the wind, but if she started allowing her imagination to be as overactive as Ruth's, she might lose her nerve too, and panic wouldn't help any of them.

This damn place; the trees; the storm. . .

She cursed her idea to come here as she slipped out into the hall and peered into the black space at the top of the stairwell. Yet how on earth would Ruth have coped with all of this alone? Anna's arrival, at this time, to this quiet place, where normally nothing remarkable happened, in time for the arrival of the stranger, seemed part of her destiny.

Anna's bare foot found the first stair. It was an old house and she prayed the floorboards wouldn't provide a fanfare of creaks to announce her arrival, but if there was a God and he was listening, he had a sense of humour as warped as the wood, for it screeched loudly as she shifted her weight onto it.

If there was anyone waiting in the darkness above, she had totally forsaken the element of surprise.

Regardless, she tried to keep the noises her body made to a minimum, and moved slowly through the shadows, until she stood anxiously in the gloom above. She gripped the heavy vase in her right hand and then kicked the door of Ruth's bedroom open with her foot, snapping the light switch instantly.

Inside, flooded with light, Ruth's room was as calm as ever, pretty as a picture, decorated in pink and scattered with ornaments and wide-eyed soft toys, a menagerie of teddy bears, rabbits and porcelain dolls with delicately painted faces and glossy nylon curls. A plethora of tacky religious statues invaded the stuffed jungle, watching over the cuddly multitude like the eyes of an omnipotent creator.

There were no dark corners for an intruder to hide in. The space within was silent, still and empty; everything remained in its proper place, waiting for Ruth, a shrine to the woman who slept here as much as to her God.

A noise in the spare room to her left made Anna's skin prickle. It was the place she had slept last night; for the last week it had been her private haven, where she had tried to deal with her grief, wrestling with it like Jacob with the angel whilst her sister slept in the next room.

There was nothing to hold her here, in this room, other than fear of what she might find in the next.

Forcing herself to confront it, she spun around to face the open door which led back out into the black corridor, still clutching the vase as if it were an amulet to ward off evil.

She entered the world of shadows again.

The door to the guest room stood ajar. Anna thought she could remember closing it, but was uncertain. Her hand rested on the handle for a moment, then pushed inwards, and with a flick of the switch she gave light to the world inside.

This space, like the one she had visited before, was empty. The décor was plain and sparse; the curtains were still open and she could see her pale reflection in the glass, dissected by daggers of rain.

There was no-one here.

They were alone in the house, except for the stranger.

3

It was just after seven in the morning when the storm loosened its grip, although there was still drizzle in the air.

At a little before ten, Anna opened her eyes to find her sister tapping her shoulder repeatedly.

'What? What's the matter?' Her fingers fought to remove the crusty residue of sleep from the creases of her lids.

'He's gone.'

'Who?'

The memory of the stranger and the night which had passed trickled slowly through her senses, a sluggish process. Anna inspected the crumpled remains of a quilt on the couch, the only evidence that the tall man had ever slept there.

'Did you hear him leave? Were you awake?'

'No.'

'Have you looked for him?'

'Not yet.'

'Well how can you be sure he's gone then?'

Anna tensed and stretched her limbs awkwardly, forcing her muscles awake. She had slept in her clothes and felt stale and uncomfortable.

'I didn't want to look for him by myself.'

'Don't worry, Ruth. I'll go.'

The blanket Anna had slept under, which was fashioned from her sister's knitted patchwork design, slipped onto the floor as she stood up. She wanted to shower , change her clothes and urinate a lot more than she wanted to hunt for the missing stranger, who had spent the night wandering around her dreams, a tall, awkward, inexplicable shadow. However, the anxious expression which had taken shape on Ruth's face told her that it would be wise to make a quick search first, and attend to her bodily needs afterwards.

Wearily, Anna started her mission in the kitchen.

The back of the long narrow room ended in two French doors which overlooked a neatly clipped lawn, enclosed by an equally tidy hedge. The glass through which a view of the garden was provided had fogged up due to the clash of temperatures inside and out. In front of the pane, the stranger stood with his back to Anna, a tall silhouette, framed by the grey light which penetrated the shadows inside. He stared out at the morning, seeing, yet unseeing. Her father's sweater hung on his frame like the rags of a forlorn scarecrow. He did not stir or flinch when the kitchen door slammed shut behind the newcomer, breaking the chapel reverence of the quiet room.

Bare feet finding the cold terracotta tiles, she crossed the room to stand next to him, and watched the garden for a few moments, trying to locate the point on the horizon which held his attention, but without success.

'We can try and contact someone now. The phone lines should be up and running again, but if not, we can run you into the village in the car.'

The stranger's eyes did not leave the misty glass, and, as she had anticipated, his expression did not show any new design as a response. This silent game tired Anna, although she did not blame him for it, or suspect the logic behind it as Ruth did.

'I'll go and try the phone.'

He lifted his arm suddenly, causing her to start before she realised what he was doing. The index finger of his right hand pressed the surface of the glass, making a damp print which spoiled the misty layer. Slowly, he created a new work of art.

Straight lines.

Anna watched, transfixed, as the same pattern she had seen emerge on the jotter took shape in front of her. Disturbed, the layer of steam began to dissolve, and the lines began to bleed into wet trails, like the painted tears upon the face of a circus clown.

'What are they?' Her eyes attempted to search his and extract meaning, but they were as hollow as the pit of her stomach.

Frustrated, she walked over to the telephone and lifted the receiver. Instead of a dialling tone, an unpleasant crackle entered her ear canal, and sent her senses jittering.

'Damn it!'

She had left her mobile on the kitchen table, forgotten in the confusion of the night before. It came as little surprise to discover that there was still no reception. Slapping the instrument back onto the grained surface, discarded as useless, she left the stranger to contemplate the misty pattern as if trying to divine the future, in order to explain the situation to Ruth.

Her sister had put on a pale blue cardigan, an indication that at last the cold had found her bones too. 'I can't stand having him here anymore.' she told Anna, her face ashen, and with no regard for the fact that the man might hear her through the open kitchen door. 'He's giving me the creeps. Look at him, I can see him from here, just standing there, making those awful lines!'

'Ruth, the poor man hasn't done us any harm; why can't you show some compassion?' Anna snapped, with words which had not sounded half as harsh inside her head. 'It's late; I can't believe we slept for so long. I'm going to shower and change into some fresh clothes. Make yourself useful and see if you can make him something to eat and drink, and then we'll get the car out. The surgery in the village will be open by now, so we can take him there. You'll have your wish to get rid of him at last.'

When the hot water hit her skin, standing naked in the white cubicle, Anna realised this was the first time she had been truly alone since the stranger had entered their lives. Privacy was something she had always treasured; Michael had been the only person she was happy to share every inch of her personal space with.

God, how she missed him.

Each night, when she closed her eyes and sleep found her, she had spent the day trying to accept the fact that Michael was gone forever. Yet every morning when she woke she was overwhelmed once more by the knowledge that he was not there. Assuming that waking each day in the bed that they had shared contributed largely to her inability to absorb the loss and adjust to a life alone, she had thought that by coming out here, to stay indefinitely with Ruth, who she had barely seen for the past five years, she could grow accustomed to being without him.

Now she missed him more than ever.

She remembered the jagged bloody wounds which her eyes had probed on the stranger's body.

He was not her husband.

Everything about the man was different; the colour of his hair and eyes; his height; the shape of his face. He looked . . . empty. Only the wounds gave them something in common, a shared suffering, a communion of hurt which they had taken together.

His presence in the house, wounded as he was, silent, proud, reminded her so much of her loss that it felt like a thousand tiny sharp fragments of glass being thrust simultaneously into her heart.

Yet despite the way in which these shards penetrated the nucleus of her pain, Anna knew that when he was gone, she would miss him.

She would miss him because at least whilst he was here, she could hurt because he reminded her, but take comfort from the fact that with him near her she could not forget, and so the memory of Michael would not fade, disappearing down a dark corridor as the stranger had slipped away into the fog in her dream.

Her tears had merged with the water and become one, washing over her like an incoming tide.

She did not want to hurt anymore.

But she did not want to forget either.

In spite of her resolve not to be infected by Ruth's paranoia, Anna found it difficult to be at ease when she returned, freshly showered and wearing a clean sweater and jeans, to find that the stranger had not neglected his silent vigil at the glass.

'He won't touch it. I tried to persuade him.' Ruth said almost apologetically, with reference to a bowl of oat cereal and a mug of tea left undisturbed on the table.

'He did yesterday. Do you think it's the shock coming out?'

'Only Jesus knows. I don't. Maybe. '

Anna translated lack of knowledge as lack of concern in this instance. She knew Ruth's moods only too well; she loved her sister but it was the difference in their personalities which had placed a distance between them as they had matured. Yet Ruth's insensitivity still came as a surprise.

'Then we need to get him to a doctor.' She started to lace her boots briskly. 'You go out and start the car- I'll bring him out.'

'Are you sure?'

'Well, as he's fit enough to stand there all morning I'm sure he can make it out to the car.'

'Alright.' Ruth looked suddenly cheerful. 'It's not that far, and I've got a First Aid kit in the boot just in case. There's bound to be someone at the surgery who knows what to do.'

Ruth's flip-flops applauded the suggestion merrily as she made her way outside. Anna stood next to the stranger and looked through the haze of condensation into the garden. 'We have to leave now.'

He turned and regarded her for a second, taking in the shape of her, calculating the sum of her, and having concluded the total amount, removed his eyes and set them upon the task of watching the watery illusion of the world once more.

Anna sighed.

'You have to come with me. Ruth will drive us into town. We can get help there; we can try and find out where you belong.'

He did not hear, did not understand, or chose not to do either.

For the first time, it occurred to Anna that perhaps his silent world was not the result of any trauma, impediment or imposed condition. Perhaps he just chose to remain mute, and if so, why?

Regardless, she was tired of trying to communicate with him in the way one might address a very young child.

'I know that you can hear.' she began slowly. 'Whatever Ruth thinks, I know it. I think you understand every word, and you don't answer me because you don't want to.'

'Anna!' Ruth dashed in, breathing heavily, her sand coloured hair in disarray, strands escaping from the blue crinkled band that normally secured it. 'Anna, the car!'

'What's the matter with it? It was fine when we came back from shopping yesterday.'

Tears were starting to prick Ruth's eyes.

'Come and see.' she blurted out in an unsteady voice, casting a derogatory glance towards the watcher at the window.

Anna hurried out after Ruth, through the front door and out onto the gravel drive, where the smell of damp earth and soggy leaves permeated the morning and the sky was the dirty bland colour of filthy dishwater. The bonnet of the Land Rover was already propped open. As she drew closer, she noticed that the air was still decorated with a light rain, which clung to her hair like clammy cobwebs. The trees stood proud and observant against the horizon at the edge of the drive.

Nothing for miles but trees and sky.

Through the drizzle, she peered down into the belly of the machine.

It was no surprise that the engine wouldn't start. The wires were cut and every connection severed, torn out. The vehicle had been gutted like a freshly hunted deer.

A lump of nerves collected in Anna's throat as she sought for a logical explanation.

'He's done this!' screamed Ruth across the gravel, her voice echoing through the waterlogged forest, her face the image of a frightened animal caught in headlights. 'It's him! He must have done it before he knocked the door, whilst we were talking in the kitchen.'

Anna stood up straight and closed the bonnet, although she knew damn well there was no need to keep the engine dry now. Her sister's breath was coming out in short gasps against the clammy air.

'It's him!'

'Ruth, don't be bloody stupid! How do you know that?'

'Well, who else could it be? You just tell me that, Anna, who else could it be? We're miles away from everybody else, there's nobody out here but us and him.'

'What about the person who attacked him?'

'What person? There's nobody else out here.'

'His stomach was cut to shreds.'

'What different does it make? He could have done that himself, to make us take him in . . .'

'That's ridiculous! Nobody could do that to themselves.'

Ruth blinked rain out of her face with tears. 'Anna, you've got to stop feeling sorry for him just because of what happened to Michael. You've got to see the truth.'

'I want to see the truth.' Anna breathed against the rain. 'I just don't want to jump to any conclusions.'

'We . . . we've got to . . . to make him. . .'

'Make him what?'

Anna started towards her sister, a cocktail of frustration and anxiety causing her pulse to drum loudly in her ears as if she were being marched to her execution.

'Make him tell us the truth; where he came from; why he came here.' Ruth answered, almost defiantly, as they came face to face in the rain.

'And how do you propose to do that exactly? Which methods of torture should we employ? Should we start off gently with sleep deprivation and ice cold showers, or should we head straight for the boiling oil and branding irons? Be serious, Ruth.'

'I am serious. We're out here alone with him. He could do anything to us.'

'He could also be as much as victim as we are to whatever is going on.'

'For God's sake, Anna, when will you stop defending him? He's not Michael!'

Anna had slapped her sister's cheek before she had time to check herself.

They had never fought, even as youngsters. They had been raised in a house where violence was a taboo; their parents were strongly opposed to any form of physical punishment, regardless of the misdemeanour. Striking her sister felt like breaking an unwritten law, like desecrating the memory of all the good things they had been taught as children; like kicking sand in the face of their parents' ideals.

Ruth's cheek had flushed crimson. Everything became still for a moment, except for the persistent drip of water falling from heavily laden tree branches onto the forest floor. Anna expected her sister to cry, but to her amazement only a tiny stifled sob came out of the older woman, and then emptiness.

They stared at each other for a few moments.

Anna considered their options; the twenty mile hike into the village; further waiting until the phone lines were up again or she could get reception on her mobile.

'I'll try and talk to him.' she said at last. 'I'm not going to go in there and accuse him of anything- he's still not in good shape and the last thing someone in his condition needs is to be interrogated. If he doesn't talk then I'll have to walk into town to get help.'

'But I can't stay here alone.'

'You'll have to. I'm quicker than you are- your ankles swell if you stay on your feet too long, you know that. I still don't believe that man is any danger to us. Whatever his motives are, if he intended to harm us we'd know it by now. Come on.'

The trees watched them as Ruth locked the car and they filed back into the house in silence.

Anna wondered why she had ever wished for this kind of solitude, and how she had thought it would help her.

It didn't feel like freedom; it felt like being caged, but without bars.

Trapped by trees and sky.

When they entered the kitchen, the stranger was sitting at the table, but still facing the French windows so that he could stare out into the garden. The inside of the house seemed even colder, and Anna watched Ruth button her cardigan. She checked the telephone line and her Mobile again, but all she discovered was a complete sense of isolation.

Ruth stood in the doorway, arms folded, watching the proceedings unfold.

Her sister pulled out a chair and sat down opposite the stranger, blocking his view of the window and thus interrupting his contemplation of the dreary land beyond.

'The car won't start.' she told him 'Somebody ripped the inside out during the night. If you know who did this, you have to tell us.'

His eyes fixed on her, attempting to penetrate through her skin and seek the thoughts and loves and losses that moved underneath, as if he wanted to peel back the layers of flesh and see her true bloody inside.

'We have no other way of contacting anybody. The nearest village is twenty miles away. It will take me hours to walk there. I'll do it if I have to, but I don't want to leave my sister out here if she's in danger.'

Anna forced herself to meet his stare, her senses unsettled by the connection between them.

'You have to tell me what you know. If I leave her here with you, will she be in danger? Will she?'

The dragging chair made her pulse skip as he stood up and broke the tension between them. He appeared uncertain for an instant, perhaps weaker than he had seemed moments ago when he stood at the window, and his hands gripped the edge of the table top as if for support.

He crossed the room and picked up a box of matches from the worktop next to the stove.

Ruth's eyes shadowed him across the room suspiciously. 'What's he doing?'

'How should I know? Answering my question hopefully.'

The stranger sat down again, heavily, and with a sharp intake of breath which told Anna that his injuries were still a source of discomfort. He placed the box in front of him on the table, and stared at it for a few minutes, leaning his head in his hands, his elbows on the wood, contemplating it as if it contained the evils of the world which the inquisitive Pandora had unleashed. His fingers finally pulled out the tray and turned it over so that the contents spilled out in an untidy heap. Taking a handful, he cleared a space and started to lay the matches out vertically in a perfectly straight line, ensuring an even space between each one.

'Oh Lord have mercy, either he's the fool or we are!' Ruth wailed.

'No.' Anna shook her head. 'It's the only thing he's done since he came here. It's an answer to every question. It has to mean something.'

'What? What can a line of sticks mean?'

The stranger's eyes caught hold of Anna's and glittered sharply at her before falling back to the pattern, taking another handful of matches and starting over again.

'I don't know.' Anna said softly. 'But I do know that working out what they mean is the only way we are going to find out what the hell is going on here.'

4

After a brief moment of silence, Anna made her decision. She was unsure if it was really the best course of action, but it was the only one she could think of.

'I'm leaving.'

Ruth's eyes looked startled again, constantly flickering between rationality and hysteria. The arrival of the stranger had unearthed so many things Anna had been hiding, and had forced her to examine them in the cold light of morning. She had discovered that she could not come to terms with Michael's loss here anymore than she could anywhere else. She had also been forced to admit to herself that she and Ruth had always been at opposite ends of the personality spectrum; other than shared childhood memories they had nothing in common. They were sisters biologically, but strangers in reality.

Right now, she was increasingly worried about Ruth's mental state. It had become apparent to her overnight that despite managing to hold down a position of trust in the local community, her sister was incredibly fragile. Ruth had spent most of her life in the shadows, lacking confidence and dealing with it by avoiding any deep relationship, either platonic or intimate, and using Christianity as a shield behind which she could hide from the reality.

Anna felt partly responsible. Since the death of their parents, she had barely kept in touch with Ruth. She had known that Ruth had chosen somewhere fairly remote to establish herself, but had never noticed just how isolated Ruth had become emotionally. She had allowed her sister to shut herself away here, a virtual hermit when she was not at work in the village. Nobody had noticed her transformation into a nervous, frightened sociopath because it had happened so quietly, in keeping with Ruth's nature.

'I'm going into the village.' Anna reiterated. 'It might take me the best part of the day to get there, but I don't see any alternative. We can't just assume that the phone lines will come back up again today, and I for one don't want to wait it out. He may not seem to be in any immediate danger, but we can't know that for sure. . .'

'The wounds really aren't that deep.' Ruth interjected meaningfully.

'He still needs to be checked over by a doctor.'

'I'm a midwife.'

'It's not the same, Ruth, and you know it!'

'Anna' Ruth's voice sounded as weak as a feather tossed in the wind. 'If you leave, I'm coming with you.'

'You'll slow me down.'

The tall man swiped his hand across the matches, destroying the sequence, scooped them into a little pile and then began laying them out again, like a fortune teller with a set of Tarot cards.

'You just said we ought to work out what he's doing, try and find out what it means.'

'We should, but you'll be able to do that while I'm gone. Give him some more paper and get him to keep writing. Eventually we might see some kind of pattern.'

'Anna, I don't want to stay here alone. I don't feel safe. Please. . .'

The stranger shot a glance at Anna, as if her response to her sister's childlike whimpering was of interest to him, but she remained silent, watching his fingers lay out the matches.

'How can you leave me here alone?' Ruth blurted out tearfully. 'I'd never do that to you. When we were children we always stayed together; we always looked out for each other. Why are you so different now?'

When no answer to her question was offered up, Ruth walked away, slamming the kitchen door behind her. Her flip-flops bumped upstairs, echoing down through the ceiling, and then the house shifted uncomfortably, like an old man turning over in his sleep, as the door to her bedroom closed.

Anna ran her fingers back through her hair. She watched the sticks run like liquid through the man's fingers, for a moment mesmerised by movement rather than concerned by its meaning.

Did Ruth have a point? Was she selfish and inconsiderate to even contemplate leaving her vulnerable sister alone with this stranger? Ruth might slow her down, but could probably manage the trek as long as they stopped to rest at intervals along the way. The man seemed strong enough to survive alone for a few hours while they went to fetch help together.

What if he wasn't? What if he suddenly took a turn for the worse and died alone, denying her the opportunity to help him that seemed to have been gifted to her in his coming here, an opportunity to exorcise her pain and guilt at losing her husband?

'He's not Michael.'

Thud-thud-thud.

She looked up from the table; the stranger let a handful of matches slip between his fingers.

Another visitor.

Anna threw him a glance. She wanted to believe that there was something positive waiting on the porch to enter and make sense of the confusion within, yet there was an awkward empty feeling spreading through her belly, a slow, swarming dread. It was the same sensation which had eaten away at her nerve-endings hungrily last night, while the stranger with the hollow eyes had pounded on the front door in the rain.

Now he was sitting here in front of her, and she was still unsure if he was angel or demon.

Thud-thud.

'I'd better. . .'

He grabbed her arm, gripping her flesh so firmly that she felt a sudden twinge of pain.

'Let go!' Anna said aloud, attempting to rise from her seat.

The stranger pulled her back down, fixing her with a cold, hard stare.

'I said, let go!'

Thud-thud-thud.

Perhaps she should have listened to Ruth. Perhaps they should have left him outside in the rain to die, callous as it would have been. It occurred to Anna that her sister might have been right all along; he had to be responsible for the gutting of the car, and now he wanted to keep them here, to isolate them, and she had been too blinded by the fresh acidic sting of her grief to notice. Now he didn't want her to open the door in case help might come from outside, and release his hostages.

Fear had risen into her throat, but she refused to be paralysed by it. Instinctively, Anna slapped the stranger hard across the face.

He let her go instantly, more readily that she had expected.

Not waiting around to see his reaction, she ran out into the hall, choked by anger and a sense of disappointment, desperate for the promise of help on the other side of the door. Her fingers worked on the latch; it seemed momentarily jammed, and for an instant she found herself imagining that the man in the kitchen had used some unearthly power to prevent her escape.

The door opened suddenly, and Anna stepped outside, eager for contact with another human being; a friendly face who might make sense of everything; a connection with the outside world she had left behind; a key to unlock the chains which bound her here.

Instead, she found herself alone on the porch.

A light drizzle was still suspended in the air. The barricade of trees which prevented their escape barely moved, and the hushed expectancy which often preceded a storm only heightened the sense of remoteness which awaited her.

Uncertain, Anna stepped off the porch and studied the narrow barely used track which led up onto the main road and towards the village. Her eyes slipped into uneven spaces between the huge torsos of trees, searching for a space where someone could hide. Discovering no-one, she decided to carry out a patrol, walking around the outside of the house, checking the back garden, and even opening the garden shed to check for intruders.

All her investigation revealed was that they were still alone; the situation appeared to remain constant.

It was only on the completion of her second circuit of their borders that Anna realised she was wrong.

Something had changed.

The car had disappeared.

Anna locked the front door, rubbing her arms against the increasing cold. Inside, her perception of everything had been rearranged by this latest development. Ruth was still upstairs, and in her nervous condition, Anna was unsure if revealing the disappearance of the car was wise.

Now, she must confront the evidence, and face a truth both she and Ruth had refused to confront. There was someone else out here with them, someone other than the stranger, someone who had trashed the inside of the car.

Someone outside who wanted in.

How had they towed it away, so quickly, so quietly?

Back in the kitchen, the stranger was busy making his matchstick patterns again. His left cheek had turned crimson and he did not look at her when she entered the room.

He had known, Anna concluded. He had known that there was something wrong, and had tried to stop her from going outside because he knew that there might be something darker waiting there.

'They've taken the car away.' she said aloud.

A shadow flickered across his face, and then dissipated, like ripples fading in ever decreasing circles across a still pool, until calm resignation remained.

'Why? You know why, so tell me. Are you in some kind of trouble, is there someone after you?'

Thud-thud-thud.

'Oh my God!' Anna said aloud.

The stranger looked up at her. His eyes spoke wordlessly.

'I shouldn't go out there, should I?'

Thud- thud- thud-thud.

'What will happen if I do? You know who's out there, don't you?'

The sound was growing louder, thundering through the house, as if someone was hitting the front door with a sledgehammer, like a demon child playing pranks, knocking and then running off to hide.

The stranger didn't answer, fixing her with a deadly serious expression. He wasn't asking her not to answer the door; he was ordering her, and the look on his face implied the danger which lay waiting outside in a way which required no verbal cue.

A chill had descended, so intense that her jaw began to tremble and she had to clench her teeth in order to stop them from chattering wildly.

The banging sounded through the house again; a battle of frost giants throwing rocks, and the whole structure seemed to be shaking.

'Okay, okay, I'm coming.' A voice echoed down the stairwell, accompanied by the familiar clip-clopping of flip-flops.

'Ruth, no!' Anna almost screamed aloud.

The stranger laid his hand on hers, his eyes imploring her to stay inside, speaking to her wordlessly.

She mustn't let them in . . .

'Ruth!'

Anna tore away from the man at the table and ran through the house, almost tripping over furniture as she tried to reach the front door ahead of her sister.

When she reached the hall, Anna already knew instinctively that she was too late.

The front door was wide open, and spots of water had covered the hall carpet in a haphazard design. She stood on the doorstep. Nothing appeared to have moved, but Ruth could not be seen anywhere in her line of vision outside.

Bewildered, Anna ran up the stairs two at a time, slamming open the doors of the upstairs room and yelling her sister's name. The rooms were empty, scenes vacated by the actors, only the stage props lay waiting to be used again. A bible lay open on Ruth's bed, her place kept by a set of rosary beads which Anna recognised as their mother's.

'Ruth!'

Running back down into the hall, Anna realised that for all their differences, there was a bond between them, and that losing Ruth would feel like having a limb amputated, torn off without anaesthetic, leaving gaping jagged tissue. ..

She practically tumbled out of the front door again, her boots skidding on the gravel.

'Ruth! Ruth!'

The trees and earth and sky, the walls of her prison, stared back at her vacantly, denying any involvement. She jogged the perimeter again, speckles of water hitting her face and biting her skin. The road was quiet and still, damp gravel undisturbed since last night's rain. It occurred to her distractedly that there ought to be tyre tracks in the mud where the car had been taken, but there were none visible.

Anna peered into the woods, the pungent smell of damp overgrowth entering her lungs with each breath. The trunks were too densely positioned for her to see anything more than a few metres under the lush canopy. She could have charged into the undergrowth looking for Ruth, but in which direction, stranded as they were amid acres and acres of unforgiving wilderness?

She screamed her sister's name over and over into the forest, listening for a response, but hearing only the patter of water.

Defeated, she turned back towards the house, tears clogging her throat and staining her cheeks.

The stranger was standing on the doorstep, resting his head against the frame wearily, eyes scanning the horizon.

Anna climbed up onto the porch.

'Where is she? What's happened to my sister?'

He did not answer; could not, perhaps.

'Where is she?'

Frustrated, Anna grabbed hold of him, her fingers sinking into her father's soft sweater, and started shaking him. She wanted to hit him, to beat him, to tear the truth out of him with her bare hands, but all the fight had been taken out of her, and she collapsed on his chest sobbing, as if somehow she had known all along that he had never been their enemy.

He held her for a moment, whilst she cried like a baby.

It felt as if something had broken inside of her, fractured, like jagged glass left hanging in a broken window frame.

It felt as if a part of her already knew that her sister was dead.

The stranger placed his hand under her chin and lifted her head up, forcing her to look into his eyes for a moment, then took her hand and led her back into the house.

Once inside, he closed and bolted the front door firmly.

Anna understood why.

He was trying to keep something out.

5

The world had grown darker.

Somehow, the light had faded, leaving a deeper shade of grey, although it was still morning. Alone in this monochrome nightmare, with a silent actor for a companion, Anna felt as if she was living in a stark expressionist movie.

She had tried to use the telephone, and been greeted with a disjointed and unsettling cacophony of creaks and rustles. The screen on her Mobile was blank too. The rain had started to come down heavier again, and the leaden sky was dissected occasionally by finger of lightning probing down through the clouds.

Frustrated, she had turned on the small portable television in the front room, in an attempt to discover if there was any news, any glimmer of hope that might reach them from the world outside. Instead, the annoying hiss of static had greeted her, a white screen covered by dots that resembled multi-coloured bugs writhing in unison.

They had sat alone together at the table now, barely breathing, motionless, for half an hour. Her eyes traced the grain of the wooden table top distractedly, searching for meaning in the patterns, concentrating so hard that knots in the surface became twisted grotesque caricatures acting out a macabre tableau.

Thud-thud.

At first it was a vague, distant stirring, echoing at the furthest shores of her consciousness, barely loud enough to tear her from the trance of hopelessness into which she had descended.

Thud-thud-thud.

Scarcely aware of her surroundings, Anna emerged from the coma of grief slowly, registering at first only the face of the stranger in front of her. His skin had lost any trace of colour as the temperature in the room plummeted; he displayed the first signs of being truly affected by any exterior stimuli since she had found him on the porch. He was shivering visibly.

A loud cracking, snapping sound broke the heavy air behind them.

Anna craned her neck around just in time to watch the moisture of condensation which covered the French windows instantly freeze into a layer of thin ice.

Her eyes widened, her heart bouncing against her ribs as terror descended with the cold.

Something rattled close by.

Her attention turned to the table. She watched as the stranger's trembling fingers placed the matches in straight lines, his jaw clenched with determination as he tried to contain the shivers which moved through his limbs.

Thud-thud-thud-thud.

The hammering echoed through the house again, breaking the air and filling the space inside each room, causing the building to shudder uncontrollably.

A rage began burning inside Anna, driving out the advancing chill of cold and fear.

She was tired of trying to read his thoughts. She was tired of trying to make sense of what was happening, of the series of disjointed inexplicable scenes which had presented themselves to her since the moment he had turned up on the doorstep. It was impossible for anyone to have taken away the car without leaving tracks. It was impossible for ice to form on the outside of the windows in the middle of a summer storm. It was impossible for her sister to have simply disappeared so quickly. Yet all of these things had happened, and although she did not believe the stranger was the cause of them, she could not put his arrival in conjunction with them down to sheer coincidence.

Anna had never believed in ghosts, spirits, angels or demons. A teacher, she had been trained as a rational human being. Choosing the solidity of the here and now over the promise of eternity in another life, she had rejected religion for the logic and reason she conveyed to her pupils. Now she was being forced to try and make sense of a situation which had no explanation which could be based in her scientific, earthy understanding of reality, and it terrified her.

The stranger knew the answer, hidden, buried deep somewhere.

Her hands slammed down on the table, making him start and forcing the matches to scatter in all directions.

'You know what this is!' she screamed at him, tears filling the spaces behind her eyes, struggling to break free but always contained. 'You know what's out there! You know what took Ruth, so why won't you tell me? Why?'

He stared at her, half bewildered, half surprised, then grabbed her hands and squeezed them hard in his, as if by making this contact she could somehow feel the answer through his skin.

'What does it want? Is it here for you? Does it want you? You brought it here, it took my sister, the least you can do is least tell me why!'

She closed her eyes against the memory of losing Ruth, of hearing Ruth's voice echo down the stairs, of Ruth disappearing into thin air, as if swallowed by the fog as the stranger had been in last night's dream.

'If I go out there . . .' Her voice came out in a jumble of disjointed syllables '. . . it will take me too, won't it?'

She winced as he gripped her hands, harder, harder, as if he wanted to grind her bones to dust.

Why had he tried to stop her from running outside, now and earlier, yet had done nothing to prevent Ruth from opening the door into the unknown? Why had she not been taken first, when the car disappeared?

Thud. Thud.

Slower, louder, heavier.

There was a splintering sound, like the cracking of wood.

'It's coming in!' Anna yelled. 'It's going to break through!'

Then silence, suddenly, swiftly, silence returning to the corners it had been driven out of. She felt her skin tingle, and her muscles relax as the room grew warmer again.

Her eyes flicked open.

The stranger let go of her hands. She stared at them, half expecting to see the imprint of his fingers burned into her flesh.

'Gone.' she murmured 'But it'll be back again, again and again, until finally it finds a way in.'

His fingers set the matches out again, using what was left on the table. She watched idly. There were exactly nine matches, a space, and then another nine.

The sound of the clock striking the hour in the other room, reminding them that it was two o'clock, disturbed her concentration. As the mechanism completed its mission, when both chimes had been completed, the stranger paused. He looked past Anna at the window, where the ice had melted into little rivers of uncertainty, and then carried on making little groups, eight sticks this time, then a space, then another eight, over and over.

Anna frowned.

It was like a tally chart, just as she had first suspected. He was counting something after all.

'It's the time.' she said quietly to the atmosphere, a startling realisation seeping slowly through her senses. Finally, it seemed she had fallen upon at least part of the answer to this nightmare puzzle. 'You're counting the hours down. You're marking the hours that are left.'

He looked up at her across the table.

'Left until what?' she asked, although fully aware that he would not respond.

She knew the answer already anyway.

'Until they come for us too.'

The light seemed to be fading still.

Two hours had passed and they had continued a silent vigil, rigid and still like two forgotten mannequins in a bizarre shop window display.

The stranger had given up spreading the matches out like a set of archaic runes, but had left the pattern set up in front of him, and studied it, as if searching for the meaning. The tap dripped steadily, and the occasional burst of rain played a restless tune on the window, but other than this background music, they breathed against the air in a quiet, frozen world.

Until a familiar sound entered, finding them through the gap under the kitchen door.

Thud-thud-thud.

A string of disjointed syllables tumbled from Anna's lips.

'Not again, please.'

The sudden rush of air made her ears pop like child's toy gun as the temperature shifted rapidly, attempting to force their bodies into a state of cryogenic limbo. Glancing behind her, she realised that the house was wearing a shroud of ice once more.

Thud-thud.

Scraping noises sounded overhead.

'It's in the house.' Anna screamed into the stranger's eyes.

The memory of her search of the rooms above during the small hours came flooding back. Had it been here with them then, filling the empty scenery in the rooms above, while the three of them slept, innocent against this darkness?

Yet the tall man's eyes told her more.

They told her he had glimpsed the dark heart of the creeping chill which stalked the upstairs rooms, a stealthy, sleek predator.

She remembered the slashes across his stomach she had seen when they first brought him into the house. It had let him escape, so he had come to them for help and brought it here. He had carried it to their door with him, a malign shadow, which had reached in and taken her sister.

What the hell was it?

Thud-thud-thud-thud-THUD.

Louder, harder, faster.

Scrape-drag-scrape-drag.

The skin of the stranger's face was rendered corpse grey by the cold. His lips were set against the chill, but his eyes held her, like Svengali hypnotising the ill-fated Trilby, as they had from the moment she had found him on the porch.

Thud- thud.

Drag-scrape-drag.

Louder, louder, louder. . .

'No!'

She stood up, arms tense at her sides as if she was straining against invisible bonds.

'No!'

Rising heat caused her flesh to prickle with the sensation of something cold and heavy, which had been crushing her spirit, being lifted away.

They were alone again.

The stranger buried his face in his hands as if to shut out the world.

All along, as the darkness had crept up on them, steadily moving closer, Anna had assumed that he knew the answer to the riddle, that he was the keeper of keys, the bearer of secrets. Yet now she suspected that if he were able to speak to her, all he would convey was a litany of fear, a lament of terror, an account of the nature of the thing which pressed against their world, a world now limited to the confines of the house. She did not think he knew anything which could help them.

Except for the straight lines, on his flesh, on the white paper, on the table in front of them.

If they were marking the hours, if they were an indicator of how long they had left before whatever was outside penetrated their defences, it meant he must have some insight into its nature, its motives, its intentions.

The possibility twisted and turned, reshaping itself inside the whirling vortex of fear rotating inside her head.

She came to a conclusion which ate away at the remainder of her hope.

Whatever the relevance of the straight lines, the fact that they were his only method of communication threw up a stark possibility. Perhaps whatever waited out on the porch had simply ripped his mind to shreds, torn out his reason, and left him a voiceless shell, a hollow reminder of the horror which awaited Anna at the brink of her sanity if she was forced to face it too, and of what her naïve, immature sister might already have seen.

Death or madness.

The devil or the deep blue sea.

Anna closed her eyes and wept silently.

'I'm going to look for Ruth.'

Anna proclaimed her intention with the knowledge that leaving the safety of the house, perhaps even the room, might be the equivalent of staring into the eyes of death.

Assuming he had already glimpsed that dark, loveless place, that precipice on the edge of madness, the stranger's reaction came as no surprise. His eyes reproached her without voice.

'What does it matter to you if I go out there? What does it matter to you if they take me? You didn't try to stop Ruth; you let her go running out there. Why stop me?'

Although she had become accustomed to attempting to fashion an answer out of the silence he gave her, weaving meaning out of invisible threads, the empty space which lay between them presented no clues this time.

Only that she mattered to him somehow.

'It doesn't matter what you think. I can't just sit and wait until they come for us. I have to do something. I have to find her. We don't know for certain that she's . . . beyond help. We ought to be out there searching for her. If you had any feeling, any humanity left in you at all, you'd help me.'

Frustrated by his apathy, she stood up, throat dry, skin still tingling, stomach churning, her whole system infected by the disease of trauma.

'I'm going. I'm not coming back until I find her.'

A sigh escaped his lips, a heavy clot of carbon dioxide bleeding into the air.

She was afraid to leave him, in case he was gone when she returned.

If she did return.

'I'm sorry. I don't want to leave you here alone. I don't want to go out there alone myself. It's part of the human condition, isn't it, our fear of death? We fear crossing over into the black, but most of all we fear slipping away without a hand to hold, or a lover's arms to cling to. That's why you came here to us, isn't it? You came for help, you came although you knew we could offer you no protection, because you wanted comfort from somebody, anybody. I want to stay here with you, but I can't just let her go.'

He stared at the drizzle outside, his eyes moving though her and past her, beyond the window, beyond the rain, to focus on a place unknown.

'I'm sorry.' she reiterated, shredded by guilt suddenly. 'I have to go.'

Anna severed the connection between them, the unseen cord which held them together, strangers, yet as interconnected as lovers, and walked out of the room.

Outside the kitchen, the grey light cast shadows across the room where they had slept the night before, whilst the storm raged outside. Everything remained in place, just as Ruth had left it. The house was quiet and still, immersed in an early Sunday morning hush.

Perhaps this was the calm before the storm returned, a maelstrom more malign than anything in her understanding, a freak of nature, another beyond her comprehension which was swarming, pressing, thrusting, against the perimeters of her world, penetrating slowly, like a hypodermic syringe sliding into flesh.

If she waited, she would lose all hope. She would retreat and hide; a shivering tangle of shattered nerves.

Determined to fight for survival until the last breath, she attempted to make her exit through the front door.

The stout oak construction was still in place, hinges intact, handle firmly closed, lock secure.

Everything was in place.

Except for the huge split running vertically down the door, following the grain, where the surface had buckled against the weight of the intruder.

Anna stared at the ruptured timber, temporarily turned to stone by fear. Everything she had experienced so far had been subtle; a sound, a vibration, a rush of air, objects moved by unseen hands. The physical manifestation of the presence which lay in wait for them chilled her to the core. Perhaps she had been still clinging to a shred of logic, to the vain promise of an explanation for everything which had happened in the last few hours that could be considered mundane. Perhaps she had been hoping that she might wake in the guest room and discover that she had been the subject of a bizarre nightmare, or better still, back in her old apartment a few weeks ago, with Michael sleeping soundly at her side.

Seeing this concrete evidence of the attempt which had been made to enter the house tore away this last vain hope, pulling the metaphorical rug from under her feet, uncurling her desperate fingers from the ledge of sanity.

Yet she couldn't let fear overcome her now. Despite the growing damp cold dread inside of her, despite her assumption that Ruth was already lost, she had no way of being certain. She couldn't face life, or even face death, until she had tried to find her sister, whether still living or a clammy corpse becoming rigid and hollow in a dark place somewhere.

Gingerly, she placed her hand upon the bolt and drew it back slowly.

The metal felt like ice beneath her fingers

When the defences were down, she paused before opening the door, remembering the moment when she had found the stranger on the porch, remembering the moment when her sister had run out into the unknown.

The door creaked open, jarring uncomfortably against the hall carpet before opening fully, perhaps as a result of its distorted condition.

Outside, a world of trees and rain and colourless sky still waited, unchanging.

Anna surveyed the panorama, preparing to step out into the rain in only her shirt.

The branches waved in a slow undulating fashion, almost hypnotic, a sea of misshapen limbs, beckoning her out and into the woods.

'Anna.'

Every muscle in her body tensed, and she became so still that it felt as if her blood had frozen in her veins.

'Anna, help me.'

It was Ruth's voice, but different, ethereal, echoing from between the trees to find her on the porch and call her out to play, just as she had heard it so often coming to her from beneath the apple trees in the garden of their childhood home.

'Ruth!' she yelled back into the shadows, and yet was reluctant to leave the transient safety of the porch.

'Anna, I'm lost. Help me find my way back, Anna, please.'

A cold grip of apprehension had tightened around her heart.

The heaving mass of green surged with a force far stronger than the wind, writhing and hissing, a deafening roar of splintering wood and slithering foliage. It was as if the trees themselves were beckoning her, twisting and shaking in an orgiastic ritual, designed to draw her out among them.

'Help me, Anna.' Ruth's voice wailed, descending into madness. 'Help me!'

'Ruth!' Anna screamed and headed out towards the perimeter of the trees.

She didn't make it.

The stranger's arms grabbed hold of her and held her back, bound so tightly around her that she felt her ribs would break.

'She's out there! She's out there, let me go to her, let me go! '

He tried to drag her back inside but she wrestled with him, tears blurring her vision, intent only upon being released and running out towards her sister's desperate cries. Frenzied, she clawed and bit at his flesh, beyond control, but he would not release her.

The air around them became strangely still.

The woods stopped moving.

Anna froze, as the tall man still held her, and listened.

Something heavy shifted in the overgrowth ahead of them. It sounded like a large trunk falling, but her eyes, still rooted to the place in the shadows from which Ruth's voice had echoed, could see nothing to explain the cause.

The rippling treetops continued their frenzied dance, faster, faster, leaves flying up in a whirlwind spiral, carried away by the breeze.

Something was coming towards them, invisible, moving through the forest unseen.

'It's coming!' Anna whispered.

Silent as always, he clenched her arms in his fists and hauled her back inside.

She watched as he bolted and locked the door with trembling fingers, whilst she stood beside him, shivering, rubbing the places where his hands had clamped down hard upon her flesh.

The stranger had stepped back from the door but a second when something heavy hit the wood straight in the centre. Anna started, staring at the place where the split had started, watching, transfixed, as the wood splintered further with each fresh blow.

He pulled her by the hand and led her back through the house into the kitchen, the foundations shifting around them as the door was continually battered by the trespasser. Once inside, he dragged the chair out violently, sat down, and closed his eyes, breathing rapidly.

He had known.

He had known it would not allow her to leave, that it would find a way to strike terror into her heart and prove she was helpless against it.

This was the reason for his lack of emotion, his inability to display any interest in her plan of escape.

He had known she would never make it.

He had know they would die here together, crushed into this room like sheep on their way to the abattoir, black eyes staring towards death in a cramped claustrophobic container.

Anna stood in the kitchen, watching the stranger. She wanted to take him apart in order to see what was inside and know why he had come here, knowing that death was his companion.

But even if she could dissect him piece by piece, like all creatures, the secrets of his heart and mind which inhabited a place beyond flesh would remain out of her reach.

Thud-thud.

She closed her eyes defiantly against the invading cold, but there was nothing she could do to keep it from coming at her, raking her skin, freezing the windows, sending a message deep inside, reminding her that each time it came, it moved closer to them.

Drag-drag-shuffle-drag.

Footsteps were dancing up and down the stairwell, so heavy that the owner might have been wearing concrete boots.

If she ran to look for them, she would find the rooms above empty.

For now.

Until the black found its way to seep between the cracks and fill the spaces in the rooms, in her flesh, in her head.

It was growing stronger.

It was almost here.

Only a few hours now until it burst in and devoured them whole.

Then the madness would find her too.

6

When the air turned black and the woods were strangely still, brought alive only by a symphony of raindrops, the noises became quiet.

They had been waiting in the kitchen for hours which had seemed like forever, barely moving, listening to the unseen hands pressing harder and closer, feeling the temperature rise and fall, each attack accompanied by a growing dread. It felt as if they were been watched somehow, as if they were imprisoned in a transparent cage, to be watched and prodded by the outsider, for its amusement, like a sideshow attraction.

Anna found herself thinking about Michael in the midst of all of this, as they waited, listening.

She could still remember their last moments together vividly.

It had been such an ordinary day. Bearing no sign or trademark to distinguish it as the day upon which her heart would be torn to pieces, how could she have seen it coming? There had been no premonition, no vague foreshadowing, nothing which she could have gleaned from their existence together, to let her know that the kiss she had given him on his way out, her eyes still clogged with sleep, would be the last they ever shared.

Now the stranger sat before her, laying out his pattern, keeping time.

The order had changed now.

His fingers placed the wooden sticks in pairs.

Two hours left.

Why couldn't they at least try and run instead of waiting to die?

Perhaps her mistake had been to try and go alone, blinded as she was by the loss of what had been her closest living relative. The fear of not knowing what was waiting for her out there in the woods was too strong for her to overcome, and she felt ashamed of this weakness, because it even surpassed her desire to find out what had happened to Ruth. This man had been touched by the darkness, and she had interpreted his silence as an illusion of the void it had left behind inside his head, but what did she know? Nothing made sense in this nightmare parody of reality; for all she knew he might know a way to escape it, as he had before no doubt, if only she could find a way to prise it out of him.

The telephone rang, a shrill sound emerging out of empty air.

Anna leapt to her feet, desperate for contact from the outside world, the world where logic and reason still prevailed.

She lifted the receiver.

An odd crackling hiss came at her down the line.

'Hello.'

There was something, distant, beneath the static, barely audible, but present if she strained her ears.

'Is there someone there?'

'Anna! Anna! Anna, help me!'

The voice was her sister's voice, but not her sister's voice, it was strange and low and disjointed, like the voice in the woods which had tried to lure her out.

'Ruth, is that you? Ruth.'

Her name was repeated, a dull hum, over and over again, under the interference and distortion.

The sound of the stranger standing up in the room next to her alerted her momentarily from the trance which the voice lulled her into, providing a vain hope that her sister might still be alive somewhere.

He crossed the room and stood in front of her, staring at her, and reached for the receiver.

'No!' she stepped back angrily and pressed it against her ear. 'Ruth, can you hear me?'

Her companion bent down to pick up something, retrieved the object of his desire, and held it in front of her.

It was the connecting wire, the tiny plug which should be inserted into the phone socket dangling on the end of it. She observed it, bewildered, whilst the eerie crackling grew louder on the other end of the line, and Ruth's voice tried to compete with it, resounding her name over and over until it became a roar, thundering out of the handset and making her ears ring.

But the line wasn't even connected.

Reason and logic had disappeared now, fading into the distance, slipping into the fog. Stunned, she allowed him to take the receiver from her, and put it down.

Instantly, it began to ring again.

Anna started anxiously as the stranger ripped the machine off the wall and slammed it against the tiles, causing the casing to shatter and the wires to become exposed, internal parts spilling out into the grey light.

Insides churning, she went over to the sink and almost vomited, but nothing came up from the pit of her stomach but water. She knew Ruth was dead now. What was left for them but to wait here to die too?

After a few minutes of leaning over the faucet, she ran the tap, gulped down a few mouthfuls of fresh water and splashed a little over her face, then turned back to face the stranger, who was sitting down again, playing with matches like a disobedient infant.

'Why don't we make a run for it, both of us?' Her voice was a ghostly thin sound in the middle of suffocated stillness. 'I can't tolerate waiting for it to come for us. Don't you understand? You escaped before, why not now? It's not that far into town, and you're stronger now. I think we could make it.'

As if in response to her suggestion, something shifted so violently that it made the whole room stir.

The blood seemed to turn to solid inside her veins.

A loud gurgling sound issued from the sink behind Anna's back.

It was a familiar noise; the sound of blocked pipes perhaps, a lump of leftover food causing an obstruction in the network which carried waste away from under the basin.

Yet the faucet had not been used for hours, and the low guttural grunt which had leapt out of it was far louder than it should have been.

The tap dripped; a fat blob of water falling through time and space.

As if in response, the plughole grumbled.

Anna edges away nervously. The stranger stood up, staring hard at the source of the vibration as if fascinated, like a child with a new toy.

Something was wrong.

Another water droplet escaped the tap, bigger, fatter than the one before. It fell heavily, and the pipes groaned back.

Anna watched the tall man move closer to the drainer and peer cautiously over the edge into the drain. She moved closer again, reluctantly, and stood behind him, waiting.

Each time the tap unloaded a cargo, the result seemed bloated, swollen, like a pregnant woman's belly. The drain wailed in response in a slightly higher pitch, a banshee cry reminiscent of the howl of the wind which had accompanied the storm and the arrival of the stranger.

He reached his hand behind him and pressed her arm, urging her back against the table.

'What . . .?'

Her eyes were frozen to the faucet as she observed a watery shape emerging. It was growing, yet did not fall down into the dark pipe below like its predecessors, but continued to expand and swell like a balloon being inflated slowly.

The drop became the size of a small potato. Its outer surface shivered and shifted as it grew. An occasional bump appeared during the change, which reminder Anna of the way in which the limb of an unborn child causes its mother's skin to bulge and ripple as it shifts in the safety of the womb.

The shape was as big as a grapefruit now, and still developing.

Stumbling over one of the kitchen chairs, Anna backed away behind the stranger. His expression was one of terror, but he did not look away. Another moan issued up out of the drain. The gurgling became a roar and the rush of water being thrust up from below, drawn back up from the sewers by some invisible force, filled the kitchen. Dirty dishwater, foul smelling, leapt up from the plughole to form a glistened bubble blown from an unseen wand, reaching up to embrace and taint its cousin above.

Both forms were taking shape now.

Fingers appeared, the contours of claws being drawn from rippling water flesh.

For the first time since this darkness had descended, a scream was ripped from Anna's throat.

Thud-thud-thud.

Behind them, the unseen visitor had begun hammering at the front door again.

Drag-scrape-drag.

The house was alive with the assault, with the fall of unseen feet in the rooms above, with the persistent knocking, with the gurgling hiss as a pair of deformed hands reached out towards the tall man with the hollow eyes from out of the sink.

Anna was pressed against the kitchen door, desperate to run but afraid of what might be outside.

The stranger stood his ground, watching the liquid apparition as it moved closer, sleek arms glistening in the half light, stretching out of the metal enclosure until the fingertips were inches from his face, poised to sink into his eyes and gouge them from his flesh.

As she stood, transfixed by fear, Anna realised that whatever happened in the brief time they had left, she was unable to watch him die in front of her. She was unable to allow him to walk into the eyes of death the way that Michael had walked out of her life that morning. This time, she had been given the foresight, she could see the reaper waiting, and she knew that even if it meant risking her own life, she could not allow the axe to fall again.

Too much had been taken from her.

In a sudden fit of desperation, she launched herself across the room towards the swaying, slithering transparent apparition.

Her body did not fall into its watery grasp. She felt her belly jarred against the edge of the sink as the water was rapidly sucked back into the pipes, disappearing into the darkness from which it had emerged, leaving her gasping for breath in the still, silent house.

She turned back to her companion.

'We can't just give up. Don't you see that's what it wants? We have to try and find a way out of here.'

He stared at her as if she were more incredible than the thing which he had confronted, a silent question posed by his eyes.

Anna answered it, despite her reluctance to expose the raw bleeding places where her loss was still tender.

'I lost my husband a short while ago.' she told him. 'He was stabbed to death. It appears. . .' She paused for a second in order to prevent her grief from breaking the surface. '. . . that I've lost my sister. I don't intend to let anyone else go without a fight. I refuse to just sit here and watch you die too.'

Without waiting for his response, and satisfied that the rest of the house had been vacated by the intruder, she resolved to make plans.

'I'm going to fill a bag with supplies.' Anna announced. 'Then I'm leaving, and you're coming with me.'

Time seemed to have elapsed far more swiftly than Anna had anticipated as she carried a rucksack downstairs, past the battered front door and into the kitchen, the slammed it down on the kitchen table. It was already dark outside, so she rummaged through the kitchen drawers and finally found a torch to add to the provisions. The walk into the village wasn't far, and she had a local map, but she wasn't under any delusions about the kind of danger they might face on the way.

This thing wouldn't just let them walk away.

The only weapons she could find were a couple of carving knives with worn white handles which looked like old yellowed bones. She doubted any physical ammunition would prove reliable against the kind of assailant they were likely to encounter, but at least some means of defence might make them feel more confident.

As she gathered the last pieces of equipment, the stranger ignored her, contemplating a single match placed in front of him on the table as if it were the last light source on earth.

Anna threw a worn anorak she had found upstairs on top of the bag which she had judged might be big enough for him. If the rain came down as heavily as it had last night they would both need protection from the elements.

'Put this on. Let's go.'

He looked up at her, eyes shrouded by a dark knowledge of things she had only briefly glimpsed.

'Now.'

His refusal to obey made her uncomfortable, although she was accustomed to this response by now.

'We're going. We need to go now before it starts again. If you're too afraid, then that's a good reason to leave because there's a lot more to fear in staying.'

Ignoring his silence she went back into the main room and pulled on her coat. A tension hung in the air, a crackling invisible force, like electricity; the feeling of something waiting to happen.

The television suddenly flickered to life, although the plug remained out if the socket. A white screen alive with swarming static illuminated the room. The little squiggles started to gather together, taking on a vaguely humanoid shape in the middle of the display.

Without waiting to see the finished result, she ran back into the kitchen.

'For God's sake, come on!'

A low rumbling echoed down from the ceiling above.

'It's coming!' The words burst out of her lungs sharply. 'It's coming! We have to get out of here now, please.'

Wood scraped the tiles as he stood up, pulled on the anorak and picked up the rucksack.

Relieved, Anna hurried over to the French windows and unlocked them. The attack always seemed to start from the front of the house, as if the invader wanted to appear like a regular visitor rather than a skulking burglar, so she thought they might stand a better chance leaving this way.

Her fingers worked the handle, aware of the man waiting behind her.

An odd stuttering sound echoed in the pipes under the kitchen sink. A series of short, sharp dragging sounds entered the room from above.

The handle squeaked as her fingers worked it, but the door did not open.

Perhaps it was just stuck.

Frustrated, she turned to her companion. 'It won't move. You try.'

He stared at her blankly.

'Open it!'

His fist clamped around the metal as she moved aside for him to take her place. She watched his knuckles turn white as he wrenched it back and forth anxiously, but they remained imprisoned.

Thud-thud-thud.

Something made the room shake, like the tremor caused by a small earthquake. The single match the stranger had left behind flew off the table.

'It won't let us go!' Anna yelled 'It's trying to stop us, but that means it's afraid we'll escape it if we leave the house, it means we might have a chance outside. Break the glass!'

The stranger stopped wrestling with the jammed door. He froze, his back to her, looking through the window into the dark garden where his reflection loomed out of the black, dissected by tributaries of rain.

Something was rearranging the room above.

Something was hammering at the front door.

Water instantly began gushing from the faucet.

There was no time to wait for his fractured senses to comply with her request. Anna lifted up one of the kitchen chairs and hurled it against the window.

It bounced back, like a child on a trampoline, and fell onto the floor, fractured, with one the legs sticking out at an awkward angle beneath it.

Frustrated, she repeated the action with its twin, and watched in despair as the second chair smashed back down against the tiles, remarkably still intact. Picking it up, she battered it against the glass relentlessly, over and over, until her arms ached and she let it fall.

The stranger was still watching his doppelganger in the door.

A low rumble was moving under the house, a sound like a juggernaut approaching on a quiet country lane.

Thud-thud-thud.

Something slammed hard in the other room. It sounded like the front door finally coming off its hinges.

Furniture was being overturned upstairs. The tinkle of breaking glass filtered down through the atmosphere

The roar below their feet grew louder.

Anna screamed as a split began to open in the floor, from the corner near the kitchen door. She watched in horror as it zig-zagged across the room towards her, throwing up tiles, exposing the black foundations, the heart of the house.

Stepping back to avoid being caught in the middle of the room as it was ripped apart, she found herself in the stranger's arms. He took her hands into his, staring at her blankly as if the end which faced them was of no consequence.

They were going to die here together.

He had always known it. Perhaps this was why he had made no effort to escape with her.

Insides swirling with the rapidly spreading disease of fear, the tears had dried on her cheeks as she slipped into shock. The house was coming apart around them now, but it seemed vague and distant. Only his eyes mattered, boring deep inside, seeing all of the hurt, feeling each of her losses. She realised that they had always been connected, since the moment she had found him on the porch in the storm. There had been an invisible cord, a telepathic line, which held them together in a permanent state of silent understanding.

At last, she understood the message he held. It was he who had trapped her here. He had been the outsider all along.

A low sound escaped his lips, the terrified murmur of a frightened child. He looked down, and lifted his sweater, staring at his stomach. Her eyes followed his, and watched in morbid fascination as the slits in his flesh ripped open, blood dripped down onto the tiles and splashing against her skin. A pair of dark writhing hands squirmed out into the light, glistening with the remains of tissue and shredded intestine, reaching out, to pull her in.

Finally, she knew what he really was.

Death.

Something razor sharp brushed her skin, creeping in between the folds of her coat.

A sudden pain gnawed at her belly, too intense to bear, a dull sting, like the burning of an avenging angel's sword searing through her flesh. The black shapeless shifting thing crawled out of his belly and slid comfortably inside her womb.

Everything faded, and although she tried to hold onto him, to stay awake, she swayed and collapsed, her head filled with an eerie bright light.

The outsider swarmed through her senses, invading each cell.

The world was still and black.

Darkness had found her at last.

The storm was rising again, wind howling through the woods and clouds of lead bumping each other in the atmosphere.

The stranger stood in front of the kitchen sink, inspecting the incision in his stomach, which had congealed already, starting to heal and fade. He washed his hands, and pulled on his sweater. Stepping over the body of the dead woman, he briefly regarded the place where her belly was split open from chest to pubic bone, and the remains of punctured vital organs draped like rags across the tiles. He opened the rucksack she had left on the table and withdrew the local map. His fingers flicked through the pages, and he studied them intently before closing the book, and dropping it onto the floor casually.

The rain had started to fall, hitting the window, tapping gently at first, a long lost friend come back to haunt him.

He could already feel something dark shifting and growing inside him. Something hungry.

The village was close, just a few miles walk away.

He opened the back door and looked out at the night, illuminated by the first flashes of lightning dissecting the horizon. Throwing a brief glance back at the ruins of the house, he stepped into the rain, and then wandered out into the woods, in search of another sanctuary.

James Howlett

THE DEVIL'S DOORSTEP

'Willie. Willie, come and look at this,' Jake urged impatiently.

Willie looked down from the top rung of the stepladder he was standing on at his young apprentice. He still kept his hammer in his hand and started to swing at the metal pipe he was trying to dislodge again.

Jake hopped from foot to foot, like he was standing on hot coals. 'Willie, I'm serious. You've got to come and look at this,' Jake pleaded. His voice was loud, but not so loud that the rest of the people working on this floor of the old hospital could hear him.

'Jakey, if it's another bloody great spider, I'm really not all that interested,' Willie replied whilst continuing to knock the pipe with his hammer. He reversed the head of the hammer and began to use the claw to wrench the pipe away from the concrete slab. 'Damn this bugger is stuck on here tight,' he said to himself.

'Why don't you just unscrew the clip?' asked Jake, his sudden urgency replaced by the matter immediately in hand.

This time, Willie did stop, resting the hammer against the top of the stepladder and turning round to face Jake. 'Because, numb nuts, the screw heads are rank. You can't get a driver in them. Give me some credit, please.'

'Right, okay,' Jake mumbled. 'But shit! You've got to take a butcher's at this!' Jake's eyes widened as he begged his mentor to leave the pipe alone for a few minutes and come with him.

Willie sighed, his shoulders sagging slightly as he did so. 'You're not going to leave me alone unless I do, are you?' he groaned. He began to climb slowly down from the stepladder. Once at the bottom, he dusted the front of his overalls down and faced the youngster. 'Okay, what is it?' he demanded.

'Follow me!' Jake cried and dashed off towards the stairs that led to the basement, picking his way deftly through the patches of debris that littered the floor like mines.

Willie followed, shaking his head, watching the thin frame of Jake skip through the rubble like he was playing a game of hopscotch. No-one paid him any attention as he crossed the litter strewn concrete floor, stepping over bits and pieces of broken furniture, concrete and light fittings. He squinted one eye shut and put a hand to his grey temple as someone started up a hammer drill and began taking lumps out of one of the walls. He had the early indications of a headache coming, and the hammer drill was like ringing the dinner bell. Clouds of dust enveloped the user, like he was being swallowed whole by some monster. Perhaps it was just as well he was taking a quick break, he hadn't got his ear defenders on him anyway. Jake was waiting for him at the top of the sweeping stairs that glided down to the basement.

'Jake, what have you been doing there anyway? We're not working on that floor until next week. We've got to have these two floors stripped out by Friday, and I doubt we're going to manage that on our own without any help. Do you wanna go and ask Geoff for help?' Willie placed his hands on his hips as if to emphasise his point.

Jake looked down at his feet and then dismissed Willie's negativity. 'Well, no, I don't. But just spare me a few seconds okay? Then we'll get right back to work.' Jake scuttled down the steps.

'Jesus Jake,' Willie grumbled under his breath and followed the young apprentice. Willie had given Jake the task of stripping out the light fittings ahead of the builders, who could then start their work. Surely the kid hadn't gotten so far ahead on his own that he had started on the basement? Sure, there was a reasonable pile of lights stacked in the corner, but Willie could see he hadn't finished this floor yet. So what was he doing poking around the basement? Well, at least he wouldn't have been on his own. He was pretty sure there would probably be a pair of plumbers down there too, but as he didn't really know any of them he just kept out of their way. As he got to the bottom of the stairs, he could see a pile of old light fittings and switches, sockets and the like all heaped together, which at least proved that Jake had been doing something. Willie gave them a cursory look as he walked past, over to where Jake was standing.

'Jake! I told you not to go near that thing! It hasn't been switched off yet!'

Jake was standing by the main switchboard for the whole building. They now four floors of the abandoned hospital: four floors which their company had won the contract for the refurbishment of the electrical services. But first, all the old redundant installation had to be removed, and fast if they were to keep on programme. The foreman, Geoff, had assigned one working pair to each floor of the building and Willie and Jake had got the first and ground floors. They worked well together as a team, and as such, had stripped the vast majority of the services out on the ground floor already. Most of the stuff that required two bodies anyway. Once this had been achieved, Willie had sent Jake down to the ground floor to get a head-start on things. The way things were going, it wouldn't be long before they would be finished and off-site for a few months whilst the builders came in and did their thing, erecting a wall here, creating a room there. However, Willie preferred to relax when he was on top of things, when the back was broken of the work to be done, not when they were half-way through. And things like his apprentice running off half-cocked and stripping things out here and there were an unwanted distraction. Still, he didn't want to curb the boy's enthusiasm. At least he seemed interested, unlike some of the other apprentices he had worked with.

The only thing that was staying in the building was the main switchboard, which provided power to everything within the old hospital. Of course, it was all but switched off, save for the fact that a power supply had been taken from the board to a nearby records building, which was to remain operational. People still worked in there, although Willie wondered how they put up with the noise at times. So they couldn't switch the board off until an alternative supply had been connected to the records building, which, according to Geoff, was scheduled to happen this weekend.

'You better not have been poking around in there, Jake. It's dangerous. 415 volts, it could kill you boy,' Willie said sternly. The switchboard was huge, around six metres long and three metres high. A lad such as Jake could easily have climbed inside if he wanted to, touched the busbars, and *bang!* No more Jake. Of course he was trusted not to, they must have taught him that much at college, Willie thought. Jake was a first year electrical apprentice and shouldn't be left unsupervised. Willie had taken a chance letting him out of his sight, but he had given him strict instructions not to go anywhere near the switchboard, or indeed anything that resembled a switchboard. Damn, the thing was covered in warning labels anyway, telling any idiot that might wander down here that the thing was still live. Still, Willie was both annoyed at himself and at Jake, for letting him down.

Jake looked hurt, as if he could read Willie's thoughts. 'I haven't been inside it, I promise. But look what's coming out of it!' he turned round hurriedly and went to one end of the board.

The only thing that should be coming out of the board was the supply cable to the records office and Willie could see that. It emerged from the steel side of the board at the other end and was clipped along the wall before disappearing into the respective basement of the records office. All of the other supply cables hung limp, disconnected, like a dead spider above the board, before disappearing through the ceiling slab and off to the other floors. So what was Jake so excited about?

Willie peered down the end of the basement and could see Jake's scaffold tower down there. It must have been where he was currently working, taking light fittings off the ceiling. 'Is that as far as you've got?' asked Willie, jerking his thumb in the direction of the tower.

'Err, yeah Willie,' answered Jake.

'Been taking your time, haven't you?'

'Well, they're big fittings to handle by yourself, you know.'

Willie laughed and shook his head. He couldn't be too angry, they were ahead of schedule after all. 'Heavy, right,' he commented.

Jake, meanwhile, had dashed off toward the scaffold tower.

'Now where are you going?' protested Willie.

'This is where I first saw it!' shouted Jake, who was almost at the tower already.

'For goodness sake,' Willie said and trudged off toward Jake. He was right about the plumbers, there were some down here, taking radiators off walls and removing the old air conditioning by the look of it. A few of them were looking in Willie and Jake's direction, the boy's shouting having grabbed their attention. Willie gave them a perfunctory nod as he walked past them, on the other side of the basement.

Willie made it over to Jake and stood next to him. 'Keep your voice down, Jakey. Whatever it is, I don't think it's wise if everyone knows about it just yet, okay?' Willie was scared of the boy making a fool of himself in front of this lot, site operatives could be a pretty unforgiving bunch sometimes. Even worse, he might make a fool out of both of them, and Willie didn't really need that. It was bad enough being called Willie, the name alone came with a lifetime's supply of knob gags that he had had to endure ever since the age where he could understand what was being said to him. Occasionally he was surprised by the odd original joke, but mostly, he had heard them all before.

'Look,' said Jake, pointing to the ceiling, which was pretty dimly lit down this end. The builder needed to rig up some more of that festoon lighting if they were going to make any significant progress down here. He would probably end up doing it himself.

'It's some ductwork,' Willie said flatly. 'If it's in your way, go and make a start somewhere else, the air conditioning boys will get round to it eventually.'

'No, look behind the ductwork,' Jake urged.

Willie squinted behind his glasses but couldn't make anything out. He climbed onto the scaffold tower, which was only three metres in height. He craned his neck around the ductwork, leaning across the outside edge of the tower and looked behind the duct.

There was a large cable clipped behind the duct. It had been sat in a channel carved out of the brickwork and the duct sat over it, almost as if the installer had wanted it to be concealed from sight. In fact, that must have been the reason, as no-one would put a piece of ductwork knowingly right over a large cable like that, it made no sense. Maintenance purposes for one thing. 'Wow, he's a big boy,' Willie commented. He looked away from the switchboard, along the length of the ductwork and the cable was running all the way behind it, right to the end of the basement, or so it seemed, as it was too gloomy down there to be really sure.

'Come back this way,' Jake said waving at him, and then scampered back to the switchboard.

Willie slowly clambered down the tower, dropping the last few feet to the ground. His ankle popped as he did so, reminding him that at fifty-two years of age, he really ought not to be jumping off scaffold towers, no matter how small they might be. Following the line of the ductwork back the way they had come, Willie knew what the big deal was before he got there. When he eventually did arrive, his suspicions were confirmed. It appeared that the cable was still connected to the switchboard, so must be drawing power to somewhere. Willie walked over to the front of the board and looked at all the fuses that protruded from its metal skeleton. Everything was neatly labelled, providing information on its former purpose, when the hospital was in use.

'Do you reckon it's still live?' Jake asked.

'Stand back,' said Willie and opened the switchboard door. Inside, it was quite dark, so Willie slipped his pocket torch from the front pocket of his overalls and switched it on. He crouched down low, and peered right inside the cubicle. He could see the busbars, and the protective devices that the supply cables would have been connected to. He shone the torch to his left, and there he could see the cable that fed the records office disappear into a fuse holder, which came out of the front of the board with a padlock on it, so it couldn't be accidentally switched off. That all made sense so far. He swung the torch to the right, and guessed at the spot where all the other cables came in. He was able to find that easily, as all the holes that the glands of the cables had been screwed into were now of course open, and letting in dim pools of light. Next, he shone the torch into the far corner of the board, trying to see where their mystery cable had been terminated. Eventually he found it, and to his surprise, it was connected straight to the busbars, without any fuse protection. Someone didn't want this cable to be turned off anytime soon, it seemed. So much so, that they were prepared to forego the protection of fuses and connect straight to the bars. This was highly unusual. He lurched back out of the cubicle and sat clumsily down on his arse, onto the floor.

'It's in there, isn't it?' Jake asked eagerly, crouching down beside Willie.

'Yep Jakey, it sure is. Connected straight to the bars too. Very naughty,' said Willie, switching the torch off and slipping it back into his pocket.

'Why would someone do that?' asked Jake.

'I can only think of two reasons. One, they didn't want anyone to be able to switch it off, and two, judging by that ductwork, they probably didn't want anyone to know it was actually there at all.'

'I did find something good, didn't I?'

'You've hit the jackpot, Jake my old son,' said Willie, getting back to his feet and swatting the beige coloured dust from his backside.

'How do you mean?' said Jake.

Willie laughed and clapped the boy on the back. 'Jake, you have indeed got a lot to learn. This here is what we in the trade call 'Bluey'.'

'Never heard of it.'

Willie began leading Jake back toward the scaffold tower. He wanted to try and figure out where this cable was going. 'We've been told everything bar that cable to the records office and this switchboard is coming out of this shithole, haven't we?'

'Yes,' confirmed Jake.

'Now, a survey must have been conducted to find that records office cable, and that's the only thing that is staying. The rest is junk. Of course, the guys back in the office know about all the other supply cables that are coming out, so we can't sell them for scrap money. But...' Willie trailed off.

'They don't know about this one?' Jake finished for him.

'I'm betting they don't,' Willie smiled. 'How would they know? It's connected into the back, there's no record of it on the circuit chart pinned to the front of that board. And he's a big bastard too. Gotta be at least a 185mm four core massive industrial cable, wouldn't you say?'

'Um, if you say so. I wouldn't really know.'

'No you wouldn't,' Willie agreed quietly. Jake felt that he wasn't really talking to him, he was deep in thought. He was saying words, but his mind was going ten to the dozen in some other place. For the moment, Willie was lost someplace else, someplace that perhaps Jake would learn the path to if he finished his apprenticeship. 'No, you wouldn't,' Willie repeated. Then, he frowned whilst looking at the ductwork that was concealing the cable from the general view. 'Jakey, go grab my hammer would you?'

'Yeah, sure!' Jake turned tail and sped off toward the stairs.

Willie hoisted himself back onto the scaffold tower and began knocking the ductwork with his hand. It was like he was listening for something. He put his hand on his chin and pondered. He looked both ways along the length of the ductwork. It came from the floor above in the same area as the supply cables and seemed to disappear through the wall at the far end of the basement, along with their mystery cable. Now Willie scratched his head and climbed back off the tower. He made for the stairs where only seconds ago his apprentice had scampered up.

Back on the ground floor, Willie waved a hand in acknowledgement at Jake who was jogging back to him, hammer in hand. Willie walked over to the riser cupboard where all the supply cables entered the ground floor. Sure enough, there they all were, thick black liquorice stalks popping out of the concrete and going straight up into the next floor.

Panting slightly, Jake stood next to him. 'Here's the hammer Willie. What you doing back up here? You could have got it yourself.'

'Cheeky bloody sod. You're the apprentice remember? Anyway, I'm an old man by site standards, a whopping fifty two years old and this is a young man's game, or say they keep telling me. Whatever. What's wrong with this picture, brain of Britain?' Willie gave Jake a friendly nudge.

'I dunno,' said Jake, shrugging his shoulders.

'Come on boy, think!' prompted Willie.

Jake stuck his head in the riser cupboard and abruptly jerked it back out again. He looked, non-committed, at Willie.

'Geez. Youth of today, eh?' he propped his hands on his hips, his favourite stance that let Jake know he was not performing up to scratch. 'Where's the pipe work?' he asked.

'What?' said Jake.

'Jakey, the pipe work comes out of the floor in the same spot as the supply cables down there. So where is it?' Willie said patiently.

'Maybe the air conditioning boys already stripped it out,' Jake suggested.

Willie rolled his eyes. 'So where is the hole, dickhead?'

'Hey,' said a hurt Jake. He looked back in the riser cupboard. Willie was right. There was no ductwork and no sign that any ductwork had in fact ever been there.

'What's going on, Willie?' he said, looking at his mentor for answers.

Willie hefted the hammer in his hand. 'Let's go downstairs and find out, shall we?'

Together they walked back down into the basement, passing the plumbers on the way down. They exchanged glances and managed a couple of 'All rights?' between them. 'Probably a good idea that we're on our own,' said Willie quietly, as they reached the bottom of the stairs.

'Oh no. they warned me about you. They told me never to get myself alone with you in a dark spot,' Jake laughed, backing nervously away.

'That's right,' said Willie, joining in the joke. 'I like to murder apprentices, smashing their heads into a bloody pulp with my special claw hammer.' He menacingly stalked Jake, hammer held aloft.

'You'll never catch me, old man!' teased Jake.

Willie dropped the hammer to his side. 'Not so much of the old, huh kid?'

Jake trotted back to Willie. 'I'm only joking, mate.'

'Yeah, I know, you little bastard,' Willie smiled. The look of unease on his face was wiped off like a sheet of dust and replaced with intrigue once more as they reached the switchboard. 'Right, drag that tower over here Jakey,' he instructed.

Jake gave him a mock salute. 'Sir! Yes sir!' he cried, before running off.

Willie looked after him, shaking his head. He liked Jake, but he feared the kid was just too damn nice to make it on a building site. Willie himself had learned to toughen up pretty quick back when he was a lad, it was sink or swim. If you showed any sign of weakness and you were working with the wrong bunch of blokes, your life could be a bloody misery. They could be relentless, worse than a group of schoolchildren picking on the kid that didn't fit in, but the mentality just about the same. It didn't help the fact that he had a baby face, with deep blue eyes set into a face full of innocence. That would be a great help with the ladies at some point, but it didn't endear him to his colleagues. The trouble with Jake was, not only was he a nice kid, but also quite naïve too. It was fine whilst he worked with Willie, but Willie wouldn't be around forever. He was going to have to have words with him, no doubt, for his own good, but not now. Right now, he was just as excited as Jake was about their find. This could be big. Copper prices were going crazy right now, just as bad as steel. The booming economy in the Far East was eating all steel and copper in its wake, driving prices back over in Britain crazy. A hideous scraping noise gate crashed his thoughts like a bunch of drunken yobs in a teenage slumber party and Willie looked over in the direction in which it came from.

Jake was furiously dragging the tower over to him, bumping over the debris and crushing it underfoot as he came.

'For Christ sake, take the bloody brakes off the thing Jake!' he yelled.

Jake had a wonderful baby look of stupidity come over his face for a few seconds and then he stopped, turned around and kicked the brakes off the tower. Suddenly, the tower glided much more smoothly along the ground.

Again, Willie shook his head to himself. The kid was hopeless sometimes.

Then he was there, the tower beside them. 'Right,' said Willie. 'Watch this.' He climbed onto the tower and leant across to where the ductwork gave the impression that it was coming through the floor. Then, he swung his hammer as hard as he could at it. There was a terrific *klang!* sound, and the bend of the pipe work came crashing to the ground.

Jake dodged quickly to one side as the pipe work landed, crashing onto the roof of the switchboard first, and then dropping over the edge to the floor. Nothing came out of it, no water, no hissing sounds of escaping gas. 'Bloody hell…' said Jake.

Willie stood proudly on the tower, swinging the hammer like a baton in his right hand. 'Thought so,' he said smugly. There's nothing in this pipe, never was, Jake. It's there purely to conceal this cable, I'll bet.'

'Why would someone go to such lengths to hide this cable?' asked Jake.

'That,' Willie said, 'I don't know. But let's see where it goes, shall we?' he dropped down from the tower, knees not ankles popping as he did so. He said, 'Come on,' and walked off toward the end of the basement, whistling tunelessly through pursed lips. It sounded like he was attempting a rendition of 'Dad's Army', but Jake didn't want to pick holes in his older colleague's whistling abilities.

As they walked down the basement, neither of them spoke. Jake kicked an empty Coke can along for a few metres, before finally running up and taking a hefty kick at it and sending it across to the other side of the floor with a noisy rattle. Gravel crunched under their feet as they walked, and every now and then, Willie, still whistling, would look up to his left as if checking the pipe was still there, although you could plainly see it was, going all the way to the end of the floor. The lighting down here wasn't that great, but there was nothing else on this side of the basement. The majority of the gear down here was heavy plant, and as such, it all sat on concrete bases in the middle, allowing access to it from all sides. Giant pieces of dulling metal with buttons and meters fixed to the front of them. Huge pieces of ductwork rose from the top of these machines and snaked their way along the ceiling to some greater purpose within the building. Their days of service were gone, and they were being honoured with retirement. Apart from the main switchboard, the electrical services down here were fairly minimal. Occasionally, a cable dropped down the wall to a socket outlet, but apart from that, it was just lighting and the pipe, but more importantly, what lay behind it.

As they neared the end of the basement however, it became apparent that the cable did not disappear through the wall like Willie had expected it to. Instead, hidden before by the lack of luminance, the cable snaked down the wall in its remora like state, still hidden behind the fake pipe and then vanished through the floor.

Silently, Willie aimed a kick at the pipe, and it broke away easily, leaving behind no trace of a hole in the floor and thereby completing its act of deception.

'Huh,' Willie grunted to himself. It was a good job he was wearing steel toe-cap boots, otherwise he would never have so blithely kicked at a six-inch piece of steel pipe. He could still feel the vibrations echoing through his toes, though.

'This is the basement, right?' said Jake.

'Last time I checked,' agreed Willie, bending down and running his fingers over the plastic sheath of the electrical cable. It felt warm, but that was probably the ambient temperature down here; after all, it was the middle of August and they were in a basement with no ventilation.

'So where does this go?' sighed Jake. He was tiring of the mystery quickly. He had been initially excited at finding it, but like most young adults, he was struggling to feign interest already. What was the big deal about a stupid lump of bloody cable anyway?

Willie meanwhile, was getting more intrigued by the second. But, he could tell his mate needed something to do, otherwise he was going to go in search of another bloody empty drinks can. And he wasn't sure his head was up to that. 'Jake?' Willie asked.

Jake turned around, hands in overall pockets.

'Do me a favour and pace out the distance back to the switchboard will you?'

'What for?' moaned Jake, sounding more like a two year old instead of a seventeen year old.

'So I know how much of this bloody cable there is, okay? Look, don't grumble, just get on and do it, will you?' coaxed Willie, trying not to lose his temper with the reluctant youth.

'Okay,' mumbled Jake and set off, taking huge dramatic strides as he went. He looked like a contender for the 'Ministry of Silly Walks'.

'Keep up those big strides now, no sissy steppin',' Willie teased.

'I know,' whined Jake.

Willie turned back to the cable, and the floor it seamlessly slipped into. He leant back against a large boiler, redundant, but as yet to be removed. The boiler moved a little behind him with his weight, and he very nearly toppled backward, which could have had some nasty consequences for a man of his age. Instead, he managed to get purchase on a steel upright and save himself from not only physical injury, but at least two weeks worth of piss-taking from Jake and no doubt, the other guys on the site. The boiler had given way to reveal the latest part of this conundrum; He could see the outer edge of a large trap door set into the concrete base, previously obscured from view by the boiler sitting over it. This was starting to turn into real *James Bond* stuff. Secret passages and everything.

Made of heavy wood, the door had a very succinct old feel to it, as if it had been set in concrete for centuries, as opposed to decades. This building was constructed back in the late sixties, so whoever had made these modifications and put that cable in must have done it sometime since then. Willie laid his hand on the wood and recoiled almost instantly, his heart skipping a beat. Unlike the cable, the wood was cold, a deep seated cold like holding a frozen lollipop in your mouth for as long as you could bear it. He knelt there for a few seconds, clasping his hand and looking accusingly at the door as if it had just reached out and struck him. Perhaps it had, a voice whispered in his ear. Stop it he ordered, right now. Frowning, he placed his hand back on the grain and traced his fingers along the knots in the wood. The coldness was still there, curling around the tips of his fingers and prising underneath his nails. He half expected to see vapours rising from the wood, but of course there weren't any. Stop scaring yourself old man, he chastised himself. He gradually acclimatised himself to the chill and inspected the door more closely. The door had no lock, and Willie supposed there was no reason it needed to, given the circumstances of its positioning. There was a large brass handle set in the middle of the wood, partially green with age and tarnished. He lifted it up with his hand and let it clunk back again. This sure was odd. Before he could explore any further though, he heard a yelp off to his right and from the direction of the switchboard, which sounded an awful lot like Jake. Willie straightened up and turned around to see what the matter was.

It was Jake all right, but more importantly, it was who was with him. Grabbing him roughly by the ear and jerking him back against the switchboard was Derek Sherman, who by a clear country mile was no doubt the biggest arsehole that Willie had ever met, let alone had to work with. He hadn't known whether this situation they had found themselves in would require Derek's involvement, and given a choice, Willie would rather have kept him out of it altogether. That wasn't possible now. This wasn't going to be pretty, but it had to be dealt with all the same. Willie began to walk over to them.

Derek was a tall, lean thirty year old electrician, with a pinched face and pursed lips that gave him the perpetual look of always being pissed off. Which he pretty much was. He was one of those people who looked like an arsehole and actually was an arsehole. What you saw was what you got with Derek.

'Hey Willie! What're you and the little faggot up to then, huh? Got something to hide have you?' Derek snarled, still pinning Jake by his ear to the metal frame of the switchboard.

Jake, ignoring the pain, roughly wrestled his ear free and glared defiantly at Derek. 'Geez you're a bastard Del,' he said.

Derek turned from Willie's direction and looked squarely at Jake. 'Shut up faggot,' he growled.

'I'm not a faggot,' mumbled Jake under his breath, absently rubbing his ear.

Derek's attention was fully on the approaching Willie now though, and for a moment or two, Jake was forgotten. He knew the old man and the little faggot were up to something when he couldn't find them on the ground floor where they should be. He hated Willie, he was a dinosaur who worked slowly and still thought things worked on a building site how they did twenty years ago. And he hated the faggot even more, cowering under the wings of the old fart, learning how to be a product of a bygone age from a teacher who should have retired or fucked off somewhere else a long time ago. It was saying something that Willie had never been a foreman in his life and now took orders from people younger than himself. This would never happen to Derek, he would make sure of that. And then he would be giving the orders to the old bastard and the little faggot. And then would their lives would be hell.

'Shouldn't you be upstairs Willie? What the fuck are you doing down here? We'll never get this strip-out done on time if you and the faggot are scuttling down here for some bum love will we?' Derek snarled.

Willie glared at Derek and then his eyes softened as he glanced toward Jake. 'You okay?' he asked the boy.

'Yeah,' grumped Jake defiantly, staring at Derek who did not bother to return the favour.

Derek stood his ground, not giving an inch as Willie walked right up to him. 'Come on, let's hear it Grandad. I've been looking for you for twenty minutes.'

'Leave the kid alone Derek, for crying out loud,' said Willie. 'You can't treat these kids like this. You've been warned before. The office will have your job.'

'Fuck the office. Who's going to tell them anyway?' Derek spat. 'You?' he said, looking at Willie. He turned to Jake. 'You? Don't make me laugh.'

Jake continued to lean against the switchboard and keep his mouth shut, which is what Willie would want him to do. He jammed his hands into his overall pockets and began playing madly with the handful of old screws he had amassed in there since he began taking the light fittings down.

Willie's face remained impassive. 'I'm trying to give you some advice is all.'

Derek snorted derisively. 'I stopped taking your advice five years ago.'

'You never took it in the first place actually,' Willie retorted. 'You don't listen to anyone.'

'Fuck you,' Derek countered, and began masticating wildly on the chewing gum doing the tour of his mouth, as if it was the only thing stopping him from killing them both.

'Look, for once, just listen to me, will you? Jake here has made a bit of a discovery,' said Willie, stepping away from Derek and over to the wall.

'Oh yeah? He's discovered he's gay?'

Willie let out a huge sigh. 'Derek, for fuck's sake, come over here will you?' Willie motioned Derek over with his hand. 'Look at this,' he said, pointing to the cable.

Willie then proceeded to explain to Derek what they had found whilst they walked the route of the cable, finishing up with the door in the floor. 'How many metres clipped to the wall, Jake?' he asked.

'Thirty, I'd say. Why's that?' Jake enquired as he brought up the rear.

Derek rolled his eyes at Willie and turned to Jake. 'Because, dickwad, I'd say that thirty metres of that cable is worth around six hundred pounds, melted down. Possibly even more, with copper going the way it is.' He turned back to Willie. 'Am I right?'

Willie nodded. 'Yep. And there's more down here, but I don't know how much yet,' he said tapping on the top of the door.

'Let's go and find out,' said Derek, leaning across for the door handle.

'Shouldn't we tell Geoff first?' said Jake.

'Shouldn't we tell Geoff first?' mocked Derek. 'We'll fuckin' tell him when we know how much of this stuff there is, hey Willie?' this was put as more of a statement rather than a request for someone's opinion.

Willie shrugged his shoulders. 'I don't suppose it matters either way, Jake. Probably is best to tell him when we know exactly how much we're dealing with.'

'Okay,' said Jake. 'Six hundred pounds? Awesome!'

Derek shook his head and tugged at the handle on the door. It lifted up easily and swung right back on itself, clattering against the concrete base as it landed. A small cloud of dust billowed up from it and joined the rest of the general dust that was circulating around in the basement like lost souls since the strip-out started.

Willie was surprised the hinges didn't creak, so old looking was the door. But it didn't make a sound and swung open as if it couldn't wait for them to come inside.

Before they could crane their necks and peer down into the hole, the darkness seemed to jump out at them, accompanied by a rush of cold air that took Derek by surprise but not Willie, given his earlier encounter. 'Shit, there must be some lights down there,' said Jake, who was standing behind the two men who were kneeling. The hole left behind by the door was deceptively large; roughly about two metres by two metres, two people could easily slip in at the same time if that were possible, which it wasn't, because the only visible means of access to whatever lay beneath was a rusty, not entirely safe looking metal ladder. It was roughly bolted to the concrete and looked sturdy enough, until that was, you noticed its rustiness.

'The plot thickens,' said Willie in a dramatic voice.

Derek meanwhile, had leant right in and was blindly groping around for a light switch. Although the top of the ladder was visible, the darkness seemed to eat everything else right up in its path. It curled up his arm and looked like it may try and pull him down there.

Suddenly, Derek lurched backwards with a yelp and a massive black spider came scuttling out of the gloom over his leg and into the shadows of the far reaches of the basement in a flash. The whole thing was over in a matter of seconds, such was the speed of the huge arachnid, but both Jake and Willie had recoiled in horror. Neither of them minded spiders, they kind of came with the job when you were stripping out. Lord knows, Jake had seen what he thought were some beauties on this job, but they paled in comparison to this bloody great thing. But this one was so big, you could actually hear the thing running away from them. Jake had only got a glimpse of it, but it had looked like a huge black hand fleeing for its life from some unseen predator. It had not even stopped to take a look around its new surroundings, instead it had simply seemed eternally grateful to be let out of whatever was down there and wasn't stopping to look back.

Derek, on the other hand, hated spiders. He got to his knees, looking in the direction of the gloomy recesses of the basement, trying to find the thing. 'Mother fucker,' he whispered as he started off in the apparent direction in which the spider had scrambled.

Willie caught his arm. 'Leave it Derek, you'll never find it in here. Besides, we've got bigger fish to fry, right?'

Derek looked down at his arm and then at Willie before nodding and turning back to the trap door. 'Mother fucker,' he repeated, as if swearing profusely would re-establish himself as the alpha-male in this trio. He leant into the gloom again, a little more cautiously this time, and there was an audible *click!* and Jake could have sworn he heard the murky shadows scream as they were torn apart by light.

'Ah, found the switch,' said Derek.

'And there's our cable,' said Willie, pointing to the left of the ladder.

Sure enough, the cable came through from the concrete slab above and was clipped down the wall. Now that the lights were on, you could see that the ladder must have been around ten metres in length before it hit the floor below. Then all you could see was bright light, trailing off into whatever lay beyond down there. The cable dutifully followed the light and disappeared also.

'Well, that's another ten metres, ain't it?' Derek declared, grabbing the top rung of the ladder and preparing to shimmy down. Within seconds Willie and Jake heard Derek plop onto the floor and shout, 'Old man and faggot, come on down!'

'Didn't realise we were in 'The Price is Right', did you Jakey?' said Willie, staring down the ladder also. He looked up at Jake, standing at the threshold. 'What's up kid?'

'What is this place, Willie?' asked Jake, looking apprehensive.

'Don't know Jakey, but you'll never find out standing there will you? Come on!' Willie disappeared from view.

'That spider was scared of something,' protested Jake.

'Yes Jakey. It was scared of *us*, now come on,' Willie urged.

Jake shook his head and followed his mentor into the depths beneath the hospital building and onto this secret floor they had discovered carved into the bowels of the earth. He carefully and methodically made his descent, rung by rung. Partially because the bloody ladder didn't look safe, despite it already handling the weight of Derek and Willie, both of whom weighed more than he did, but also out of an unpronounceable fear. He didn't know why, but his heart felt heavy and his mind was trying to tell him something, like a small child tugging at his sleeve, but he couldn't put his finger on it and the last thing he needed right now was Derek on his back again. The chill was still in the air, like he had stuck his head in a chest freezer. The rungs of the ladder were cold to the touch and felt like they were burning into his hands as he continued downward. Eventually he landed and let out a breath, which misted in front of him and wafted upwards. Was it really that cold? Jake breathed out again, but this time, he could not see his breath.

Jake was gob smacked by the sight that unfolded in front of him. Ahead, he could see his colleagues slowly following the route of the cable whilst soaking in their surroundings, which were amazing considering what had been built on top of it. They were in a room which resembled more of a tunnel in length, it must have been at least thirty or so metres long, but guessing the lengths of cable had never been his strong point, something which Willie forever teased him about. The room was like a vault, with a high ceiling that was richly decorated with various plaster sculptures and designs. There was a picture rail running at around six metres from the floor and it was above this rail that the unmistakable thick, black form of their cable was running. The picture rail certainly did not conceal it, more like take your attention away from it, as it was out of contrast with the older style décor of the room. There was no carpet, only floorboards that had a thick coating of dust laying upon them, showing up their footfalls, so the otherwise eerie silence was broken up by their echoing footsteps. You couldn't sneak up on anybody in here, that was for sure. The lighting they had found by flicking the switch by the trapdoor earlier was provided by hanging pendants, yellowy globes that hung from the dark ceiling like dying suns. It was enough to see the cable by, and to walk through, but little else. The other thing about this room that struck Jake was that it had no contents whatsoever. It was completely empty, devoid of any furnishings. It turned the room into more of an access tunnel, because at the far end, where the others had walked to, were another two doors. By the gesticulating that was going on, it looked like some kind of debate was opening up between Willie and Derek. Jake hurried over to see what was going down.

Both men glanced at Jake as he appeared next to them.

'Well Jake, what do you make of this place?' asked Willie, spreading his arms out wide like a circus grandmaster of ceremonies. 'Isn't it fantastic?'

Jake didn't think so. He thought it was downright bloody scary, but he wasn't about to admit that, especially in front of Derek, the arsehole.

Derek, as always, looked suitably unimpressed, and was in fact lighting up a cigarette. He sucked in a huge lungful of smoke and slowly exhaled it, tilting his head backwards as he did so. Jake looked back at Willie.

'What the hell is this place?' he asked both men, bewildered by his surroundings still. It was kind of like stepping back in time; the only thing he could begin to liken the room to was the entrance of the local museum, reeking of age and hinting at splendour past.

'I can only think it's some kind of secret floor,' said Willie. He sounded a little surprised, but not in awe like Jake was.

'Of course it's some kind of secret floor,' chided Derek, taking another hefty drag from his cigarette, like he came across them all the time.

Jake tilted backwards, looking overhead, lost in the sheer height of the room. 'How old is this place?' he asked, still craning backwards. Jake wondered where the constant undertow of cold could come from. Perhaps it was because the room was so big and so empty. Maybe that was it.

'Christ knows,' Derek interrupted. 'But let's not take our eyes from the prize, shall we?' he dropped the cigarette to the ground and crushed it underfoot. A small cloud of dust celebrated the cigarette's demise and Derek gave it a suitable send-off with a hacking cough. 'Our cable's going into this room,' he said, thumbing toward one of the doors they were facing. Indeed, the cable snaked downwards and passed through the wall to the side of the door. Derek tried the handle of the door and to everyone's surprise, it opened without even so much as a creak or complaint of any sort.

'Well, the surprises just keep on coming, don't they?' said Willie.

Derek just grunted and stepped inside. Jake waited behind, as there was only enough room for one person to enter at a time. Ahead, Derek had obviously found another light switch, as the harsh repeating *ting!* of a starting fluorescent tube could be heard, followed by a burst of light.

This room was much smaller and a more familiar sight to all three of them. It was around six metres by six metres and had bare walls, floor and ceiling. The single light fitting was enough to adequately illuminate the room and apart from the light switch by the door, was the only visible furnishing. The cable was here though; but all it did was run neatly clipped along the wall and out the other end.

'For fuck's sake,' announced Derek, spitting on the ground in disgust. He was not a patient man. 'At least we don't need no bloody scaffold tower for this bit.'

Willie nodded in silent agreement. 'Where's Jake?' he asked, turning around.

Meanwhile, Jake had been drawn from the room and to the other door. He wasn't interested in looking at more electrical cable, he wanted to know what the hell this place was, what it used to be. The room leading them here gave nothing away, apart from an indication of age perhaps.

Now, he stood at the front of the other door, which gave no clues as to what lay behind it. For some reason, Jake felt a heavy cloak of trepidation settle around his shoulders, like a teacher coming up from behind you and catching you in the middle of some naughty deed, as he placed his hand on the doorknob. Suddenly, his heart felt like an impossible weight in his chest and he wanted to sag to his knees. He straightened up. This was nonsense, stop it.

Just like its neighbour, the door swung soundlessly open. Before Jake could find a light switch, the lights came on by themselves. He jumped back, startled. Something pushed him forward, roughly.

'Relax dickhead, movement detectors,' Derek growled, shoving Jake into the room and pointing at the ceiling at the same time.

'This place is bizarre, isn't it?' Willie said as he stepped inside. 'First it looks like we've gone back in time to the sixties, then we're standing in an office with lighting controlled by bloody movement sensors. What next?' He laughed to himself in amazement.

This room, which by far was the largest thus far, was more in keeping with the décor of the floors above them which they had been stripping the services from. Another large open space, but this time broken up by small workstations positioned in every space. The whole floor was open plan office space, filled with desks, chairs and filing cabinets. The lights fitted into the suspended ceiling above their heads. Jake walked over to a desk and ran his finger over it. There was a heavy layer of dust settled over everything. No-one had been in here for a long time, it seemed.

'Christ, it's a whole other floor,' gasped Willie.

'Like a secret operations floor or something,' added Jake.

'Fuck off kid. This isn't *James Bond* for God's sake,' snapped Derek. 'It's just a disused fucking basement, all right? Now where did that cable go?' he walked over to the wall that met with the smaller room on the other side and looked up at the ceiling. He leant over and grabbed one of the dusty chairs from a nearby desk. 'Hold onto this,' he ordered before stepping onto it, lifting up a ceiling tile and poking his head above the suspended ceiling.

You're braver than I am, Jake thought to himself.

Willie, who had walked over to the chair and was bracing it, made a mock gesture to Jake of pushing the chair away, which would have sent Derek crashing to the ground.

Jake smiled silently and nodded eagerly.

Willie smiled and winked back at him.

Despite his friend's attempt at humour, Jake was not happy. It seemed to have gotten colder in here and he felt very apprehensive. Despite the lighting, shadows still managed to snake and coil in the corners, as if plotting something. The feeling that held him the strongest was that something had happened here, something bad. Of course he didn't know what, but he couldn't help the way he felt. He was beginning to wish he had never found the bloody cable in the first place.

Derek came down from the chair and kicked it away with his foot. The chair wheeled off and bumped into a desk. 'Yup, it's up there all right. Runs the length of this fucking floor too. Christ, we must be coming on for around eighty metres of the fucking stuff. Shit.' He took out his cigarettes and lit one.

At the end of this room, which was best described more as a floor in its own right, there was a corridor off to the right. They headed off in that direction, walking the central aisle down the middle of the floor. Deserted desks and chairs stared unseeingly at them as they went past. There must have been a lot of people working down here at some point, Jake thought. They're gone now though, a sneaky voice whispered inside his head. Stop it, he ordered himself immediately. For Willie's sake, if not your own.

It didn't help matters that judging by the state of some desks, it seemed as if people may have left in a hurry. There were overturned mugs, notepads with various scribblings and opened desk drawers everywhere. People didn't generally leave their workspaces in that state, Jake was certain. But the dust covered everything and gave him some assurance that if something had happened here, it had happened some time ago, leaving only whispers and echoes behind it, suggesting and hinting that something was once here. On one desk, there was a day-by-day calendar, and all three of them exchanged glances when the date it had been left on was 15/08/72. Had this place really been deserted that long? How come nobody had come back and cleaned the place out? They had just left, and even forgot to turn the bloody power off. This just didn't feel right to Jake, it was downright creepy. On the plus side though, he could probably sell most of this vintage stuff on eBay. There was bound to be some bloody collector of old office shit out there somewhere. Everything was collectable these days, you only had to watch television to see that.

So Jake just walked down the aisle, following the back of Willie's overalls and being careful not to tread on Derek's heels. That wouldn't go down well. He didn't need to see anymore of this stuff around him, he was on the verge of freaking out. So instead, he concentrated on the dusty imprints their footsteps were making and trying not to choke on Derek's cigarette smoke, which seemed to be hanging in the air for an interminable amount of time, almost like it was waiting for Jake to catch up to it, so it could drift into his lungs and make him cough.

Willie stopped and Jake bumped into him. 'Sorry,' he mumbled. They were at the intersection and to the right after a few metres, was yet another door. There was no need to check above the ceiling for the cable this time, however. The door had an electricity warning notice stuck to it.

'I'm betting our cable ends up in there,' said Willie.

Derek opened the door into another spectacularly undecorated room.

Except for one thing.

One entire end of the room was taken up by a huge switchboard, similar to the one upstairs that they had left some twenty minutes ago. Several green and red lights blinked on it, indicating that the power was very much still on. Willie and Derek studied the front of the board.

'All of the switches are off,' Willie remarked. 'Is it feeding anything?'

'Who cares?' sneered Derek. 'It's where our cable terminates.' He pointed to the cable which plugged into the top of the board.

'Uh-huh,' noted Willie. 'So it is. But is this board doing anything, Derek?' he placed a hand on its metal exterior and felt a mild vibration run through it. Electricity. How could this thing still be here, drawing power? Surely someone must know about it?

'How the fuck should I know, Willie? And anyway, no-one knows about this place, do they? Let's just rip this fucking cable out and go.' Derek stood back, facing the board, hands on hips. 'This thing is nearly as old as you, though.'

'Thanks,' mumbled Willie.

'It's feeding the lights,' put in Jake, standing alongside the two men.

'We know that fuckwit,' snarled Derek. 'We'll have to rig up some power down here, get some lighting in.'

Willie was nodding whilst still pondering over the purpose of a switchboard that had been left running for possibly some thirty years or so. 'This isn't going to be a five minute job, Derek.'

Derek looked at him with some hostility. 'I fucking know that. I fucking know that,' he repeated, looking at the cable. 'There's gotta be one hundred metres of this thing, man.'

Willie knew what was running through Derek's mind, but first, they had to actually get the thing out. 'We'll need Geoff's help. And Daniel's,' he said.

Derek didn't look pleased at this piece of information, but knew that Willie was right. He didn't have a problem with Daniel, he was his apprentice anyway and would do as Derek told him. But Geoff as well? Shit, that was a five-way split. He walked around the small room, pacing furiously and rubbing his chin.

Jake just watched him. He had seen Derek like this before, and knew he was on the verge of throwing a fit.

Willie continued, 'It's a five man job, Derek. Face it. There's still a hundred metres of the stuff, that's a pretty nice pay out for all of us.'

Jake was uneasy, and wasn't entirely sure what the big fuss was all about. It was only a little bit of scrap money, after all. This whole hidden floor was another deal altogether. Shouldn't people be notified about it? 'Um, don't you think we maybe should tell the office about this? We don't want to get into any trouble,' he ventured cautiously.

Quick as a flash, Derek roared and threw Jake up against the switchboard. 'Don't you fucking tell anybody you little prick!' he spat. He took hold of Jake by his lapels and had nearly lifted him off his feet. Jake did a mad pirouette on his toes as Derek snarled in his face like an angry tiger. Spittle flecked Jake's face.

'Let him go,' Willie commanded sternly.

Derek didn't even look at Willie. He was breathing heavily.

'What's the big deal?' Jake choked.

Somehow, Derek's grip got tighter around Jake's lapels as his fury doubled itself. 'You know how much that cable is worth?' he growled.

'That's enough!' said Willie and hauled Derek back by grabbing his shoulders. Derek released Jake and stumbled backwards, but kept his balance. He whipped round and faced Willie.

'Don't even think it,' Willie said calmly.

Derek glanced between both Willie and Jake, as if sizing them up. He was like a caged animal, looking for someone to take his anger out on.

Willie held a hand up toward Derek and turned to face Jake. 'Jakey, take a guess at the copper value of that cable when it's stripped and taken in to the scrap merchant.'

Jake shrugged his shoulders. Derek shot daggers at him, but said nothing.

'Come on Jakey,' Willie pressed.

Jake kicked his feet on the floor. 'Shit Willie, I don't know. Six hundred pounds?'

Derek snorted in disgust and Willie smiled. 'You're right Jake. Six hundred pounds, that's right.'

'So why the big fuss about...' Jake began.

'Each,' Willie finished.

Derek nodded.

Jake's eyes widened in realisation. Each? Six hundred pounds each? Now he was beginning to see what had got Derek so excited and why Willie was playing along with him. 'I see...' he said.

'That's *our* money faggot. You don't tell anyone about it. It's bad enough I've gotta split three or four thousand pounds worth of scrap with you, let alone you run around and tell everyone you come across. We'll end up with nothing,' said Derek.

Willie sighed. 'He's right Jake. It's a nice thing you want to do, but if everyone finds out about this cable, it'll be worthless. We'll spend hours stripping it out and end up with no more than fifty quid. The five of us can handle it, we just need to keep it quiet.'

Jake nodded, whilst re-adjusting his overalls from the mauling Derek had given them. He was wasting his time trying to reason with them. Derek he expected no more from, but he was surprised at Willie. Money corrupts, he decided. The thought of a six hundred pound unexpected bonus was a gratifying one, but it just didn't feel right. Quite clearly, they and nobody else was ever meant to find this place and he felt it should remain undisturbed.

'I know what you're thinking, Jake,' said Willie.

'Oh yeah, and what is that?' replied Jake, wincing at the spite that had crept into his voice.

'The cable would have been found sooner or later, and probably by other people,' said Willie, folding his arms. 'The switchboard is being retained, yeah?'

Jake just looked at him, rubbing his throat although the constriction inflicted by Derek earlier had long since departed.

'When the new cables were connected, whoever did it would have found the cable then. And they would have got the scrap money. How would you feel about someone like *The Happy Peanut* getting it?'

Jake frowned. He hadn't really looked at it like that before. *The Happy Peanut* was an arsehole he had worked with before being paired up with Willie. He was called Happy because he never was, and Peanut because his head was shaped like a peanut. And he hated apprentices, in fact, he seemed to hate anyone younger than himself.

Willie had known the right button to push. He didn't want The Happy Peanut to get anything other than his comeuppance. He still had the nagging persistence that they were doing something wrong, though. But now was not the time for this debate, he would speak to Willie in private about it later, he decided. He nodded quietly and walked over to Willie, making a deliberate show of keeping away from Derek.

'You with the programme, faggot?' Derek asked as they left the room.

'Shut up Derek,' Willie flared without looking at the other man. 'Let's go and show Jake's little find to Geoff and Daniel, then work out a plan of attack.'

Derek mumbled something inaudible under his breath as they walked back the way they had come.

It wasn't until they re-traced their steps that Jake spotted the steel door. At least, he assumed it was a door as it had architrave set around it, but no other indicator that it was an opening into another room. It was just a sheet of steel set into the wall with an ornate wooden frame. It was on one side of the floor, roughly in the middle, but set between two filing cabinets, one taller than the other, and depending on which part of the floor you looked at it from, sometimes it couldn't be seen. Jake also seemed to be the only one really interested in it too. He tugged at Willie's sleeve and pointed him in the direction of the gleaming door.

'Hold on a second Derek,' said Willie.

Jake and Willie picked their way around some desks and stood in front of the door, which contained no further evidence that it was a door, not even a handle or keyhole. Perhaps it was a blocked up hole.

'I wonder what's behind there?' asked Jake.

'In this place? Who knows?' said Willie, running his fingers over the architrave, which from this distance, Jake could make out was etched with dozens of intricate symbols and pictures. It must have taken a carpenter hours to carve that lot into the wood.

'Nice architrave though,' added Willie. 'That would look good in my living room, don't you think Jakey?'

'Suppose. I wonder what it's for though,' mused Jake. He leaned in to take in the wooden masterpiece more closely. The symbols and pictures meant nothing to him, they just looked like a load of mathematical equations gone wrong.

Just then, Derek's fist slammed into the metal sheet making Jake nearly jump out of his skin. Willie either didn't hear it as well as Jake or he had seen Derek coming up behind them.

'We ain't ever gonna know anyhow. We ain't got no machines that will poke a hole in this shit,' he commented while rapping his knuckles in various places on the door as if looking for a hollow point. There was none. 'We're only after the cable so who cares?' He turned and walked away.

Jake suddenly realised that there was a gentle but persistent waft of freezing air seeping out from around the edges of the door, as if it opened up to the arctic on the other side, and the arctic wanted in. The feeling of unease swelled in his stomach at this thought, like a balloon being blown up. Fortunately, before anything else unsettling could lay claim to Jake's senses, Willie made their move for them.

'I've had enough of mysterious doorways for one day, haven't you Jake?' He looked at his watch. 'It's time to put the kettle on anyhow, and I could kill for a cup of tea.' Placing his arm around the boy, he led them away and back out of the giant sized room.

Jake allowed himself to be sequestered, grateful for the welcoming embrace of the older man. All of a sudden, he felt like a very small boy and very, very afraid indeed.

They all sat in the site hut drinking tea whilst Derek and Willie explained to Geoff (and Daniel, but mainly Geoff as he was the foreman) about Jake's find. Derek had tried to put a spin on it by saying they all found it, but Willie made sure that everyone knew Jake had found it. It might help Jake's cause in the long run and besides, he had found it anyway. Derek and Daniel and maybe even Geoff needed to respect that.

'Found it whilst he was looking for some place to whack off probably,' grumped Daniel. He was a couple of years older than Jake, a senior apprentice and someone who had spent way too much time with Derek. In other words, he was an arsehole. He looked to Derek for gratification after insulting Jake, and duly got it in the shape of a friendly punch in the arm from Derek.

Geoff, a portly man of around forty years of age, removed his hard hat (some of the blokes reckoned he went to bed with the thing on) and ran his fingers through his tangled, sweat-laden brown hair. He set his mug down on the table, spilling its contents a little and walked over to his desks where he had all the plans and drawings of the building pinned to the wall. 'Around here, you say?' he said, pointing to the area where he thought the door in the floor was located.

Willie came and stood next to him. 'Yeah, that's about it.' He then proceeded to trace the route of the cable with his finger and showed Geoff where he thought roughly the sub-basement extended to. It seemed to be larger than the original footprint of the building, but it didn't matter.

When Jake had climbed up from the ladder and back into the original basement, he had instantly felt better, as if he had unburdened himself with some great secret and now he was finally free of it. He swilled the dregs of his tea around in his mug and stood up. 'Don't you think it may be better if we leave it?' he said.

Daniel spat his tea out on the table. 'What? One hundred metres of two-forty four core cable you stupid little shit? No way!'

They had mutually agreed from the size assessment given to them by Willie and Derek that the cable was probably a size larger than they had originally thought, and worth even more money. Geoff had said he would go down there with a tape measure later and find out for sure, by measuring the diameter of the thing.

Derek put his head in his hands and grumbled, 'Not this crap again.'

Willie shot Jake a look that said 'shut up' and turned to Geoff and said, 'Jake here is a little concerned that we may have stumbled onto some secret government place or something, and that we should leave it alone, that maybe it's still serving some purpose.'

Geoff just nodded and looked at Jake. 'And you think?' he said to Willie.

Willie lowered his head and stopped looking at Jake. 'The place is deserted, like I told you.' He then looked back up at Jake with eyes that felt their betrayal.

Geoff walked over to the table where Jake was and motioned for him to sit down. Jake did as he was told. He didn't know much about Geoff, hadn't heard much either, which was probably a good thing. Derek was always moaning about him, but then again, Derek bitched about everybody. Truth was, he was a little intimidated by the man, as he had direct links with the office, and the office could fire Jake. If they wanted to. So by and large, Jake had kept out of the man's way, but now he was sitting directly opposite him.

'Jake,' Geoff began, 'our contract here is to practically gut this place and start again, do you understand?'

Jake slowly nodded. Of course he understood that, he just didn't feel right about taking that cable, even if the place was deserted. How could he explain that to these guys? He had a notion that Willie knew what he was talking about, but he was blinded by the sums of money on offer. All of them were.

Geoff carried on undaunted. 'That's because this place hasn't been occupied for at least twenty years. That's why the stuff you saw looked old, because it is old.'

Derek and Daniel exchanged glances and rolled their eyes upward.

'You don't have to patronise the boy,' said Willie. 'He's not stupid.'

Geoff closed his eyes and let out a sigh. 'Fine,' he said in a much sterner tone of voice. 'I won't sugar coat it.' He leant forward, arms crossed across his chest. 'This is the deal, Jake. Well done for finding the cable. But we are going to strip it out no matter what you say, and you can either help us and take your share of the money or you can help us anyway and get none. Which is it to be?' he leant back as he finished.

Jake looked at the graffiti embedded into the fabric of the table from previous sites, trying to look distracted. Steve is gay, one scrawling announced. Jake went to college with Steve, and he didn't think he was gay. It seemed to be an obsession with people working for this firm.

'Jake, it's a five man job for sure. If you don't help us, we may not be able to get the thing out and stripped down to the copper before the rest of the other site guys come back and then it's all shot to shit,' Geoff implored, changing his tract. 'Or worse, the gypsies will come in and get it.'

'Ain't that the fucking truth,' Derek chipped in.

'He's right there Jake,' added Willie.

Indeed he was. There had been a growing number of people breaking into building sites this year, stealing mainly power tools and cable, for the copper value. They would really hit the jackpot with this one.

'Come on Jake, let me have a holiday somewhere decent for once,' laughed Willie.

'It's not like we're hurting anybody for fuck's sake,' whined Daniel, as Derek nodded his silent agreement at his statement.

The emotional blackmail he could do without, but it worked. Disgusted by their greed but ashamed of himself as he instantly thought about what he could do with six hundred pounds or so, he nodded and said, 'Okay.'

'That's settled then,' smiled Geoff and stood up. 'Now why don't you show me this big mother and we'll work a plan of attack out.'

During that afternoon, Derek and Willie went back down into the sub-basement with Geoff and showed him the pot of gold that was their cable. They were only gone for twenty minutes, but Jake had to admit he was relieved to see them come back up. Well, Willie for sure. The jury was out on Geoff but Derek he most certainly did not care about.

Geoff had left Daniel and Jake to take down the rest of the redundant light fittings in the basement and both apprentices did as they were told without speaking a word to each other, silently stacking them in one corner of the basement for the site labourers to remove at the end of the day. That was fine with Jake – as far as he was concerned, Daniel was just an apprentice arsehole, and nothing more. Besides, he didn't want the distraction of idle conversation when he wanted to keep an eye out for the world's largest spider. Several times he thought he had spotted it, but it always ended being a coil of electrical cable in a shadowy corner or niche, twisted stalks of copper that resembled huge legs to the over-active imagination of a seventeen year old boy.

They reconvened back in the site hut as Geoff outlined their course of action and who would do what. They all sat round the table, steaming mugs of tea in their hands. Jake had never drunk so much tea in one day on site, this must have been really something, he thought.

'Right, well the best day to do this will be on Saturday,' announced Geoff.

There was an audible groan from both Derek and Daniel.

'Problem?' frowned Geoff, bringing his mug to his lips and taking a huge throat searing gulp of tea. That was another indication of someone who had been on site for a while – the ability to take massive chugs of piping hot tea or coffee. An iron constitution came with the job.

'Arsenal are at home,' grumbled Daniel. Both Daniel and Derek had season tickets and were fervent supporters of the cause.

Geoff rolled his eyes and held up a hand. 'Look, it's the only way. The Electricity Board are putting on the new supply to that other office on Saturday, which means I can disconnect that cable from the switchboard...'

'...and our cable too,' Willie finished, as Geoff looked at him and nodded before taking in more tea.

Geoff wiped his mouth with the sleeve of his overalls. 'I don't fancy disconnecting that thing live, do you?' he asked the two football fanatics.

Both of them shook their heads in silence.

'It'll be on telly guys,' Jake offered, thinking he was being helpful, but he just got death stares for his trouble, so he turned his back on them and shrugged his shoulders.

'Do you want the scrap money or a home win?' asked Willie.

There were more mumblings from the pair and Jake thought he could make out the words 'scrap money' and he must have, because Willie finished with a 'Well, then.'

Geoff continued. 'It's roughly an eight hour job people. I reckon we can start on it at eight in the morning and if we crack on, we'll be done by four, maybe even earlier if all goes well.'

There was a murmur of approval at this. Perhaps the weekend was salvageable after all.

Geoff cocked a half-smile. 'After I've disconnected it, we can be as rough as we want with her. If Willie and I start unclipping it, Derek will manage the slack, Daniel, you can chop it into pieces with the chop-saw, and Jake, you strip it.'

All of them nodded as they were given their respective duties.

'Managing the slack isn't an all day job,' said Derek.

'How many two-forty four cores you stripped out, Derek?' asked Willie, smiling. Geoff snorted a laugh at Derek also.

'Haven't,' admitted Derek begrudgingly.

'Managing the slack won't be easy,' said Geoff. 'But you're right; there will be a few times when you've got nothing to do, so you can strip the insulation with Jake, okay?'

Derek looked over at Jake. 'Keep your hands to yourself, right faggot?'

Daniel sniggered.

Jake just looked at him. It wasn't worth responding to. Jake wasn't gay, and even if he was, Derek would be the last person on the earth he would consider doing anything with.

'Right, well the other thing we need to do is rig up some lights and power for the chop saw down there. It'll black as all hell when we disconnect that mother. It's gloomy enough already in places down there,' said Geoff.

Jake shuddered at this thought.

Geoff continued, 'Tomorrow is Friday, so I say Jake and Daniel go down there and rig up some festoon lighting and a socket for the chop saw, okay?' With that, Geoff stood up and walked his mug over to the sink in the corner of the site hut and began rinsing it out.

Jake's heart sank. He didn't want to go back down there anyway, let alone without Willie. Daniel, if he knew how scared Jake was, would do nothing but play cruel jokes on him the whole time. He had to try and get out of this predicament, but save face at the same time. He needn't have worried, because once again, Willie came to his rescue.

Draining the last of his tea, Willie stood up and went over to the sink, where Geoff was still standing, water splashes marking the front of his overalls like he had just pissed himself. 'Do you think it will be all right if I help Daniel, Geoff?' he asked, matter-of-factly.

Geoff looked as if he didn't give a damn, but still felt the need to question the logic. 'What on earth for Willie, that's a boy's job,' he commented.

'I know,' said Willie and then started grimacing and feeling around the base of his spine. 'But I think I tweaked my old back today, and it might be better if I just stick some cable to a wall then heft redundant light fittings around, don't you think?'

'How the fuck can you deal with that thing down there then?' snapped Derek. 'That bloody thing will weigh a ton.'

'Several tonnes, actually. He's right, Willie. Think you can do it?' Geoff asked.

'Yeah, yeah. I just need to rest it for a day, that's all Geoff. You know my old back. Just give it a day's rest and I'll be as right as rain, God's honest,' said Willie, making a slight show of walking to the door. 'Best I don't risk it, y'know? Besides, I want that bloody scrap money just like the rest of you lot.'

'Whatever. Fine, you and Daniel go and rig the juice up. Just make sure you get it done and we can see what the fuck we're doing down there,' said Geoff, lazily rinsing his mug out and setting it on the drainer with a thump.

'Hmph,' grunted Daniel. He looked at Derek, but he simply shrugged, looked away and pulled a cigarette out of the top pocket of his overalls.

'Right then, early shoot, people. We've got a big couple of days ahead of us, so let's rest up and get ready. It's half four now, but book the day. I'm going to get some quotes in for the scrap value of that cable and book ourselves in to deliver it on Saturday afternoon. I'll see you all in the morning.' Geoff ambled off into the tiny cellular office stuck in the corner of the site hut and shut the door, the nude calendar gently swinging from side to side like the pendulum of a grandfather clock as it closed.

'Laters chumps,' barked Derek and skulked out of the hut, followed closely by his lackey, who loped obediently behind him, like a dog following its master. He shot Willie and Jake a demented grin and then they were gone.

Willie stepped outside the hut and leant against it, fishing around in his pocket. Eventually, he found a cigarette and leant forward, cupping his hands to fend off the light breeze as he lit it with his lighter. He then resumed his leaning post, gazing out over the site that unfurled in front of him. Diggers, JCB's, bright orange plastic fencing and the sound of a hundred machines and various banging floated around his ears. It was a building site, and he loved it. Every so often, you could catch a glimpse of a fluorescent jacket as the workmen went about their trades, snatches of laughter and shouts competed briefly with the din of the tools they wielded. He turned his head to the sky and expelled a huge lungful of smoke.

Jake stood next to him, wanting to speak, but letting him enjoy the peace of his only cigarette of the day. He had given up, so to speak, when Jake had first met him, but had found it impossible. He had settled for a trade with himself. He stopped all the cigarettes bar one, which was at the end of his working day. He said it helped him to relax and that his wife would have a fit if she knew, as he had told her he had cut them out completely. Jake smiled at this story when Willie told him it, appreciating the little imperfection that Willie had confessed to him. There were too many people these days who thought they were never wrong, but Willie wasn't one of them. Jake's mother had always told him that a little humility didn't hurt anyone, but the way some people carried on, you'd have thought it would kill them. Still, smoke or no smoke, Jake had to speak to him. He walked around to the right hand side of Willie, so he would appear in the older man's view line.

Willie took another slow, deliberate drag, squinting one eye as the smoke drifted into it. 'What's up Jakey?' he asked.

Jake audibly huffed and looked at the ground, kicking the grit about with the tip of his boot. He managed to unearth a shiny silver screw that must have wriggled free from one of their overalls' pockets at some point. This screw became the focal point for Jake, as he concentrated on what he had to say to his mentor.

'I wanted to say thanks, Willie. Thanks for taking that job off me.' He finally managed to lift his head that suddenly weighed so much and look at Willie, who was smiling through the smoke at him.

'It's no problem, Jake,' he said. 'Any fool could see you didn't want to go back down there, especially with a snot like Daniel.' He took another measured drag from the cigarette.

'Well, thanks. But how did you know?' Jake said, feeling more comfortable now that the subject was out in the open.

'Because I know you, boy. But you'll be fine when we're all down there, won't you?' Willie's expression changed to one of concern.

You don't know me that well then, thought Jake. I'll never be fine down there, there's something wrong down there, much more wrong than monster spiders. 'Yeah, I'll be fine on Saturday,' he lied, putting on a false smile.

'Sure you will,' said Willie, dropping his cigarette and crushing it underfoot. He came forward and playfully cuffed Jake around the ear. 'Bloody boys,' he laughed. 'Let's go home.'

Friday came and went without much incident, the only notable thing being that Geoff showed them all a quotation he had obtained from City Cables, informing them that they would pay a total of three thousand three hundred pounds for the copper in their cable. It had taken them all a moment to take it in, seeming more real now it was written down on a flimsy piece of fax paper. Even Jake, who hadn't been all that interested in the money, had found himself during the day thinking about what he could spend six hundred and sixty six pounds or so on. He could give everyone a hell of a Christmas, that was for certain. Once this notion had caught in his mind, he suddenly didn't feel so bad about trespassing so to speak, and taking something that didn't feel like it belonged to him. His parents deserved a good Christmas, didn't they? And with the money, he could really spoil them. Yes, maybe it wasn't such a bad thing to do. He would do it for them.

Willie and Daniel fixed the lights and socket down in the mystery floor and Willie made no mention of it to Jake, save to say 'That boy worries me sometimes,' which was an obvious reference to Daniel.

Geoff went down and inspected their work and described it as 'sufficient.'

They had all made their respective stories to their partners and families about why they were working on a Saturday, and Willie agreed to pick Jake up outside his house at seven in the morning.

They were all set and ready to go.

'Okay, we're off,' signalled Geoff with a wave of his hand in the direction of the empty old hospital. He snapped his mobile shut and shoved it in his pocket. 'The electricity board boys have stuck the new supply in, so we can disconnect our cable and get the bugger out,' he added.

They shambled out of the site hut, the tea they had just drunk warming their bellies as it sloshed about. Although it was only September and what with global warming and all, there seemed to be an unnatural chill in the air. Jake hated to think what it might be like down in that spooky deserted floor they were about to descend into. Armed only with two pairs of stepladders, screwdrivers and Stanley knives (to strip the cable) they walked into the vacant, empty building. There was no overtime to be had on this job; they were completely alone.

Jake, being the youngest of the five, got the wonderful shoulder straining job of carrying the chop saw, which was bloody heavy. He tried to make it look like carrying it was no effort at all, but after twenty metres or so of uneven ground leading into the building, he had to change arms just to give his shoulder a break.

Willie looked behind him and said, 'You okay Jake?' which was an obvious reference to the chop saw and nothing else, except that his eyes asked a different question altogether. Well, it was the same question but it had a different meaning.

'Yeah, no problem,' Jake huffed, in-between taking in great gulps of air whilst manhandling his heavy load and trying not to trip up.

'Come on, keep up faggot,' Derek said without looking around.

'Keep up,' Daniel repeated.

Jake spoke Daniel's words back to him silently in a mocking parrot fashion and nearly did stumble over a broken piece of a wooden pallet.

When they descended the ladder into the sub-basement, Jake really did think his shoulder was going to dislocate itself. He had to carefully take one rung at a time whilst holding the chop saw down by his side. Willie eventually reached up from below and took it off him when he neared the bottom. The relief that flooded through his shoulder was nearly as great as when you finally get to piss after hanging on for a long time.

The first thing Jake saw when he touched down on the floor was a small portable generator that Willie had rigged up the day before. There were two leads coming off it, one that looped onto the wall where it was hastily clipped and disappeared in the direction of the cable. Around every three metres there was a light bulb protruding from it, and this would be their light from which they had to work by. It had been fixed above the cable, so when it came down, it wouldn't hit any of the bulbs, as the weight of the cable would smash them to pieces. There was one other lead coming from the generator, and it snaked along the floor in the same direction as the other one. This must have been the socket for the chop saw. Also placed here were several buckets, meant as receptacles for the stripped copper, Jake suspected.

Jake did not feel any better about being in the sub-basement for a second time. He looked around, buoyed slightly by the company, but unease still managed to creep beneath his jacket and infiltrate his skin like a draft coming under a closed door. Come on, he urged himself. It's going to be okay. There's five of us here after all. Nothing's going to happen, dammit. He jumped suddenly as Geoff spoke, and realised that this place was really getting to him, getting under his skin and into his mind.

'Okay, give me ten minutes and I should have this baby disconnected. When the lights go off, we'll know it's safe,' said Geoff, taking the first rung of the ladder to make his way back up.

'Sure thing,' replied Willie.

They stood in silence while Geoff clunked about above them. Jake took in more of their surroundings and in the distance, he could see the office area. The door leading to it had been propped open and he could make out the edges of desks and chairs. He kept expecting to see someone standing there and looking back at them, but he saw nothing. It was no good – he was determined to give himself a full-on case of the creeping willies come hell or high water it seemed.

Derek lit up a cigarette and began discussing the potential first team selection of the Arsenal side that afternoon with Daniel.

Willie turned to Jake. 'You okay mate?' he asked.

Jake nodded.

'That's my boy,' said Willie and patted Jake's shoulder.

'Faggots,' grunted Derek.

'Yeah, bloody queers, aren't they Del?' copied Daniel, desperate for Derek's approval.

'Well, considering you do everything that Derek does, I'd say that makes you the strongest case for homosexuality, Daniel. Do you love him or something?' Willie asked politely.

Daniel looked mortally offended and confused at the same time. Derek's eyes narrowed in Willie's direction but he said nothing and continued to work on his cigarette.

'Come on, do you?' pressed Willie, now turning to face Daniel full-on.

'No,' protested Daniel, looking to Derek for help and getting none.

Willie stepped up, nose to nose with him. 'Then shut the fuck up then arsehole,' he snarled through gritted teeth.

Derek stuck his arm between them both and pushed Willie away. 'Back off old man,' he warned.

'I've just about had enough of you too, fuck-head. Leave Jake alone,' Willie said.

'Or what?' growled Derek.

Jake did not like where this was going. He had never seen Willie like this, so angry. And it made him feel worse because he was defending him. These two bastards could do a right number on Willie if they wanted to, and it would be all Jake's fault.

Before it could escalate any further though, they were suddenly plunged into partially lit darkness, and it was enough to jolt them all back to their senses and remind them of why they were all here.

Derek leaned back toward the bottom of the ladder and shouted up, 'Yeah! That's it Geoff!'

Jake was not impressed with the standard of lighting down here. Sure there was enough to see the cable by, but only just enough to keep the liquid pools of shadows at bay. It seemed as if the blackness had now been compressed into one side of the room, rather than half of it being extinguished by the light. It was so black it almost seemed alive somehow. He didn't like to think about what may be lurking and prowling in the gloom on the other side of the room. At best, it was more monstrous spiders, at worst, well, it was God knows what. Jake was reminded of the film *Pitch Black*, where the monsters lived in the dark and the heroes had to stay in the light to survive. He'd be okay as long as he stayed in the light. He decided to stop looking around so much as well, he was frightened at what he may see.

Geoff came back down the stairs and joined them. 'Let's go,' he said.

Jake picked up the chop saw, Daniel picked up the buckets and they walked into the office section of the floor. It was a little way into here that the power lead finished. It was some twenty or thirty metres away from where they would be starting to pull the cable out.

'Ran out of extension leads,' Willie said as way of explanation for the extra walking distance that had been incurred.

'Fucking great,' moaned Derek.

'You'd rather have the lighting wouldn't you?' snapped Geoff.

Derek said nothing.

'Okay then,' said Geoff, point made. 'Jake, plug the chop saw in. Willie, Derek, let's go.' The three men walked down the office and turned the corner, to where the cable was connected into the switchboard in the tiny room.

Jake bent down and plugged in the chop saw. Daniel set the buckets down and fished in his pockets for a cigarette.

He couldn't help it; Jake had to look around. He could still make out the shapes of the filing cabinets and assorted pieces of furniture on the other side of the office, but part of it was only because he knew they were there. It was then that he noticed it – the door was gone. But it couldn't be.

Looking down at his feet, he shuffled to the outer vestiges of the illumination that was thrown from the temporary lights they had rigged up and squinted his eyes in the area of where he believed the door was. He looked back at Daniel, but he was merrily puffing away and glancing upwards at their cable. Jake looked back again. He could make out the two filing cabinets that had framed the doorway, but there was no door there anymore, only a huge black rectangle of darkness, a solid lump of jet black that was denser than the gloom surrounding it. Then it struck him, and as it did, a feeling like ice cold water flooding through his stomach blossomed in him and pooled at the bottom, freezing his intestines. The door was still there, except one thing had changed. It was open. It was open – and what had come out? His mind raced at a thousand miles an hour – it was shut before. How could it be open now? He knew, no matter how scared he was, that he had to go over there and see what lay beyond that black rectangle. Trouble is, he also knew that he couldn't go over there alone, he was still gripped by the childish notion that if he stepped beyond the light boundary, he would be swallowed up by the darkness forever. Perhaps, if he could go over there and see that there was nothing there to be scared of (but what if there was) he would settle down and get on with the job in hand without glancing over his shoulder every five minutes. He wiped his hand nervously with his mouth, and despite the chill that hung around down here like an invisible fog, there was a line of sweat on his upper lip. He had to ask for Daniel's help, there was no way of avoiding it. But he had to be crafty and get it in such a way that Daniel didn't cotton on to the fact that he was scared shitless. He noiselessly cleared his throat and said, 'Well bugger me.'

Daniel turned around and took the cigarette out of his mouth. 'What's that?'

Jake turned and looked at Daniel then back away again, trying to give the impression that he wasn't even talking to him. 'Huh? Oh, well, when we came down here before, there was a bloody great steel door over there,' he pointed into the gloom with his finger.

Daniel came and stood next to him. He peered into the dark. 'Don't see nothin,' he declared.

'That's because it's open now,' said Jake. 'It was shut before and now it's open. You know, that door was really thick and Derek said we'd never be able to open it.' Jake was deliberately baiting him.

'Really?' said Daniel. 'Whoever was down here must have been keeping something valuable in there, don't you reckon?'

Yes, thought Jake. Hooked him. 'I reckon,' he agreed.

'Wanna take a look-see?' said Daniel. 'We can keep it between us, if there's something good in there,' he said.

'Yeah sure,' replied Jake, doing his best to sound nonchalant, but he just sounded scared to himself.

Daniel stamped his cigarette out and produced a small penlight from his pocket. 'This should do us,' he said and walked off without a care in the world, into the roiling blackness.

'Wait for me,' blurted Jake. He was happy that Daniel was leading the expedition if he was truthful.

Daniel banged into a corner of a desk and momentarily stumbled. 'Fuck,' he said to no-one in particular. 'Almost a bloody dead leg there.'

Jake just made sure he kept safely behind him and didn't look around. Suddenly, he bumped into the back of Daniel, who had stopped in his tracks.

'Watch it you bloody mincer!' he snarled.

'Sorry,' mumbled Jake, not knowing what else to say.

Daniel shone the narrow beam of his penlight around the intricate architrave that surrounded the doorway. 'Well here's your answer, man. Your door is still here, only it's open, see?' Daniel aimed the light at the top of the frame.

Jake could make out the gleaming metal bottom of the door. It had slid upwards, like a portcullis. He looked into the blacker-than-black and it looked back at him. Cold flowed over his face like running water, but Daniel didn't seem to notice it. Either that, or it didn't bother him. Jake had the unshakable feeling that they were being watched.

'Here's why too,' Daniel said, now shining the light along the inside threshold of the doorway. Jake could see three magnetic locks, all open. When they had been released, the door had shot up. There were tiny neon indicators built into the locks, but none of them were illuminated.

'Shit,' said Jake, worried. When they had turned the power off, it had opened this door. He took an involuntary step backward, recoiling from the cold that seemed to be telling him it was okay to go in. The light came directly into his face and he held his hand up, shielding his eyes from the intensity.

'Fuck, you scared faggot? What the fuck are you scared about?' Daniel taunted. 'There ain't nothin' in there man. See?' with that, he shone his light into the gloom of the doorway. Jake followed the beam as it darted around the door and into the room beyond. And, to the naked eye, that's all it was. Another room, and empty too. There was something about this narrow little space though, that was different to all the others. Well, two things really. Firstly, there were no wall coverings, just bare stone, giving the room a resemblance to that of the insides of a well. Secondly, and more disturbingly, the only thing in the room was a manhole of some kind set into the floor. It looked very old, no council markings it seemed, although it was difficult to tell with only Daniel's penlight for illumination.

'Waste of time, man. We better get back,' sighed Daniel. 'Bollocks. Got my hopes up, that did.'

Jake cautiously stepped to the threshold of the doorway, a little confidence gained by the lack of anything materialistic in the room. So why was he so scared? It was fast becoming clear to him that this room, this threshold, was the source of his unease. But there was nothing there. Just then, he felt two hands shove him roughly in the back, and he staggered into the room, like an evicted drunk onto the street. Before he could think, he involuntarily let out a small scream, and he could hear Daniel, the bastard, laughing behind him.

'I knew you was scared, you little cocksucker! Have fun!' he laughed.

Jake came to a lurching halt at the other end of the small room, hands banging against the cold stone and jarring his wrists. He could hear Daniel walking off, as he banged into another desk on his way. He was absolutely shit scared. Then, he became aware of a scraping noise that seemed to be coming from underneath him. Ignoring the pain in his wrists, he knelt down, groping blindly in the darkness. The cold was coming from the floor and no doubt the stones that lined this room. Ice plunged into his kneecaps like daggers as he felt around the floor. His hands came upon what must have been the lip of the manhole. The noise had stopped, but he was sure it had come from beneath him somehow. Adrenaline had seized him and for the time being, had control of his fear.

The manhole rattled.

The brief adrenaline rush ended abruptly and Jake jumped up from his knees and ran, just ran. Within seconds he was out of the room and falling headlong over a desk, winding himself as it caught him in the midriff. He tumbled completely over it and landed in a heap on the other side. He didn't stop to worry about the pain that flared in his ankle though, he scrambled for the other side of the room where that arsehole Daniel was bent over, hands on knees, laughing at him. Jake careered into another desk and a couple of chairs before he finally felt the gentle heat of the temporary lighting bathe him. It was only then that he allowed himself to look back. There was nothing there, and if there was, he might not see it in this light anyway. Despite his fury at Daniel, he was nonetheless comforted to be in the presence of another human being, even if this one only just qualified as a human being.

'You fucking bastard,' he hissed at Daniel. Jake hardly ever swore, only in exceptional circumstances, and this certainly qualified as one.

'Don't be such a baby, you poof,' was the reply.

Jake was determined to make him see that he wasn't afraid. To admit to anything else to this tosser would be virtual suicide. 'You startled me is all,' he shot back defiantly.

'Yeah, right,' Daniel mocked. 'Startled you? You practically shit yourself! You should have seen it when you came outta there! You looked like you had seen the devil man!'

Perhaps I nearly did, thought Jake. It was no use trying to tell Daniel what had actually happened to him in there, though. He would never believe him, and it would just add fuel to the fire. Not to mention what the others would say when he invariably told them, the git. So instead, he settled for a plain old 'Fuck you,' and a two fingered salute.

Daniel just shook his head, and then turned in the direction of a noise in front of the two boys. From the far corner of the room, Derek appeared, grappling with a huge black snake, in the form of their cable. Jake had to suppress a snort - it looked like Willie was right; it was giving him quite a struggle. Shame.

'Don't just stand there fucking gawking, give me a fucking hand!' roared Derek, clearly annoyed that his struggles were a source of amusement.

Daniel started to move forward to help, but in that split instant, fear came crashing down like a badly fixed bookshelf on Jake's head, at the thought of being alone in the vicinity of that doorway. Before he knew what he was doing, he breathed 'I'll go,' and dashed ahead of Daniel, along the string of lights and toward Derek, who was an even bigger arsehole than Daniel, but was clearly the lesser of two evils at this stage. He could stand Derek's rudeness if it meant he didn't have to be alone back there, with only a strip of light to protect him, against whatever the hell it was that had tried to lift that manhole.

Jake reached Derek and placed his back under the heaving black liquorice stick that seemed to have a life of its own, and struggled in Derek's arms. Jake could see Willie and Geoff working the cable free from the position where it penetrated the switch-room wall. It was unclipped for about three metres on this side, and Derek was trying to take the weight so Willie and Geoff could have some slack with which to pull it through the wall.

'Don't...really want to have to...chop the bloody thing,' grunted Geoff in-between breaths, levering the cable upward and downward.

'Shouldn't need to...,' said Willie, gasping as he pulled on the cable.

Jake could feel the weight of the cable pushing down on him, it was a lot more heavier than he had thought it would be. No wonder Derek was struggling.

'You all right down there, faggot?' asked Derek.

Jake realised that was as close to concern that he had ever got from Derek, but it wasn't really concern for him. Derek didn't want him to hurt himself otherwise they might not get all of the cable out, which meant less money for him, Jake knew that.

'Fine,' replied Jake, tightly.

'Here it comes,' announced Geoff as the cable slowly withdrew from the hole like a penis leaving a vagina. They grappled with it briefly near the end, and then it came out completely, sagging instantly to the floor and toppling

Willie from his stepladder. For someone of senior years, Willie deftly landed on his feet, with the obligatory pop of a joint somewhere. Obviously, it was not the first time he had been forcibly ejected from his stepladder.

Without warning, Derek let go of the cable and hopped backward so it didn't land on his feet. The weight on Jake's back increased very quickly, and he pulled himself out from under it, banging the back of his head on the cable as he did so. He straightened up, rubbing the back of his neck. 'Thanks,' he said to Derek sarcastically.

Derek looked back at him and shrugged his shoulders as if he didn't give a shit.

Geoff climbed down from his stepladder and joined the three of them in looking at the fallen cable, which lay coiled on the floor like a slain sea serpent. There was about fifteen metres of it on the floor, and then it rose through the air and back onto the wall, clipped every half metre or so back in the direction of the trapdoor that led them here in the first place.

Geoff removed a grimy looking handkerchief from his pocket and wiped his forehead with it before saying, 'Warm work.'

Willie and Derek just nodded their agreement, but Jake didn't. He couldn't think how anyone could be warm down here, even if they had been straining with this monster cable when he felt so damn cold. It's because they hadn't been in that room, through that doorway, he thought. They haven't been touched by what's in that room. Haven't felt it.

Geoff put his grubby rag back in its home and turned to Jake. 'Get Daniel and bring that chop saw as near to here as you can. Drag the cable over to it and get chopping and stripping.'

Jake nodded eagerly.

'Off you go then,' said Geoff, waving his hand dismissively. He looked at Willie. 'Your back okay Willie?'

Willie gave him the thumbs up. 'No problem.'

'Then let's unclip some more of this mother,' said Geoff.

'What do I do?' said Derek, like a petulant child.

Geoff already had one foot on the first rung of his stepladder. He craned his neck over his shoulder at Derek and said, 'Those boys will need a hand managing the cable into the chop saw.'

Jake dashed back to the spot where Daniel and the chop saw were waiting, but only one of them was there, and it wasn't Daniel. The chop saw kept a lonely vigil in the languid light, like someone who had been stood up on a date. The black veil once more settled on Jake's heart like someone laying a new bedspread. The door got him, a voice whispered in his head. No! No! Jake silently replied. He whipped his head around from side to side, frantically looking for any sign of Daniel, but there was nothing. Jake started to panic, all of his fears flooding into his mind like a herd of stampeding elephants, uncontrollable, wailing and crashing off the walls of his skull. He didn't know what to do, so he yelled, 'Willie! Willie! Come here!' at the top of his voice.

It wasn't Willie who answered his call, it was Derek. He could make out his wiry frame stalking toward him and could catch snatches of some mutterings. Jake needed to compose himself and quickly, otherwise Derek would pull him to pieces.

'There a problem?' asked Derek sullenly.

'Yeah, yeah there is…,' said Jake, thinking on his feet. 'Daniel's gone.' He spread his arms out wide and turned around in a circle, emphasising his point.

Derek's beady eyes performed a quick scan of the area and came up blank. 'Little fucker,' he said quietly, and then looked at Jake. 'Bring the saw,' he snapped to Jake and then scooped down and picked up one of the buckets.

'Where the bloody hell is he?' asked an angry Geoff, from atop his perch on the stepladder. He had a screwdriver in one hand and a cable clip in the other. He carelessly tossed the clip onto the floor. Willie climbed down from his ladder and moved it to one position in front of Geoff's and began climbing up. He too had a screwdriver in his hand.

'I reckon he's gone to the loo,' said Derek.

'We all went before we came down here to avoid this exact sort of time wasting,' Willie complained.

'Yeah, we can't afford goddamn shit breaks every twenty fucking minutes,' added Geoff.

'I'm gonna kick his arse when he comes back,' Derek assured everyone. He dragged the end of the cable around in a loop and pulled it over to the awaiting serrated mouth of the chop saw. Jake levered the mouth upwards, allowing enough space for a short section of the cable to be placed in it. He slipped a pair of safety glasses over his face and started it up. His mind was going ten to the dozen thinking about where Daniel had gotten to. He hadn't gone to the toilet, Jake was sure of that. Daniel was the kind of bloke who would have just gone around the back of one of the desks or something, not walk all the way back to the Portaloo beside the side hut. Something had happened to Daniel, something bad, Jake was sure of it. It was the thing that had rattled the manhole cover. It had come out and took Daniel when he was all by himself. Jake shut his eyes and shook his head as if he was being bothered by a wasp, trying to dispel these unwelcome thoughts. He lowered the saw onto the cable and watched as it sliced through as easy as a knife through butter. There was a flurry of bright orange sparks as it bit through the copper and then it was through, the small piece of cable dropping to the floor on his right hand side.

Derek fed another piece through to him. 'We need another ten of those I reckon,' he said.

Jake just nodded and lowered the saw again, letting the grinding metallic noise fill his head and push out the ghoulish thoughts about Daniel. By the time he was halfway through, he was close to convincing himself that perhaps he simply had gone upstairs to the toilet after all and would come bounding down the corridor of man-made light any moment, full of excuses and a stupid grin. But the nagging doubt remained, only Jake gave it no room to breathe, to pollinate and infect his mind.

After ten minutes, he was through with the sawing, and sat back, pulling his glasses down to their former position around his neck. He was relieved to feel a thin line of perspiration across his forehead too. Genuine sweat this time, not fear induced sweat, brought on by the creeping willies. Derek was sitting around two metres away from him, a bucket beside him, and was busily stripping the PVC from the pieces of cable with his Stanley knife. He worked quickly and deftly, large bars of stranded copper sticking their heads out of the bucket as he plopped them in before carelessly discarding the gutted PVC husk into the gloom. He looked up at Jake and put the knife down. He stood up and dusted himself down before reaching into his pocket and producing a cigarette. 'Come and have a go at this shit,' he said, lighting his cigarette and turning his back on him. Quite clearly, it was not okay for Jake or Daniel to have a break, but fine for Derek. Jake expected no less than these double standards from such a git as Derek.

It was not long before it was time to chop up some pieces of the cable again. This time, both Willie and Geoff came down for their respective ladders and helped Derek to manhandle the cable into a giant loop, to feed it directly into the saw.

'Where the fuck is Daniel at?' growled Geoff, wiping the sweat from his forehead with his handkerchief, which looked in decidedly worse condition than when Jake had glimpsed it earlier.

Willie just shook his head and rolled his shoulders, as if to say 'Kids.'

Jake kept his mouth shut. No-one would want to hear his theory.

'I bet that little bastard has gone to the Arsenal game,' seethed Derek between clenched teeth. 'Yeah, gone home to get his bloody shirt on and sink a few pints in the local before the match.'

'He wouldn't have done that, would he?' asked Jake. Derek stared holes right through him. It was gloomy down here, but Jake could see his eyes glint with fury. 'I mean, he wanted the money didn't he?'

'Well, I thought he did, but obviously not,' said Willie.

'Fucking bastard,' put in Derek, clenching and unclenching his fists in a manner that alarmed Jake nearly as much as the thing in the room back there.

'Whichever way it is, it means two things,' said Geoff, placing his hands on his hips and admiring the cable on the ground as if he were the slayer of some mythical beast. 'One, it's more work for us, but two, it's more money for us. So come on, we've got to work harder. Daniel can go screw himself. Let's crack on.'

Derek grumbled under his breath and sulked back to his bucket to strip some more cable. Jake went to start up the saw again, but Willie stopped him. 'It's okay Jakey, I'll give it a go. You take five,' he said.

Jake got back to his feet from his bent position. 'Geoff, anything you want me to do?' he asked his foreman.

Geoff looked around him, as if he were looking for a job to spring out and present itself to him. Eventually, he turned around and said, 'Yeah, yeah Jake, I do. I've been thinking. I reckon it's probably a good idea if we don't leave any pieces of rubbish behind, you know, just in case? What do you think Willie?'

Derek looked up from his piece of partially stripped cable and said, 'Does it really matter?'

'I'm not asking you. I'm asking Willie,' said Geoff.

Derek recoiled as if he had been slapped in the face and it was all Jake could do to stop himself from laughing out loud.

'Wouldn't hurt,' said Willie. 'Just in case someone else does come down here or something. It's easier to invent a story with no evidence laying around. Yes, I think we should.' He motioned to Jake for his safety glasses and Jake took them off and handed them over.

'Right-ho Jake,' said Geoff, delving into his pocket. For a terrible moment, Jake thought the dreaded hanky was going to make an appearance. 'Here's a bin bag. Go and pick up the old cable clips and bits of stripped cable sheathing. Derek, better stop throwing it away and just leave it in a heap beside the bucket.'

Derek answered with a grunt and carried on peeling the layers of plastic away, baring the copper underneath.

Jake shook out the bag and began picking the pieces of litter up. There wasn't too much, and he was soon on top of it. He went over to Derek and bent over, picking up handfuls of waste plastic and putting them in the bag. Derek looked straight at him as he bared a huge piece of sheath and severed it quickly with the tip of his knife. He held it up to Jake as if to put it in the bag, so Jake held the mouth of the bag open for him to throw it in. instead, still looking straight at him, he tossed the sheath over his shoulder and into the darkness of the other side of the floor. Jake heard it land, bouncing off a desk before clumping to the floor.

'Fetch,' Derek whistled, and resumed stripping.

Willie started the saw up again, and for a moment, the sound was deafening. Jake stood at the threshold of the light spill and stared into the black once more. That fucking bastard, why had he done that? Now Jake had to go out there, into the dark and he knew something was in that dark. Something that belonged to the dark, was owned by the black but that wanted them. He took a hesitant step, but thought he heard something over by one of the large filing cabinets and quickly stepped back.

'You a scaredy-cat or something?' Derek taunted him. Jake could just about hear him over the noise of the saw. It was a good job that Willie couldn't hear him, Jake thought. He didn't know about Geoff yet, but Willie would have made him pay for it. As it was, he was on his own. He looked round at Derek, who was mocking him with his eyes. He knows I'm afraid, somehow he knows.

'Sod off,' Jake spat and before Derek had time to answer, stalked off into the shadows, and the black and the sudden blast of cold air that greeted his arrival on the other side.

Jake was more scared now than he had ever been in his entire life. He was desperately trying to convince himself that a draft had been the culprit of the rattling manhole lid, not some creature, some ghost, but every fibre of his being was screaming at him to get the hell out of this place, that was no wind and you're in danger. It was the body's own self-defence mechanism, the fight or flight response – and it wasn't interested in fighting one little bit.

But he had a job to do and three angry blokes after him if he left them as well. Daniel wasn't coming back – somewhere in his heart of hearts he knew that, but he had no way of explaining this to his colleagues, whose main interests lay in football and beer and things they could get hold of and stick their cocks into. But wait – he wasn't being fair on Willie, but it would be equally unfair to expect him to address Jake's childish concerns. It was akin to fretting about the bogeyman in your closet and Willie wanted that scrap money just as much as Geoff and Derek. And Daniel, but something had already ended his interest. Jake couldn't take that away from them, based on his childish notions and gut feelings. It wasn't enough.

Geoff reasoned they could still pull it off, still get the cable out and stripped and down to the scrap yard, so he couldn't be the one responsible for depriving them of their money. How he wished he had never spotted the bloody thing in the first place though. What at first had seemed an interesting diversion to him had turned into an exercise of greed and an excursion into terror, and he didn't know which one he was afraid of more. But he did, of course.

By arguing with himself and keeping in mental tune with the buzzing chop saw, Jake had managed to successfully put the brakes on the creeping willies for a bit, but now his line of logic had come to its natural conclusion, the dread started to trickle down his neck and trace an icy finger along his spine, whispering bad things into his ear. Hell, even the tiny hairs inside his ears were standing up.

In the dark, he could just about make out the edges of the desks and chairs. He put his hand out to touch the back of a chair, just to remind himself he was still in the real world and feel a solid object, but his hand passed through a spider's web, and he immediately recoiled, images of the gigantic spider of a few days ago scuttling through his mind on eight hairy legs. Surely it hadn't come back. Perhaps there were more of them, a whole nest...

Stop it. *Stop it*.

By sheer luck, his foot kicked something light, and he realised he had came across his piece of plastic cable sheath. Humming an inane tune in his head, anything to keep the fear at bay, he bent down and groped around the floor until he found his cable. He homed in on the tune inside his mind, trying to laugh at the fact it was the old 'Shake and Vac' theme. Funny what your mind does and the places it will go to to protect itself. Hey, I'm not scared. If I were scared, I wouldn't be singing this happy go lucky tune, would I?

Do the Shake and Vac and put the freshness back
Do the Shake and Vac and put the freshness back
When your carpet smells fresh, your home does too
Every time you vacuum, remember what to do
Do the Shake and Vac and put the freshness back

God that bloody advert. He had given his mum hysterics prancing around the living room with a vacuum cleaner when he was a kid, reciting that bloody annoying tune.

Something tickled his hand.

He let out a pathetic mewling sound, like a wounded dog and withdrew his hand as far back into him as he could. He cradled it with his other hand, like it was hurt. Something whispered along his knuckles and he jerked his hand up. The outline of his arm and hand were caught in the lights on the other side of the room. Jake could also see Willie, Geoff and Daniel, and mercifully, the all-out panic attack that had threaten to consume him abated enough for him to realise that draped across his hand, snarled in the crooks of his fingers, was a clump of hair. He frowned, then, that scary voice that had taken up residence in his head told him that beyond any shadow of a doubt that it was a piece of Daniel's scalp he was holding. He threw his hand down toward the floor and when he brought it back up, the hair was gone. By now, his heart had lodged a serious protest at its treatment and was threatening to go on strike. He could hear his heartbeat in his ears so strongly that he could have been on the dance floor in a nightclub. Dig that funky techno-beat, man.

Was this what it felt like to lose your mind?

Again, Willie, his saviour. Although this time, unknowingly. The saw whirring into action, cutting through the muddied waters in his head, the orange sparks leaping up, piercing the darkness like the fireworks on a November's eve. The sparks dropped down to the ground, but a red blinking light remained. It blinked on and off, on and off impatiently. Jake was in a mental fugue, but he blundered forward to try and find the source, after all, at least he was heading back in the right direction.

He was surprised however, to find the source of the red light to be right in front of him. There was an object on the grimy neglected desk in front of him that was flashing its red protests at him. The dark was even more disorientating than before. It was like he was swimming in it, and the other guys were actors under the spotlight at the other end of a theatre. You almost had to fight your way through it, it was so palpable.

It was a telephone. One of those old types, with the finger dial and the handset cradled at the top. It had a red light on it, and it seemed to be flashing even more strongly now he was closer to it. Like it knew he was there.

Someone was calling him.

Some*thing* was calling him.

And a ringing phone has to be answered, doesn't it, the voice coaxed him.

Hand trembling, bladder approaching bursting point, Jake reached out and carefully picked up the receiver. The red light stopped blinking the moment he did so.

Jake swallowed, and it felt like he had a whole apple stuck in the back of his throat. He had to swallow a second time to force the lump down. Shakily, he lifted the receiver to his ear. There was a muffled kind of static sound, like listening to a badly tuned radio station playing in another room. There were brief snatches of music trying to force its way through the white noise, but it never quite succeeded. Jake had heard nothing like it before, not even on the old radio stations Willie or his Grandparents would tune into. The only thing he could liken it to was something that might have been sung by Vera Lynn, some old wartime song or something. There was a voice warbling in there, but he couldn't tell what it was saying and an old clonky piano keeping pace with it all. There was something about it that was deeply unsettling. Then, much clearer than the music and sounding as if he were standing right next to him, he heard a voice. Daniel's voice.

'Jake, it's cold. It's so dark here and I'm cold,' Daniel pleaded. He sounded like a very frightened little boy, not some cigarette smoking foul mouthed arsehole of only twenty minutes ago. Jake tried to speak, but his mouth was completely dry and all that came out was a harsh rasp. *Do the Shake and Vac* Jake formed the words with his lips but no sound was created *and put the freshness back* and then Daniel's voice came on again, saying the same thing over and over.

'It's dark Jake, so very dark.'

The music still played in the background, competing with the white noise, but Daniel's voice overrode everything. Then, the noise pitched sharply and it sounded like someone was attempting to tune in to another station. The music faded away and gave in to a whistling static noise. Finally, there was silence. Nothing.

But not for long.

Do the Shake and Vac and put the freshness back

A sharp, brutally nasal voice screamed in Jake's ear. It didn't sound human at all. 'The door is open!' it whined. 'The door is open! One is dead! One is dead!' this diatribe was repeated over and over.

When your room smells fresh

Jake slammed the receiver down and then he noticed the blackness shifting, like a pool of ink in water. It seemed almost to part, although the surroundings were still very dark. But it seemed to somehow separate and there was a figure there. Right in the doorway. It was just standing there and Jake couldn't tell if it was looking at him or not, he couldn't make out any definition to the form at all. It lifted its arm and pointed at him. Jake didn't hang around any longer. He took two staggering steps backward, pushed into the back of a chair then turned and bolted back toward the others. He must have collided with just about every piece of furniture along the way.

Your home does too, every time you vacuum remember what to do

Dull pain throbbed in his thighs and hips from banging into too many corners and wooden angles. The din he was making got the attention of the others, who all stopped what they were doing and looked at him.

Jake, still clutching the bag of rubbish, lurched, tripped, staggered and fell into Derek, knocking his bucket over and spilling its shiny contents.

'Watch it you bloody moron!' Derek complained, rolling to one side to avoid the misplaced foot of Jake, who would have crashed into him. 'I've got me bloody knife out here!'

'Jesus Jake, what's wrong?' said Willie, taking a firm hold of Jake's shoulders in an effort to calm him. Geoff walked up behind him, a puzzled expression on his face.

Jake's eyes were wide open in fear and he couldn't form a sentence in his head. All he could manage to blurt out was, 'Do the Shake and Vac!'

Geoff laughed bitterly. Derek got to his feet, knife still in hand.

Willie's eyebrows furrowed in confusion. 'What? Jake, you're not making any sense,' he said. Willie then turned to Geoff and said, 'This lad needs a cup of tea.'

Geoff nodded and produced a flask out of somewhere. From the same magical place that Jake had not noticed before (a carrier bag slumped on the side of the wall) Geoff produced four plastic cups. He set them out on the ground and unscrewed the cap from the flask. 'Made it before we come out,' he said to everyone. 'Hope you all like sugar in your tea,' he added, pouring the first measure out into one of the cups.

'I don't,' griped Derek.

'I guess you won't want one then, will you?' Geoff replied testily, and made to take one of the cups back.

'It'll have to do I suppose,' said Derek, retracting the knife blade and tucking it into his pocket. He then produced a cigarette from behind his ear, as if he were some sort of illusionist.

Geoff set the cup back down and resumed pouring.

Willie had his arm around Jake's shoulders, but Jake still found the whole situation surreal. Here they were, taking bloody tea whilst god-knows-what out there was stalking them. He had no choice anymore, he would have to come clean and hoped they would believe what he had to say. There was someone back there, he had seen them. Already, the sensible side of his brain, the part that had been reawakened by Willie's touch was telling him it was shadows and nothing more. Fine he replied, but what about the telephone call then? Do the Shake and Vac, do the fucking Shake and Vac and put that fucking freshness back, man.

He refocused back into the world. Geoff was looking at him with a level of concern and holding out a white plastic cup with steam rising lazily from it. Couldn't they tell how unnaturally cold it was in here by now? Jake took the cup and took a small sip of its sweet warmness. It made his lips tingle and scalded the back of his throat, but Willie was right as usual. He was feeling a little better, and definitely able to tell them what had happened.

Willie took the rubbish sack from him and threw it by the wall, along with Geoff's carrier bag of plenty. 'Tell us what happened, Jake. Take your time,' he said soothingly.

Jake looked at Willie and was touched by the concern in his eyes. Willie seemed to know Jake better than anyone else at all, maybe even his parents and this sudden realisation made him want to cry. He suppressed the feeling by looking at Derek, who was watching him sideways on and blowing a thin stream of smoke out from between his lips. Geoff just stood there, sipping his tea noisily and watching Jake. He was probably pissed off at having to stop work, Jake thought. Jake took another sip of tea and attempted to make sense of what had just happened to him and in a way that he could relay it back to the guys.

Then, it hit him how to start it all. 'Willie, Derek, remember the door? The one made out of steel and with the fancy surround?'

Derek now gave Jake his full attention. 'Yeah, what about it?'

'It's open. I think we opened it when we turned the power off and now something has come out,' Jake splurted the last bit out quickly, as he felt the emotion rising up in him again. Willie rubbed his shoulder affectionately. This act did not go unnoticed by Derek.

'What do you mean, *something*?' asked Geoff.

So Jake told them about Daniel pushing him into the dank room, the manhole rattling and the telephone call. They all regarded him somewhat suspiciously, and in a way, Jake didn't blame them, not even Derek. It was a bit of a tall story, telephone calls from the afterlife. He purposely didn't mention the unease he had been feeling the whole time he had been down here, besides, Willie kind of already knew that, and it certainly wouldn't help in them believing the account he had just given them.

'I'll tell you what it is,' fumed Geoff, stalking over to the rubbish bag and dropping his cup in, 'it's bloody gypsies or the like, trying to scare us off.' He turned round, staring into the gloom, hands on hips in a double tea-pot stance. 'Well, it won't fucking work.' He stomped off into the dark, making for the doorway.

'Geoff, don't!' pleaded Jake, scrambling to get to his feet and after Geoff. Willie restrained him, and to tell the truth, it didn't take much of an effort. Jake looked at Willie. 'You don't believe me, do you Willie?'

'It's not that Jake, it's just that, well, you're...upset, is all,' said Willie, very carefully choosing his words.

Jake pulled insolently away from Willie's arms. 'You don't believe me,' he sulked.

'Of course he doesn't believe you,' put in Derek. 'Who the fuck would? What could have survived behind there anyway, if there was ever anything there in the first place? Fucking ghosts and shit. Man, you really are a faggot. Even senior faggot here,' he continued, pointing to Willie, 'doesn't believe you. You're full of crap.'

Jake looked at Willie, but Willie looked at the ground, at his feet, as if the answer may be right there in front of him.

'He won't come back,' Jake protested before slumping to the ground and finishing his tea in silence.

Willie and Derek looked into the dark, roughly at the same spot as Geoff had entered it, but he had been swallowed up. Willie knew approximately where the doorway was, some twenty metres or so ahead and to his left, but he couldn't make out much other than the edges of desks and backs of chairs caught in the soft glow of the lighting they had rigged up. Perhaps he should have put more lights up and Jake wouldn't have got spooked like this, but there simply wasn't any more left on site. Damn, something always had to go wrong, didn't it? To be honest, he felt Geoff was right. After all, they didn't know what the purpose of the doorway was, and if they had opened it by switching off the power, all they had uncovered was a manhole. It was quite likely it was just a secret passage that was used by whoever the hell worked down here at some point and they kept it locked up. Someone had found it, and when the door was opened, they were going to use it to sneak onto the floor. Possibly to nick their cable, maybe to do something else. It certainly wasn't ghosts or monsters, although he had to admit, the ambiance they were surrounded in lent itself to that theory. He was starting to see how a seventeen year old kid may have let his imagine run away with him.

Derek came and stood alongside him. 'You see him?' he asked.

Willie shook his head. 'Nope. It sure is dark around here, Jake got that much right. Didn't notice it before.'

'That's because it wasn't that dark before,' grunted Jake sulkily.

Derek grunted cynically. 'We turned the power off remember?'

'I know,' said Willie, and thought: maybe we shouldn't have. There wasn't even any noise coming from over there either. It was like the blackness had eaten that up too. Perhaps Geoff was tip-toeing, hoping to catch the invaders unawares, but how the hell he could see where he was going was another matter altogether.

Ten minutes passed.

'Told you,' Jake said smugly, but not feeling smug at all. 'He's not coming back.'

'Shut up faggot,' barked Derek. But for the first time since they had been down here, there was a trace of something in his voice, something a little akin to panic. Clearly, monsters or not, there was something going on here.

Willie thrust his hands in his pockets and paced around in a circle, muttering 'Bollocks,' over and over to himself.

'Erm, someone get that will you?' said Jake nervously, pointing to something over Willie and Derek's shoulders.

They turned around to see what Jake was pointing at.

There was a red blinking light screaming at them in the dark.

They had a telephone call.

'It's for you,' Derek jerked his thumb in the direction of the telephone, looking at Jake.

'It's for all of us arsehole,' Willie growled. 'We'll all go. Come on Jake.'

Jake got to his feet. At least he wouldn't have to face this one alone.

Keeping huddled close to each other, they shuffled into the dark toward the beacon of red light. It wasn't all that far away, it was just the density of the blackness that made it seem a long way off. They reached the desk. It wasn't the same phone as before, Jake was sure of that. They weren't as far away from the light as he had been. Derek looked around them, searching for any sign of people, but found none.

Willie reached out for the receiver, but Jake suddenly found a new lease of courage and pushed his arm out of the way. 'I'll get it. You just listen in.' He was surprised at the small shaft of steel that had crept into his voice. It didn't sound like him, he sounded more like his dad when he was in trouble at home, getting told off for coming in late at night or something. Not harsh, but showing an inner strength.

He picked the receiver up and held it loosely to his ear. Derek leaned in on one side and Willie from the other. He could hear their breathing, shallow and fast. They were scared too, but just wouldn't admit it.

The music started up again, same as before.

'This is what it did last time,' Jake whispered.

Then, a voice. It was hard to make out if it was Daniel or Geoff because now it was competing with the music which was much louder and it wasn't like that before. There were snatches of words like 'cold' and 'dark' but it was impossible to link it into anything coherent.

Then white noise drowned everything out before it was followed by the dreaded silence, and then the nasally voice was back.

'The door is open! The door is open! Two are dead! Two are dead!'

Willie placed his hand quickly over Jake's and crashed the receiver down back in its cradle. 'That's quite enough of that,' he said firmly.

They shuffled back in double quick time to the welcoming light. It was here they all felt safer in having a discussion about what had just happened. The light they were standing in wasn't the most flattering, but Jake thought that Willie and Derek were as white as sheets.

'I tell you, it's both of them fucking with us,' insisted Derek. 'Geoff set us up a treat. Him and that little bastard Daniel are going to scare us off and then get the cable for themselves.' He lit up a cigarette, presumably to calm his nerves.

'You could be right,' said Willie. He preferred this explanation to Jake's, any day of the week. 'You got one of those I can have?'

'You don't smoke,' retorted Derek.

Willie looked at the floor. 'No, I don't,' he sighed.

Come on guys,' pleaded Jake, 'it was just like I said, wasn't it?'

'Yeah, actually it was. You in on this then, faggot?' Derek's eyes narrowed and he bit down on his cigarette, gripping it vice-like between his teeth. Smoke partially obscured his face, but Jake knew what it looked like anyway. He had frequently seen Derek like this.

'Don't be stupid,' said Willie. 'We're in this together, us three,' he stated.

Derek gave up just like that, showing he didn't really believe what he had just said either, but it helped him to get mad instead of getting scared.

Jake noticed the creeping cold circling around him, like fog on a January morning. It was getting bolder it seemed.

The light didn't put it off as much as it had earlier. Put what off? He berated himself. Keep it together Jake, for fuck's sake keep it together if you want to get out of here and with your sanity intact.

Willie said, 'Let's think about this. They could have manufactured those calls, either with prior tapings or downloading some shit from their mobiles, couldn't they?'

'For sure,' said Derek, tapping some loose ash from the end of his cigarette.

'I don't believe this,' said Jake. 'It's not Daniel and it's not Geoff. They're dead, I'm telling you.'

'What makes you so sure?' asked Willie.

Jake came out with it. 'I just know,' he muttered.

'Oh, that explains everything then,' Derek chirped sarcastically. He pointed out into the dark. 'You know those two fuckers are probably standing in that precious doorway of yours and laughing their butts off listening to us, don't you?' The end of his cigarette was a little orange pin-prick against the black backdrop. 'That's where they are.' His words were not altogether clear, twisted because he had to keep a hold of the cigarette dangling from his lips. Just when it was about to fall, he yanked it away from his mouth.

'Holy shit,' Jake blurted, backing away from the chop saw and colliding with the half-filled bucket of copper bars.

'Bloody nora,' added Willie, doing the same, protectively sticking an arm across Jake's chest, nose wrinkling in disgust.

'What now?' fumed Derek, looking in the direction of the horrified gazes of Jake and Willie. 'Well, stone the crows,' he said, dropping his cigarette to the floor and stamping it out.

Sitting on the wall, just in front and above them, was an enormous black slug. It must have been at least a foot long, and Jake didn't know any kind of slug that could get that big, especially down here. It didn't seem to be moving, unlike the spider of earlier on in the week, it just sat there, stuck to the wall like some ugly child's Halloween decoration. Its antenna waved curiously in the air, like it was spying on them, listening in to their conversation. Its slimy skin glistened in the light of the bulbs strung across the wall, making it look like a giant blob of black spittle.

'Fuck me,' Derek gasped and bent down to the ground, groping for something without once taking his eyes off the creature. As if it was going to rush him, but it was a slug. Then again, with the weird events that had already taken place, perhaps it could cover the distance in a few seconds.

'Where the hell did it come from?' said Willie.

'You just answered your own question I think,' replied Jake, both of them doing the same thing as Derek, watching the monstrosity with awed horror, not daring to avert their gaze for one second. It was taking Jake's mind off the monstrosities behind him, in the dark spaces of the floor. Slowly, he found himself backing up to the edge of the light pool and it was here that he nervously stood his ground.

Between the devil and the deep blue sea.

Shit, that wasn't a good adage for the moment.

Derek finally seemed to find what he was looking for when he stood upright clutching a piece of copper in his hand. Jake just about caught the glint in time to realise what he was holding but not quick enough to stop him from doing what he did next.

'Derek! Don't!' Jake barked. He had pressed forward, but Willie's arm stopped him from going any further.

Derek gave them both a dismissive glance and then threw the copper at the slug. It smashed into the wall beside it, but still had the effect of knocking the thing to the ground. It landed with a plopping sound, like a plastic bag filled with mince.

Without hesitation, Derek picked up a length of un-stripped cable, held it high over his head and brought it down on the slug, splattering it like a devilish pimple. Black fluid whipped up into the air in gooey strips, some of it on Derek, but most of it up the side of the wall and onto the surrounding floor area. In its death throes, the slug let off a hideous shriek, similar to that of a toad's.

Jake clamped his hands to his ears, trying to shut the noise out. It was a terrible sound, not just that of a creature in pain, but something else entirely. This cry, this agonised howl stole into your head, ripped through your body and took something from you. 'Stop it!' Jake cried. 'Stop it!'

'I think it's dead Derek,' Willie affirmed.

Derek, cable held aloft, looked around at them. He was breathing heavily, drunk on adrenaline. Black spots pock marked his face and overalls. A terrible smell filled the air, reminiscent of dog shit.

Willie gagged and covered his nose and mouth with the lapel of his overalls.

Despite the disgusting notion that he was breathing that stench in, Jake managed to breathe through his mouth.

It didn't seem to bother Derek.

The slug, which by now was barely recognisable as anything that had once had a life, managed somehow to let off one last howl of defiance into the air.

This time however, the cry was answered.

It was answered by something that quite clearly was much larger, and much more pissed off than the slug had been. A booming sound, like a combination of angry whale song and metal grinding against metal filled the floor, swamping it in seconds, coming from everywhere, impossible to pinpoint.

Except Jake knew where it was coming from, and Jake knew what it was doing. It was answering the cry of one of its own. One of its own that they, or rather Derek, had just killed. Jake suspected whatever it was out there wasn't going to be choosy about finding which of them in particular had killed the slug. They had all been there - they were all part of it.

Now they all had their hands clamped to their ears, Derek dropping the slimy murder weapon to the ground. Dust shook free from the ceilings, the chairs and desks seemed to perform a quick makeshift version of 'Riverdance' across the floor. Bits of cable and copper rolled along the ground, some of them disappearing into the black, rolling under desks, never to be seen again. All three of them took small shuffling steps, adjusting their balance as their equilibrium was challenged by the screeching.

Perhaps the situation was still within the bounds of explanation, and that by intrepid fearless exploration it could all be explained, the culprits found and normality restored. But who was he kidding? Who in their right mind, was going to go stomping around down here, in the dark, looking for trouble? After everything that had happened so far, everything that had happened to challenge the way in which they saw the world and how they thought they understood everything that happened within its boundaries? Something else had impinged upon those boundaries and Jake didn't want to know what. Such an adventure was not on the cards. Because Jake had given up. He wanted out, and he wanted out now. They should never have come down here in the first place and it was only their greed that had lured them here. He was going to do the Shake and Vac and get the hell out of here.

'Oh man, what the fuck was that?' said Derek, sounding like he was about to soil himself. Jake wouldn't have blamed him – the sound did that to you.

'I have had enough of this bullshit,' stormed Willie. 'You hear me? I've had enough!' he shouted into the gloomy interior. 'Enough!' he grabbed a piece of the chopped cable and bustled past Derek and Jake, wielding it like he meant to do someone some serious harm.

Jake caught up to him and stood in his way. 'Willie, don't! Let's just get out of here, okay?' he beseeched his mentor.

Willie's eyes seemed to have lost some of their focus, as if some switch had been flipped on inside him. Or flipped off for that matter. Perhaps it was this damned darkness, but Jake thought that his friend had gone over the edge, the crazy events of the last ten minutes taking their toll on him. He guessed Willie didn't have the Shake and Vac or something like it, anyway.

'No Willie,' he pleaded again, back pedalling toward the dark and very conscious that he was about to run out of bargaining space. He loved Willie – but if he was going in there on some damn fool crusade, then he was doing it alone. Jake had seen – and heard – enough.

For a second, Willie seemed to come back to him. The old Willie, the calm Willie, the Willie that always kept Jake on the leash. The Willie that used to tip him a wink then disappear outside the site hut for a fag at ten to five every day of the week. He looked down at Jake and spoke, very softly, 'Jake. There is no such thing as monsters and devils and things that come out of manholes. Okay?' Then he was gone, and the new Willie was back. He bared his teeth in a feral snarl and forced his way past Jake.

Jake watched him go. Several times he appeared to bang into desks and chairs, but they didn't seem to slow him down any. He was heading straight for the doorway Jake guessed. And why not? If you were someone who dealt in rational theory only, then there were people out there playing games with them, and it probably was Geoff and Daniel, and they probably were hiding out in that damp little room behind the doorway. That was if you dealt in rational theory only, and Jake had given up on that a long time ago. Maybe it was the last vestiges of the child left in him, but he knew with a child's unquestioning certainty, that something evil was lurking in the black. It had come from the doorway, but now it was out, and moving amongst them.

Jake looked behind him at Derek, but Derek just looked at him and said, 'Let the stupid old fart get on with it.'

Jake leapt at him, fists flailing, all the months of torment exploding from him like the cork popped off a heavily shaken champagne bottle. He found himself calling Derek all sorts of names, names he would never have dreamt of calling anyone, surprising himself at the ferocity of his own hatred.

Derek staggered backward, shocked by the sudden attack of the one guy in the entire firm he would have bet his house on that didn't have it in him. His back foot skidded on a puddle of the slug's remains and he fell backward, banging his head on the wall.

This didn't stop Jake, who then proceeded to put the boot in. Derek covered up for a few moments and Jake wasn't sure if he had hurt him or not, but he reckoned the knock he had just taken on his head must have pissed him off some. Anyway, this was remarkable therapy, Jake could feel the pent up rage pouring out of him with every obscenity he shouted and every blow he rained down on Derek. Suddenly, Derek's hand snaked out and encircled Jake's ankle. He pulled it sharply, sending Jake to the ground alongside him. Within seconds, he was up and over on top of him. He pinned Jake's arms to his side with his knees and then Jake found his head trapped between Derek's thighs. He thrashed and bucked furiously with his legs, but he was wasting his time. Derek was larger and heavier. He was going nowhere.

'Well, got some spunk in your after all, eh faggot?' he snarled. Jake noticed a trickle of blood snaking its way along the furrows in his forehead. It came from somewhere around his hairline. Jake had obviously caused this when he sent Derek crashing into the wall.

Jake, still fuelled by anger, snarled back, 'Get the hell off me arsehole!' and thrashed his legs some more, making Derek look like the bloodied rider of a bucking bronco machine, the kind you find on seaside pier fronts.

'I will', he replied, very measured. It was similar to Willie's voice, calm yet totally crazy. This place seemed to do that to you. It had made Willie crazy, Jake crazy and now Derek, although it was arguable that Derek was crazy in the first place. He didn't want to think about what it had done to Daniel and Geoff.

Derek blindly fished around behind him and came up with his weapon of choice, the lump of slug stained cable. Clearly, he intended to dish out the same treatment to Jake, like he was nothing more than a slug to be squashed. 'Gonna smash your face in rent boy, smash it in good.' His eyes betrayed no hint of emotion or compassion and he stared holes through Jake as he slowly raised the cable over head, preparing to bring it crashing down in Jake's face.

Jake struggled once more, briefly, then shut his eyes as the cable came down. A bolt of pain, like a flash of lightning across his vision, detonated in his head as his nose exploded. He felt a warm flush across his cheeks and knew it was his own blood. Opening his eyes, he saw Derek making a deliberately slow play of raising his arm for the next blow, like a teacher from years past making an example of a pupil with the cane. 'Two more and we're done,' he said, like he was doing Jake some kind of god damned favour.

Before he could punish Jake any further though, an arm came across his throat in a clothesline and knocked him back. Derek managed to let out an 'Urgh!' before he toppled off Jake and crumpled back against the wall, clutching at his throat, trying to pull off an invisible choker.

Jake was yanked roughly to his feet, like a wimpish soldier who can't complete the assault course. He knew then that it was not Willie that had saved him.

It was Geoff.

And Geoff had looked better. His overalls were tattered, there were bloody gouges across his whole body like he had been in a fight with a grizzly bear. A large flap of skin hung from his cheek and lay there like a limp lettuce leaf. Comically enough, he still had the wherewithal to try and clean himself up with his filthy rag of a handkerchief, but he only succeeded in making matters worse. He didn't seem to notice. He looked over Jake's shoulder at Derek, and then at Jake. He was breathing heavily.

'Geoff, what the...what the hell happened to you? I mean, are you okay?' Jake asked. He tenderly touched his nose. It was still there, but it felt like a vacuous bag filled with little pieces of bone swimming around in it. The pain flared when he touched it, making his head swim, so he left it alone. It settled into a steady, aching throb, worse than any headache he had ever suffered.

'There's something back there, boy. And it's got bad intentions,' Geoff said. He looked around distracted. The mess of the slug didn't seem to perturb him either, but Jake supposed that he had already seen far worse than that already. Jake looked at his watch and saw it was only nine thirty in the morning. He thought bad things like this only happened at night, didn't they? But shit, this wasn't a bloody movie and it was as good as night time down here anyway.

'Where's Willie?' Geoff asked. That was what he was looking for.

'I think he went off to find you,' Jake semi-lied. Actually Geoff, I think he went off to kill you, but it looks like we all owe you an apology on that one. 'It's just me and Derek,' Jake shrugged.

Geoff looked over at Derek again and Jake followed his gaze. It seemed as if Derek was still struggling to get air into his lungs. He looked like he was trying to strangle himself. Geoff strode over to Derek and planted a firm kick into his bollocks. Derek howled and his hands left his throat to clutch at his throbbing genitals.

'Fuck this piece of shit. Want to come and get yourself some?' Geoff offered to Jake.

Jake was getting scared badly again. True, he had wanted to kill Derek moments ago, but that had passed. Geoff was under control of the same demons as the rest of them, it appeared. He had saved him from Derek, but how long would that last until something triggered Geoff into a murderous rage at Jake?

'Umm, no thanks man. I think he's had enough,' Jake said.

Geoff looked down at Derek who had settled into a whimper. 'Reckon?' he said, sounding surprised.

Shit, this is awkward, Jake thought. Change the subject, Jake, change the subject. 'Should we try and find Willie, Geoff?' Jake used Geoff's name in an effort to re-focus him, like people who try and talk other people from jumping off tall buildings. Like Mel Gibson in 'Lethal Weapon'.

Geoff either didn't hear him or didn't care. He landed another swift kick into Derek's mid-section. Derek let out a sound like a dog that has sniffed something it doesn't like. To Jake's ghastly despair, apart from the sound, Derek did not acknowledge the blow. He must have been in too much pain already. Jake felt a momentary weight push down on his heart that he instantly recognised as guilt, but he quickly pushed it away. He asked Geoff his original question again, and this time, Geoff seemed to hear him.

'He went to look for me, you say?' Geoff said, and to Jake's relief, sounding more like the old Geoff. Then again, he never really knew the old Geoff, and perhaps the old Geoff was capable of doing what Jake had just seen him do.

'He went out there?' Geoff pointed into the black, like it was the other side of the world, and perhaps it was. The other side of something else, anyway.

Jake nodded.

'He's probably dead then.'

'You're not dead,' replied Jake defiantly.

This seemed to throw Geoff, who had to think about things for a moment or two.

'You're right,' he said finally. 'I'm not.' It was like he was surprised at the revelation he was still alive. Then, that crazy look returned and he dashed off past Jake and into the dark shouting, 'I'm coming Willie! Hold on!'

'Shit Geoff, no!' Jake cried. He didn't want to be left alone again. And certainly not with Derek. Shit - Derek. He had forgotten about that arsehole. He whipped around but it was okay. Derek was still rolled up into a foetal position, like a woodlouse trying to protect itself.

He turned around again, not knowing what to do. He wanted to leave, but he couldn't if Willie was still alive. He had written Geoff off and he was still alive, wasn't he? Well, he was a few seconds ago. He couldn't just cut and run if Willie needed his help. He turned and stared into the dark, the swelling dark that he could have sworn was denser still, that curled and roiled like black fog in amongst the natural gloom of this interior. Keep it together Jake, he pleaded with himself. Do the Shake and Vac if you have to. He turned around into the dark, not knowing he had stepped into it (or maybe it had stepped into him) and his heart rocketed out of his ribcage and lodged itself in his throat.

Willie was standing in front of him.

Jake's Adam's apple was now competing with his heart to expel itself from his throat. Blood surged and pounded in his ears like a crashing tide trying to smash the shoreline into oblivion.

Do the Shake and Vac

'Willie?' Jake quivered.

Willie was ghostly white. He didn't seem to be injured, but the only piece of him that was visible was his face, as it was so white. The dark blue of his overalls was eaten by the black swirling around him.

Swirling around them.

And put the freshness back

'Willie?' Jake asked again. He could barely hear his own voice over the pounding in his head.

Willie's mouth opened and closed slowly. 'There are monsters Jake,' he whispered.

Do the Shake and Vac

Then, a pale white hand emerged from the dark and closed around Willie's mouth, another pale arm encircled his chest from behind him and a hideous face glided into view. It was neither male nor female and most certainly not human. The face was smooth with no crevices or formations, no eye sockets, no cleft in the chin. In fact, it didn't have a chin. Its cheek rested on Willie's cheek. It smiled at Jake, but it was an angry smile, the kind you get from a drunk when trouble is about to start. Full of malice and full of purpose. Its black eyes glittered like beetles. Then, it glided backward, taking Willie with it, like they were on roller skates and the dark just swallowed them up and it was like they had never been there.

And put the freshness back

Jake whimpered and backed up, turning around and preparing to flee.

Derek was standing straight in front of him. Jake rebounded off his chest and faced him, mind going a thousand miles an hour. Derek said nothing, but instead head butted him on his already shattered nose. The pain roared like a lion and washed everything else out of Jake's system. He fell to the floor, bouncing off the corner of a desk as he did so. He didn't have time to worry about the thing that had claimed Willie, the pain in his nose consumed everything, took his world from him.

Derek could not believe the gall of that little bastard to go for him like that. Still, he had to admire him. He never would have thought he had the guts. It was the quiet ones you had to watch out for, or so they said. He gingerly touched his forehead and winced when his fingers came away smeared with blood. Although the wound was bleeding, the pain was nothing compared to the heavy metal drummer that was rocking out in his nuts. The pain there pulsed like it had a heartbeat.

He smiled to himself as he quickly gathered up any bars of copper that he could see. He certainly wasn't going to go hunting for them, because one thing was for sure – there was some freaky shit going on down here. Just before he had nutted Jake, it was clear to him that he had seen something pretty bad, because the kid looked like he had just shit himself and it wasn't at the sight of seeing a pissed off Derek.

He pushed these thoughts to the back of his mind as he set about the task of retrieving as much of the copper as possible. He had been through a lot today – and he was not about to leave empty handed. They hadn't got through much of the cable before the shit had hit the fan, but he reckoned he had got around three hundred pounds or so wrapped up neatly with cable ties in a bundle. He could have used a cigarette to calm his nerves, but there would be time for that later. He had to get out of here before something really nasty happened to him, other than being attacked by two of his colleagues. He'd never liked Jake, but he hadn't minded Geoff all that much. Well, he was on the shit list now for sure. And Derek always got even.

He paid no attention to the warping blackness that seemed to pace with him to his right as he stumbled along the lighted path across the floor, into the hallway and toward the trap door that had led them to this nightmare. He occupied his mind with thoughts of revenge, and a plan began to form in his head. It grappled with the dull throbbing pain that had taken up residence, eventually evicting it to lay out its scheme to him. He would get out of here first, but then he would weigh the door down somehow, perhaps with a site box if he could drag it over there. There was one on the floor above, he was sure of that. Perhaps if he emptied it, he could place it on top of the door and then fill it up again. He knew where Geoff kept the keys to the boxes in the site hut. Yes, he would trap them down here, and if whatever was stalking them didn't get to them first, then perhaps insanity would. They all seemed to be going a little crazy.

Yeah, he would have the last laugh on those bastards if it was the last thing he did. He chuckled to himself as he trotted toward the ladder that led to the floor above, telling himself the whispering he could hear was the sound of his trousers chaffing against each other, and it wasn't coming from all around him, behind, left, right and in front. No sir – it was his trousers, and it didn't sound like words, it was his mind playing tricks on him.

Jake came to slowly at first, then his senses snapped back in like he had stuck his head in a bowl full of cold water. Shit! He was still down here, and alone!

Something else dawned on him as he shakily got to his feet, with the aid of a nearby desk. There must have been at least thirty or more orange glows blinking soundlessly into the darkness. His mouth dropped open in horror as he realised all the phones were going. Before, it had only been one. Now, it was all of them. He didn't realise how many of them there had been, and he could only see all of them because they were calling him. One before – now loads. This couldn't be good.

There was one benefit to this frightening development though – all those orange glows had given a partial faint illumination to the blackness that had previously enveloped the whole floor and threatened to engulf them if it hadn't had been for their paltry temporary lighting. He whipped his head from side to side, looking for any sign of an approaching monster, but could see none. But he did see Geoff.

He was standing at the threshold of the doorway, just standing there, trance like. It was hard to see if he was talking to anybody, because as useful as the light was, it did keep blinking on and off. It was like watching a movie where every other frame had been removed from the reel.

Then the music started up. He hadn't noticed any speakers in here before, but it was coming from somewhere. It was the same as the music on the telephone, some old swing tune, but now it was much louder. It wasn't on the other end of a telephone line from hell – it was right here with him.

He turned to run and then thought of Geoff. Should he try and save him? He was still standing there, looking into that tiny room with the manhole. Jake called over to him, but he got no reply. And that damn music – he had to really shout to be heard over it.

Then the music stopped to be replaced by deafening white noise and Jake remembered what came next. He looked at Geoff, at the doorway and clapped his hands to his ears at a sudden *whoomph!* noise and a resultant pressure drop that popped his eardrums. It felt like a needle had been plunged through the thin fabric of Jake's reality and through that tiny hole, something huge had forced its way through, ripping the hole into a massive tear.

The static stopped and it was like there was a charge in the air, like before an electrical storm. Something had perversely changed on this plane of their existence. The silence, in its own right, was completely deafening.

The orange lights blinked on and off.

Geoff stood looking into the door.

Jake was watching him, frozen in fear to the spot.

It was almost as if they were standing in the eye of a twister. Calm. Too calm.

A black wave pulsed out of the doorway, swamping over Geoff and swallowing him from view. It crashed into the opposite wall, splashing in all directions, and there were things in it.

Living things. Things with scrawny limbs and claw like hands, things with lolling tongues and thrashing tentacles, things that scuttled across the floor and across the walls, things that bulged forth from the black tide, bulky, massive things with black eyes that regarded him soullessly.

And murderously.

Jake stood there horrified, transfixed and unable to move. If any of the others were still down here, there was nothing he could do for them. He managed to regain control of his neck and look back longingly at the old hallway and the ladder and trap door that lay beyond it. He had to leave, but he couldn't make his feet move. The first time he looked back, there was a dozen or more of the monsters emerging from the tar and heading toward him. Some were moving much quicker than others. Some of the things, the bigger ones he noticed, oozed forth and explored their surroundings with tentacles, antennas and proboscis like curious insects. And they continued to pour forth. It was like hell had been turned upside down and all the hideous things within were dropping out. Some could land on their feet, others just splatted onto the ground and took it from there.

He could not afford the luxury of watching this dark carnival, he had to run and run for his life. The first light bulb in their string of hastily installed lights popped out of existence as a creature landed on it. Then the next one along popped too, and then the whole damned procession was coming toward him. The sound of another light bulb, this one perhaps only twenty feet away snapped him out of his reverie. He turned tail and fled.

Do the shake and Vac

Arms pumping madly in the air, running as fast as he could. Oh god, something landed on his back. He felt arms (or legs) encircling his waist and a sharp pain as the creature bit into his shoulder. He cried out and then remembered he had his Stanley knife in his pocket. Not breaking stride, crying out as the creature bit into him time and again, he tried to pull it off with one hand as he produced his knife with the other. He pushed the blade down, stumbling, nearly falling, and slashed blindly behind him.

And put the freshness back

Something screamed in his ear and he pulled the thing off. He didn't stop to see what it was, he didn't want to see. The bulbs were blowing like popcorn and they were gaining on him, the blackness was gaining on him and he didn't need to look behind him to know that whatever had been spewed out of that doorway was catching up to him and fast. He became aware of movement to both his left and right, things hopping over the desks and scuttling along the walls, staring him down with inhuman curiosity. Something tried to trip him up, but he kept his balance as he hurtled through the first door and into the old hallway.

Do the Shake and Vac

There was a multitude of screams and shrieks as well, howlings of some unearthly beasts as they closed in on their prey. More bulbs going, almost level with his head and still he ran.

And put the freshness back

He could hear voices in amongst the screams, voices snatching at his name, hissing his name, spitting his name. Something grabbed his leg and almost pulled him down. He felt a claw on his thigh and he was dragging something with him. He slashed manically at his leg, cutting himself but also cutting his attacker. Another hideous cry and the thing was off him. The blackness rearing up behind him like a monstrous tidal wave, ready to come crashing down. The light bulbs just ahead of him popping as he reached them, almost at the ladder, almost, but not quite. Shadows of grossly misshapen heads and limbs climbing the walls in front of him, rearing up like a shark from the sea. The devil's shadow puppets.

When your carpet smells fresh

Jake could feel the blackness creeping around the peripheral of his vision, something like a tentacle stroked the nape of his neck and he cried out 'No!' as he jumped and caught the fourth rung down of the ladder, shins smashing painfully into the rungs below it, nearly causing him to lose grip.

Your home does too

Something snaked around his ankle and he looked down. Black fluid broke around the bottom of the ladder and carried the creatures with it. The thing holding his ankle looked like a child, only half of its head was missing. It looked up at him with an eyeless socket and smiled. Thick dark liquid seeped from its mouth along with a collection of creepy-crawlies the like of which he had never seen before.

Every time you vacuum

Jake cried out in pain as the thing reached up and bit his foot. He felt sharp, dagger like teeth pierce his trainer and puncture his flesh. To the side of him, at head level, a massive spider scuttled across and tried to climb onto him.

It was like a spider in every way except it had a human head and a fiendishly long tongue that darted out and whipped him across his face. Jake squinted his eyes shut and kicked with all his might. He felt something else take a hold of him, and slowly but surely, began pulling him down. Something slithered across his fingers and the voices started up again, whispering, taunting, teasing him.

Remember what to do

One hand slipped so only the tips of his fingers held on. His other hand still had a good grip until he looked across and saw several tentacles snake out and coil around his forearm. In unison, they all pulled down. Jake grunted and did his best to hold on, but he knew it was a losing battle. Before he let go and succumb to the black, he looked down once more. The child-thing was still there clinging to his ankle, but for a quick moment he was certain he saw Willie rise up out of the black pool, face contorted in anguish. But right away several pale, bony arms pulled him back under.

'No,' Jake sobbed, and let go of the ladder.

He felt something very firm grab hold of him under the arms and was pulled up very quickly. So quickly, that the things trying to drag him back down had no time to react. He found himself wrenched out of the hole like a nail being removed from wood and tossed equally as carelessly aside. He landed on his side, debris and rubble bruising him but he didn't notice. He was transfixed at the sight before him. The basement was lit up by floodlights like a football pitch and the basement, which had previously been empty save for some old machinery, was now packed full of soldiers. There must have been at least six of them all pointing their guns down into the trapdoor. Some of them fired and he saw a spider scuttle out. It didn't get far as a soldier turned around and emptied his gun into it. It let off one of those awful screeches as it died.

Jake felt like he was watching a scene from a movie, that he wasn't really there, that he wasn't a part of all this.

Another group of soldiers were hurriedly laying a cable across the floor and opening up the old switchboard, where Geoff had disconnected their cable in the first place. Then they split up and began stripping either end of the cable, ready to make a connection. One of them held a gleaming silver block in his hand, that resembled some kind of heavy duty lock.

The trapdoor was slammed shut and more soldiers poured in, hammering down planks of wood, nails gripped between their teeth. Some of them lay across the door and several times it was hammered on from underneath. 'Fucking hurry up!' the soldiers laying across the door cried, sounding every bit as scared as Jake had. One of them started up a blow torch and began welding. As they did this, a small group of them parted and let a man dressed as some kind of priest come through. Jake couldn't hear what he was saying amidst all of the soldiers barking orders at each other, but he began throwing his arms at the trapdoor and chanting something. A loud knocking could be heard from the other side of the door, knocking that doubled in intensity as the priest went to work.

Another soldier came in and started chiselling around the wood. He worked very quickly and Jake could hear his colleagues telling him to 'Hurry up' and 'Make it quick.' The soldier with the lock appeared and started fixing it down and connecting the cable. They all stood there with guns pointing at the trapdoor, looking they were expecting its unholy contents to spew forth at any moment. Now, the priest was throwing water at the trapdoor, and Jake guessed that it had to have been holy water. He was still chanting away. Jake thought the caught snatches of it – words like 'You shall not pass' and 'God commands you.' The knocking was becoming weaker though.

Jake rolled onto his back and lay there, catching his breath. As he slowly regained his senses, his wounds began biting into him. He was in quite a lot of pain as it happened. He looked to his other side, where there was no trapdoor and no unearthly screeches.

The face of Derek looked back at him, a neat hole in the middle of his forehead, a flood of drying blood spattered around it. Jake saw a sharp glint in the shadows that seemed to be cuddling Derek and realised he had some of the scrap copper on him. The idiot looked like he was smiling. Had they been too late to save Derek, or had they...

A face, an older face, wearing an army helmet, chinstrap cutting into the flesh, appeared in his view.

'You okay son?' the soldier asked.

Jake nodded. He wasn't sure how mentally sound he was going to be after all this, and apart from his mainly superficial wounds, he was indeed okay.

'Good,' the soldier continued, 'because we need to talk. On your feet son.'

Jake was led roughly by the elbow outside the building. He had forgotten the tracking of time once again, and had to shield his eyes against the noon sunshine. It really must have been dark down there. He was being escorted by two soldiers, the one who had spoken to him must have been their leader as he stalked off in front and occasionally barked something at one of the soldiers that still continued to pour forth into the building like ants. Jake turned around as he stumbled forward, the soldiers not really allowing him the luxury of doing so, and he noticed the priest was following along behind them.

Once his eyes had got adjusted to the glare, he could see the old site hut in the distance, but this time, there was no Willie sneaking a crafty cigarette, no Derek or Daniel or Geoff. They were all gone. Jake hadn't spotted the huge trailer parked right in front of them. There were several more behind too, and this was obviously the transportation used by the military in getting here.

The man in front of him slid back one of the side doors and climbed in. Jake was manhandled inside also. The soldiers and the priest came in last, shutting the door again behind him. He still had his bible clasped in both hands, Jake noticed.

It was deceptively large in the trailer, in fact, it was more like a house. There was a mound of electronic equipment in there as well. Neon lights of all colours blinked their greetings to Jake as he was pushed into a chair. The soldiers sat by the door as if to block Jake's escape. The priest and the other soldier, who Jake could now see was called Sanders, took chairs also and faced him.

The priest looked decidedly harried; Sanders looked decidedly pissed off. He shook a packet of cigarettes out of his shirt pocket and pulled one out.

He stuffed one into his mouth and groped around the rest of his uniform for what presumably must have been a lighter or a box of matches. He found his lighter eventually. Before he lit up, he glanced up at Jake and said, 'You mind?'

Jake shook his head. Somehow, he felt he wasn't really in a position to argue.

Sanders lit his cigarette, expelled a large cloud of smoke and eyed Jake through it, eyes forming into slits against the sting of the smoke. Sanders removed his helmet, revealing a shaven head covered in dark black stubble. It looked like he had performed the haircut himself, with a razor. Perhaps he had.

How militarily precise, Jake thought.

'Now,' Sanders barked commandingly whilst flicking the first of several ash deposits of the end of the cigarette onto the floor, 'Mr MI5 wants to know what you boys have been doing down there.'

Jake was still shaken up by what had happened to him, but he didn't need all his wits about him to know that he may well have jumped from the frying pan and into the fire, so to speak. Still, he couldn't help but feel a little aggrieved at his treatment thus far. He crossed his arms in his chair and leant back. 'What happened to Derek? Did you kill him?' he asked.

The priest looked down at the ground. Sanders laughed. 'Hell, he was the one who came out swinging with a goddamn knife, son. What are my boys supposed to do? Let him slash them to pieces? He got what he deserved. Besides, time weren't exactly on our side, you could see that.'

Jake couldn't really argue with that.

Sanders continued, 'Now son, tell me. Tell me what in God's name you were doing down there and what in the hell you nearly brung back up with you.'

So Jake told them the whole story, from the moment he found the cable to the moment they yanked him out of the trapdoor like a thorn stuck in your side. Sanders just sucked on his cigarette and looked solemnly at him. The priest seemed to be hanging on Jake's every word.

After he had finished, the priest continued to question him on the finite points of what Jake had thought had actually come out of the doorway, like it was important to know about giant slugs and spiders with twisted human heads.

'This sound like what you were talking about?' Sanders asked the priest.

The priest nodded.

'You sure? It's the...thing?'

The priest nodded.

Sanders turned to Jake and said, 'Thanks son.'

By the time that was over, Jake was quite scared again. He had relived the whole ordeal in precise detail. He asked nervously, 'Those things can't get out of there can they?'

Sanders turned in his chair and looked at the priest. 'Well, can they?' he said.

'I shouldn't think so, I mean no, they can't,' the priest stammered. 'I put enough incantations and holy water on that hell hole to kill the devil himself,' he added. Then he laughed, as if he made some sort of private joke.

There was a burst of metallic speech through a walkie-talkie strapped to the shoulder of Sanders, and for a terrible moment Jake expected to hear that awful nasal voice that would probably haunt him forever. Instead, he caught something like 'It has been contained.' Whatever it was, it must have been good news, because Sanders leant into his shoulder and snapped back, 'Good. Bring the men back.' He then stood up and straightened his combats out before looking at Jake. 'Well, it looks like we're just about done here, son. I don't even know your name.'

Jake stood up, a dizzy wave of relief washing over him at the thought that this might finally be over. 'It's Jake,' he replied.

Sanders offered his hand. 'Good to meet you Jake. My name's Neil.'

They shook hands.

Sanders jerked a thumb at the priest. 'This here's Alex. He handles these kind of...' Sanders paused, '...things, if you know what I mean.'

'Is this necessary?' Alex asked Sanders, ignoring Jake completely and then offering him a strained smile. Jake noticed a broad Scottish accent in Alex's tones. He hadn't heard it earlier, but then again, what with the hideous screeching coming from the trap door and the sound of gunfire exploding all around him, it was hard to pick up on the finer inflections of someone's voice.

'Sure it is,' Sanders smiled, grinning from ear to ear and gripping Jake's hand so strongly it felt like it was in a vice. 'I leave you to do your part Alex, so leave me to do mine.'

Finally, Sanders released Jake's hand, but at that time, Jake felt another palpable shift in the pressure, in the atmosphere inside the van.

'You see Jake, this kind of event, well, it requires what we call a 'total slate clean'. Know what I mean?' As Sanders said this, he removed his handgun from the holster attached to his belt. He cocked the weapon.

The priest, Alex, audibly tutted and looked away.

Sanders continued, 'And I'm sorry to say that you are one very bad stain on my nice clean slate Jake. And I can't have that.' He pointed the gun at Jake's head.

'You want Alex here to say some words for you, pray for you or some crap like that?'

Jake shook his head. He was no longer scared. He was resigned. How could he have ever hoped that this situation would resolve itself and he would be home in time for tea? That shit only happened in movies, and it certainly never happened to him.

Sanders didn't even blink. Jake was looking at a machine, a killing machine, no more compassionate than that thing down in the basement, beating its fury at being imprisoned once more.

'May be the difference between you ending up back down there,' he said, pointing back towards the area where the trap door was, 'or up there,' pointing to the roof of the van.

Jake just stared at him, feeling the cold metal of the gun barrel burn into his head the way an overdose of ice-cream does.

Any last words then?' Sanders asked brightly, still smiling, but not flashing his teeth this time.

'Yeah,' Jake said, leaning into the barrel of the gun.

Sanders frowned at this sudden show of courage.

'Do the Shake and Vac,' Jake smiled.

Graham Masterton

CAMELOT

Jack was scraping finely-chopped garlic into the skillet when he heard somebody banging at the restaurant door. 'Shit,' he breathed. He took the skillet off the gas and wiped his hands on his apron. The banging was repeated, more forcefully this time, and the door-handle was rattled.

'Okay, okay! I hear you!'

He weaved his way between the circular tables and the bentwood chairs. The yellow linen blinds were drawn right down over the windows, so that all he could see were two shadows. The early-morning sun distorted them, hunched them up and gave them pointed ears, so that they looked like wolves.

He shot the bolts and unlocked the door. Two men in putty-coloured raincoats were standing outside. One was dark and unshaven, with greased-back hair and a broken nose. The other was sandy and overweight, with clear beads of perspiration on his upper lip.

'Yes?'

The dark man held out a gilded badge. 'Sergeant Eli Waxman, San Francisco Police Department. Are you Mr Jack Keller?'

'That's me. Is anything wrong?'

Sergeant Waxman flipped open his notebook and peered at it as if he couldn't read his own handwriting. 'You live at 3663 Heliograph Street, apartment 2?'

'Yes, I do. For Christ's sake, tell me what's happened.'

'Your partner is Ms Jacqueline Fronsart, twenty-four, a student in Baltic singing at The Institute of Baltic Singing?'

'That's right.'

Sergeant Waxman closed his notebook. 'I'm sorry to tell you, Mr Keller, but Ms Fronsart has been mirrorized.'

'What?'

'Your neighbours heard her screaming round about nine-thirty this morning. One of them broke into your apartment and found her. They tried to get her out but there was nothing they could do.'

'Oh, God.' Jack couldn't believe what he was hearing. 'Which – what – which mirror was it?'

'Big tilting mirror, in the bedroom.'

'Oh, God. Where is it now? It didn't get broken, did it?'

'No, it's still intact. We left it where it was. The coroner can remove it for you, if that's what you want. It's entirely up to you.'

Jack covered his eyes with his hand and kept them covered. Maybe, if he blacked out the world for long enough, the detectives would vanish and this wouldn't have happened. But even in the darkness behind his fingers he could hear their raincoats rustling, and their shoes shifting uncomfortably on the polished wood floor. Eventually he looked up at them and said, 'I bought that mirror about six months ago. The owner swore to me that it was docile.'

'You want to tell me where you got it?'

'Loculus Antiques, in Sonoma. I have their card someplace.'

'Don't worry, we can find it if we need to. I'll be straight with you, though – I don't hold out much hope of any restitution.'

'Jesus. I'm not interested in restitution. I just want - '

He thought of Jacqueline, standing on his balcony, naked except for a large straw hat piled ridiculously high with peaches and pears and bananas. He could see her turning her face toward him in slo-mo. Those liquid brown eyes, so wide apart that she looked more like a beautiful salmon than a woman. Those brown shoulders, patterned with henna. Those enormous breasts, with nipples that shone like plums.

'Desire, I can see it in your every looking,' she had whispered. She always whispered, to save her larynx for her Baltic singing.

She had pushed him back onto the violently-patterned durry, and knelt astride his chest. Then she had displayed herself to him, her smooth hairless vulva, and she had pulled open her lips with her fingers to show him the green canary-feather that she had inserted into her urethra.

'The plumage of vanity,' she had whispered.

Sergeant Waxman took hold of Jack's upper arm and gave him a comforting squeeze. 'I'm real sorry for your loss, Mr Keller. I saw her myself and – well, she was something, wasn't she?'

'What am I supposed to do?' asked Jack. For the first time in his life he felt totally detached, and adrift, like a man a rowboat with only one oar, circling around and around, out of reach of anybody.

'Different people make different decisions, sir,' said the sandy-haired detective.

'Decisions? Decisions about what?'

'About their mirrors, sir. Some folks store them away in their basements, or their attics, hoping that a time is going to come when we know how to get their loved ones back out of them. Some folks -- well, they bury them, and have proper funerals.'

'They *bury* them? I didn't know that.'

'It's unusual, sir, but not unknown. Other folks just cover up their mirrors with sheets or blankets, and leave them where they are, but some doctors think this could amount to cruelty, on account of the person in the mirror still being able to hear what's going on and everything.'

'Oh, God,' said Jack.

The sandy-haired detective took out a folded handkerchief and dabbed his forehead 'Most folks, though -- '

'Most folks *what*?'

'Most folks *break* their mirrors, sooner or later. I guess it's like taking their loved ones off life-support.'

Jack stared at him. 'But if you break a mirror – what about the person inside it? Are they still trapped in some kind of mirror-world? Or do they get broken, too?'

Sergeant Waxman said, solemnly, 'We don't know the answer to that, Mr Keller, and I very much doubt if we ever will.'

When the detectives had left, Jack locked the restaurant door and stood with his back against it, with tears streaming down his cheeks, as warm and sticky as if he had poked his eyes out. 'Jacqueline,' he moaned. 'Jacqueline, why *you*? Why you, of all people? Why you?'

He knelt down on the waxed oak floor, doubled-up with the physical pain of losing her, and sobbed between gritted teeth. 'Why you, Jacqueleine? Why you? You're so beautiful, why you?'

He cried for almost ten minutes and then he couldn't cry any more. He stood up, wiped his eyes on one of the table-napkins, and blew his nose. He looked around at all the empty tables. He doubted if he would ever be able to open again. Keller's Far-Flung Food would become a memory, just like Jaqueline.

God, he thought. Every morning you wake up, and you climb out of bed, but you never know when life is going to punch you straight in the face.

He went back into the kitchen, turned off all the hobs and ovens, and hung up his apron. There were half-a-dozen Inuit moccasins lying on the chopping-board, ready for unstitching and marinating; and yew branches for yew branch soup. He picked up a fresh, furry moose-antler. That was supposed to be today's special. He put it down again, his throat so tight that he could hardly breathe.

He was almost ready to leave when the back door was flung open, and Punipuni Puu-suke appeared, in his black Richard Nixon T-shirt and his flappy white linen pants. Jack didn't know exactly how old Punipuni was, but his crew-cut hair looked like one of those wire brushes you use for getting rust off the fenders of 1963 pick-up trucks, and his eyes were so pouchy that Jack could never tell if they were open or not. All the same, he was one of the most experienced bone chefs in San Francisco, as well as being an acknowledged Oriental philosopher. He had written a slim, papery book called *Do Not Ask A Fish The Way Across the Desert*.

Punipuni took off his red leather shoulder-bag and then he looked around the kitchen. 'Mr German-cellar?' (He always believed that people should acknowledge the ethnic origins of their names, but translate them into English so that others could share their meaning.) 'Mr German-cellar, is something wrong?'

'I'm sorry, Pu, I didn't have time to call you. I'm not opening today. In fact I think I'm closing for good. Jacqueline was mirrorized.'

Punipuni came across the kitchen and took hold of his hands. 'Mr German-cellar, my heart is inside your chest. When did this tragedy occur?'

'This morning. Just now. The police were here. I have to go home and see what I can do.'

'She was so wonderful, Mr German-cellar. I don't know what I can say to console you.'

Jack shook his head. 'There's nothing. Not yet. You can go home if you like.'

'Maybe I come along too. Sometimes a shoulder to weep on is better than money discovered in a sycamore tree.'

'Okay. I'd appreciate it.'

He lived up on Russian Hill, in a small pink Victorian house in the English Quarter. It was so steep here that he had to park his Ford Peacock with its front wheels cramped against the curb, and its gearbox in Backward. It was a sunny day, and far below them the Bay was sparkling like shattered glass; but there was a thin cold breeze blowing which smelled a fisherman's dying breath.

'Jack!'

A maroon-faced man with white whiskers was trudging up the hill with a bull mastiff on a short choke-chain. He was dressed in yellowish-brown tweeds, with the cuffs of his pants tucked into his stockings.

'I say, Jack!' he repeated, and raised his arm in salute.

'Major,' Jack acknowledged him, and then looked up to his second-story apartment. Somebody had left the windows wide open, Jacqueline probably, and the white drapes were curling in the breeze.

'Dreadfully sorry to hear what happened, old boy! The Nemesis and I are awfully cut up about it. Such a splendid young girl!'

'Thank you,' said Jack.

'Buggers, some of these mirrors, aren't they? Can't trust them an inch.'

'I thought this one was safe.'

'Well, *none* of them are safe, are they, when it comes down to it? Same as these perishing dogs. They behave themselves perfectly, for years, and then suddenly, for no reason that you can think of, *snap*! They bite some kiddie's nose orf, or somesuch. The Nemesis won't have a mirror in the house. Just as well, I suppose. With a dial like hers, she'd crack it as soon as look at it -- what!'

Jack tried to smile, but all he could manage was a painful smirk. He let himself into the front door and climbed the narrow stairs, closely followed by Punipuni. Inside, the hallway was very quiet, and smelled of overripe melons. Halfway up the stairs there was a stained-glass window with a picture of a blindfolded woman on it, and a distant castle with thick black smoke pouring out of it, and rooks circling.

Punipuni caught hold of his sleeve. 'Your God does not require you to do this, Mr German-cellar.'

'No,' said Jack. 'But my heart does. Do you think I'm just going to hire some removal guy and have her carted away? I love her, Pu. I always will. Forever.'

'Forever is not a straight line,' said Punipuni. 'Remember that your favourite carpet store may not always be visible from your front doorstep.'

They reached the upstairs landing. Jack went across to his front door and took out his key. His heart was thumping like an Irish drum and he wasn't at all sure that he was going to be able to do this. But there was a brass *ankh* on the door, where Jaqueline had nailed it, and he could see her kissing her fingertips and pressing it against the *ankh*, and saying, 'This is the symbol of life everlasting that will never die.'

She had been naked at the time, except for a deerstalker hat like Sherlock Holmes. She loved Sherlock

Holmes, and she often called Jack 'Watson.' Without warning she would take out her violin and play a few scraping notes of Cajun music on it and proclaim, ' 'The game is afoot!''

He opened the door and pushed it wide. The apartment was silent, except for the noise of the traffic outside. There was a narrow hallway, with a coat-stand that was clustered with twenty or thirty hats -- skimmers and derbies and shapeless old fedoras – and the floor was heaped with smelly, discarded shoes – brown Oxfords and gilded ballet-pumps and $350 Guevara trainers.

Jack climbed over the shoes into the living-room. It was furnished with heavy red-leather chairs and couches, and glass-fronted bookcases crammed with leather-bound books. Over the cast-iron fireplace hung a large coloured lithograph. It depicted a voluptuous naked woman riding a bicycle over a hurrying carpet of living mice, crushing them under her tires. Only on very close examination could it be seen that instead of a saddle the bicycle was fitted with a thick purple dildo, complete with bulging testicles. The caption read *'The Second Most Pleasurable Way To Exterminate Rodents – Pestifex Powder.'*

The bedroom door was ajar but he hardly dared to go inside. At last Punipuni nudged him and said, 'Go on, Jack. You have to. You cannot mend a broken ginger-jar by refusing to look at it.'

'Yes, you're right.' Jack crossed the living-room and pushed open the bedroom door. The pine four-poster bed was still unmade, with its durry dragged across it diagonally, and its pillows still scattered. On the opposite side of the room, between the two open windows, stood Jacqueline's dressing-table, with all of her Debussy perfumes and her Seurat face-powders, and dozens of paintbrushes in a white ceramic jar.

In the corner stood the cheval-mirror, oval, and almost six feet high on its swivelling base. It was made out of dark highly-polished mahogany, with grapevines carved all around it, and the face of a mocking cherub at the crest of the frame. Jack walked around the bed and confronted it. All he could see was himself, and the quilt, and Punipuni standing in the doorway behind him.

He looked terrible. His hair was still dishevelled from taking off his apron, and he was wearing a crumpled blue shirt with paint-spots on it and a pair of baggy Levis with ripped-out knees. There were plum-coloured circles under his eyes.

He reached out and touched the dusty surface of the mirror with his fingertips. 'Jacqueline,' he said. 'Jacqueline – are you there?'

'Maybe there was mix-up,' said Punipuni, trying to sound optimistic. 'Maybe she just went out to buy lipstick.'

But Jack knew that there had been no mistake. In the mirror, Jacqueline's white silken robe was lying on the floor at the end of the bed. But when he looked around, it wasn't there, not in the real world.

He leaned close to the mirror. 'Jacqueline!' he called out, hoarsely. 'Jacqueline, sweetheart, it's Jack!'

'Maybe she hides,' Punipuni suggested. 'Maybe she doesn't want you to see her suffer.'

But at that moment, Jacqueline appeared in the mirror, and came walking slowly across the room toward him, like a woman in a dream. She was naked apart from very high black stiletto shoes with black silk chrysanthemums on them, and a huge black funeral hat, bobbing with ostrich plumes. She was wearing upswept dark glasses and dangly jet earrings, and her lips were painted glossy black.

Jack gripped the frame of the mirror in anguish. 'Jacqueline! Oh God, Jacqueline!'

Her mirror-image came up to his mirror-image and wrapped her arms around it. He could see her clearly in the mirror, but he could neither see nor feel her *here,* in the bedroom.

'Jack...' she whispered, and even though he couldn't see her eyes behind her dark glasses, her voice was quaking with panic. 'You have to get me out of here. Please.'

'I don't know *how*, sweetheart. Nobody knows how.'

'All I was doing...I was plucking my eyebrows. I leaned forward toward the mirror...the next thing I knew I lost my balance. It was like falling through ice. Jack, I *hate* it here. I'm so frightened. You have to get me out.'

Jack didn't know what to say. He could see Jacqueline kissing him and stroking his hair and pressing her breasts against his chest, but it was all an illusion.

Punipuni gave an uncomfortable cough. 'Maybe I leave now, Mr German-cellar. You know my number. You call if you want my help. A real friend waits like a rook on the gatepost.'

Jack said, 'Thanks, Pu. I'll catch you later.' He didn't turn around. He didn't want Punipuni to see the welter of tears in his eyes.

After Punipuni had left, Jack knelt in front of the mirror and Jacqueline knelt down inside it, facing him, although he could see himself kneeling behind her.

'You have to find a way to get me out,' said Jacqueline. 'It's so unfriendly here...the people won't speak to me. I ask them how to get back through the mirror but all they do is smile. And it's so *silent*. No traffic. All you can hear is the wind.'

'Listen,' Jack told her. 'I'll go back to Sonoma, where we bought the mirror. Maybe the guy in the antiques store can help us.'

Jacqueline lowered her head so that all he could see was the feathery brim of her funeral hat. 'I miss you so much, Jack. I just want to be back in bed with you.'

Jack didn't know what to say. But Jacqueline lifted her head again, and said, 'Take off your clothes.'

'What?'

'Please, take off your clothes.'

Slowly, like a man with aching knees and elbows, he unbuttoned his shirt and his jeans, and pulled them off. He took off his red-and-white striped boxer shorts, too, and stood naked in front of the mirror, his penis half-erect. The early-afternoon sun shone in his pubic hairs so that they looked like electric filaments.

'Come to the mirror,' said Jacqueline. She approached its surface from the inside, so that her hands were pressed flat against the glass. Her breasts were squashed against the glass, too, so that her nipples looked like large dried fruits.

Jack took his penis in his hand and held the swollen purple glans against the mirror. Jacqueline stuck out her tongue and licked the other side of the glass, again and again. Jack couldn't feel anything, but the sight of her tongue against his glans gave him an extraordinary sensation of frustration and arousal. He began to rub his penis up and down, gripping it tighter and tighter, while Jacqueline licked even faster.

She reached down between her thighs and parted her vulva with her fingers. With her long middle finger she began to flick her clitoris, and the reflected sunlight from the wooden floor showed Jack that she was glistening with juice.

He rubbed himself harder and harder until he knew that he couldn't stop himself from climaxing.

'Oh, God,' he said, and sperm shot in loops all over the mirror, all over Jacqueline's reflected tongue, and on her reflected nose, and even in her reflected hair. She licked at it greedily, even though she could neither touch it nor taste it. Watching her, Jack pressed his forehead against the mirror in utter despair.

He stayed there, feeling drained, while she lay back on the floor, opened her legs wide, and slowly massaged herself, playing with her clitoris and sliding her long black-polished fingernails into her slippery pink hole. After a while, she closed her legs tightly, and shivered. He wasn't sure if she was having an orgasm or not, but she lay on the floor motionless for over a minute, the plumes of her hat stirring in the breeze from the wide-open window.

Mr Santorini, in the downstairs apartment, was playing *Carry Me To Heaven With Candy-Collared Ribbons* on his wind-up gramophone. Jack could hear the scratchy tenor voice like a message from long ago and far away.

San Francisco folk wisdom says that for every ten miles you drive away from the city, it grows ten degrees Fahrenheit hotter. It was so hot by the time that Jack reached Sonoma that afternoon that the air was like liquid honey. He turned left off East Spain Street and there was Loculus Antiques, a single-story conservatory shaded by eucalyptus trees. He parked his Peacock and climbed out, but Punipuni stayed where he was, listening to Cambodian jazz on the radio. *That Old Fish Hook Fandango,* by Samlor Chapheck and the South East Asian Swingers.

Jack opened the door of Loculus Antiques and a bell jangled. Inside, the conservatory was stacked with antique sofas and dining-chairs and plaster busts of Aristotle, and it smelled of dried-out horsehair and failed attempts to make money. There was a strange light in there, too, like a mortuary, because the glass roof had been painted over green. A man appeared from the back of the store wearing what looked like white linen pyjamas. He looked about 55, with a skull-like head and fraying white hair and thick-rimmed spectacles. His top front teeth stuck out like a horse.

'May I show you something?' he drawled. His accent wasn't Northern California. More like Marblehead, Massachusetts.

'You probably don't remember me, but you sold me a mirror about six months ago. Jack Keller.'

'A mirraw, hmm? Well, I sell an awful lot of mirraws. All guaranteed safe, of course.'

'This one wasn't. I lost my partner this morning. I was just starting work when the police came around and told me she'd been mirrorized.'

The man slowly took off his spectacles and stared at Jack with bulging pale blue eyes. 'You're absolutely sure it was one of mine? I don't see how it could have been. I'm *very* careful, you know. I lost my own pet Pomeranian that way. It was only a little hand-mirraw, too. One second she was chasing her squeaky bone. The next...gone!

He put his spectacles back on. 'I had to -- ' and he made a smacking gesture with his hands, to indicate that he broken the mirror to put his dog down. 'That endless pathetic barking...I couldn't bear it.'

'The same thing's happened to my partner,' said Jack, trying to control his anger. 'And it was one of *your* mirrors, I still have the receipt. A cheval-mirror, with a mahogany frame, with grapevines carved all around it.'

The man's face drained of colour. '*That* mirraw. Oh, dear.'

'Oh, dear? Is that all you can say? I've lost the only woman I've ever loved. A beautiful, vibrant young woman with all of her life still in front of her.'

'I *am* sorry. My Pom was a pedigree, you know...but this is *much* worse, isn't it?'

Jack went right up to him. 'I want to know how to get her out. And if I can't get her out, I'm going to come back here and I'm going to tear your head off with my bare hands.'

'Well! There's no need to be so *aggressive*.'

'Believe me, pal, you don't even know the meaning of the word aggressive. But you will do, if you don't tell me how to get my partner out of that goddamned mirror.'

'Please,' said the man, lifting both hands as if he were admitting liability. 'I only sold it to you because I thought that it *had* to be a fake.'

'What are you talking about?'

'I bought it cheap from a dealer in Sacramento. He wouldn't say why he was selling it at such a knock-down price. It has a story attached to it, but if the story's true...well, even if it's only *half*-true...'

'What story?' Jack demanded.

'Believe me, I wouldn't have sold it to you if I thought there was any risk attached, especially after that last outbreak of silver plunge. I'm always so careful with mirraws.'

He went over to his desk, which was cluttered with papers and books and a framed photograph of Madame Chiang Kai-Shek, with the handwritten message, *To Timmy, What A Night*!

He pulled open his desk-drawers, one after the other. 'I put it down to vanity, you know. If people stare into the mirraw long enough, it's bound to set off *some* reaction. I mean, it happens with *people*, doesn't it? If you stare at somebody long enough, they're bound to say 'who do you think *you're* looking at?', aren't they?'

He couldn't find what he was looking for in his drawers, so he pulled down a steady shower of pamphlets and invoices and pieces of paper from the shelves behind his desk. At last he said, 'Here we are! We're in luck!'

He unfolded a worn-out sheet of typing paper and smoothed it with the edge of his hand. 'The Camelot Looking-Glass. Made circa 1842, as a gift from an admiring nation to Alfred Lord Tennyson on publication of the revised version of his great poem *The Lady of Shalott.*"

'What does that mean?' said Jack, impatiently. 'I don't understand.'

'The mirraw was specially commissioned by The Arthurian Society in England as a token of esteem for *The Lady of Shalott*. You do *know* about *The Lady of Shalott*?'

Jack shook his head. 'What does this have to do with my getting Jacqueline back?'

'It could have *everything* to do with it. Or, on the other hand, nothing at all, if the mirraw's a fake.'

'Go on.'

The man pulled up a bentwood chair and sat down. 'Some literary experts think that *The Lady of Shalott* was a poetic description of silver plunge.'

'I think I'm losing my patience here,' said Jack.

'No! No! Listen! *The Lady of Shalott* is about a beautiful woman who is condemned to spend all of her days in a tower, weaving tapestries of whatever she sees through her window. She weaves tapestries of all the passing seasons. She weaves courtships, weddings, funerals. The catch is, though, that she is under a spell. She is only allowed to look at the world by means of her mirraw. Otherwise, she will die.

'Let's see if I can remember some of it.

'There she weaves by night and day
A magic web with colours gay.
She has heard a whisper say,
A curse is on her if she stay
To look down to Camelot...

'And moving thro' a mirraw clear
That hangs before her all the year,
Shadows of the world appear.
There she sees the highway near
Winding down to Camelot...'

'Yes, great, very poetic,' Jack interrupted. 'But I still don't see how this can help Jacqueline.'

'Please -- just let me finish. One day, Sir Lancelot comes riding past the tower. He looks magnificent. He has a shining saddle and jingling bridle-bells and his helmet-feather burns like a flame. The Lady of Shalott sees him in her mirraw, and she can't resist turning around to look at him directly.

'She left the web, she left the loom
She made three paces thro' the room
She saw the water-lily bloom,
She saw the helmet and the plume
She look'd down to Camelot.
Out flew the web and floated wide;
The mirraw crack'd from side to side;
'The curse is come upon me,' cried

The Lady of Shalott.'

'She knows that she is doomed. She leaves the tower. She finds a boat in the river and paints her name on it, *The Lady of Shalott*. Then she lies down in it and floats to Camelot, singing her last sad song. The reapers in the fields beside the river can hear this lament, as her blood slowly freezes and her eyes grow dark. By the time her boat reaches the jetty at Camelot, she's dead.

'Sir Lancelot comes down to the wharf with the rest of the crowds. He sees her lying in the boat and thinks how beautiful she is, and he asks God to give her grace. That's what Tennyson wrote in the poem, anyhow. But listen to what it says on this piece of paper.

' 'Several other stories suggest that Sir Lancelot visited the Lady of Shalott in her tower many times and become so entranced by her beauty that he became her lover, even though she could not look at him directly when they made love because of the curse that was on her. One day however he gave her ecstasy so intense that she turned to look at him. She vanished into her mirraw and was never seen again.

' 'The mirraw presented to Alfred, Lord Tennyson, is reputed to be the original mirraw in which The Lady of Shalott disappeared, with a new decorative frame paid for by public subscription. When Lord Tennyson died in 1892, the mirraw was taken from his house at Aldworth, near Haslemere, in southern England, and sold to a New York company of auctioneers.'

Jack snatched the paper out of his hand and read it for himself. 'You knew that this mirror had swallowed this Shalott woman and yet you sold it to us without any warning?'

'Because the Lady of Shalott is only a poem, and Sir Lancelot is only a myth, and Camelot never existed! I never thought that it could happen for real! Even Lord Tennyson thought that the mirraw was a phony, and that some poor idiot from The Arthurian Society had been bamboozled into paying a fortune for an ordinary looking-glass!'

'For Christ's sake!' Jack shouted at him. 'Even ordinary mirrors can be dangerous, you know that! Look what happened to your dog!'

The man ran his hand through his straggling white hair. 'The dealer in Sacramento said that it had never given anybody any trouble, not in thirty years. I inspected for silver plunge, but of course it's not always easy to tell if a mirraw's been infected or not.'

Jack took two or three deep breaths to calm himself down. At that moment, Punipuni appeared in the doorway of the antiques store, and the bell jangled.

'Everything is okay, Mr German-cellar?'

'No, Pu, it isn't.'

The man jerked his head toward Punipuni and said, 'Who's this?'

'A friend. His name is Punipuni Puusuke.'

The man held out his hand. 'Pleased to know you. My name's Davis Culbut.'

'Pleased to know you, too, Mr French-somersault.'

'I beg your pardon?'

'That is what your name derives from, sir. The French word for head-over-heels. Topsy-turvy maybe.'

'I see,' said Davis Culbut, plainly mystified. He turned back to Jack and held up the typewritten sheet of paper. 'It says here that Sir Lancelot grieved for the Lady of Shalott so much that he consulted Merlin the Magician, to see how he might get her back. But Merlin told him that the curse is irreversible. The only way for him to be reunited with her would be for him to be to pass through the mirraw, too.'

'You mean -- ?'

'Yes, I'm afraid I do. You *can* have your lady-friend back, but only if you join her. Even so...this is only a legend, like Camelot, and I can't give you any guarantees.'

'Mr German-cellar!' said Punipuni, emphatically. 'You cannot go to live in the world of reflection!'

Jack said nothing. After a lengthy silence, Davis Culbut folded the sheet of paper and handed it to him. 'I can only tell you that I'm very sorry for your loss, Mr Keller. I'm afraid there's nothing else that I can do.'

They sat by the window in Steiner's Bar on 1st Street West and ordered two cold William Randoph Hearsts. Their waitress was a llama, with her hair braided and tied with red-and-white ribbons, and a brass bell around her neck.

'You want to see a menu?' she asked them, in a high, rasping voice that came right from the back of the throat. 'The special today is saddle of saddle, with maraschinos.'

Jack shook his head. 'No, thank you. Just the beers.'

The waitress stared at him with her slitted golden eyes. 'You look kind of down, my friend, if you don't mind my saying so.'

'Mirror trouble,' said Punpuni.

'Oh, I'm sorry. My nephew had mirror trouble, too. He lost his two daughters.'

Jack looked up at her. 'Did he ever try to get them back?'

The waitress shook her head so that her bell jangled. 'What can you do? Once they're gone, they're gone.'

'Did he ever think of going after them?'

'I don't follow you.'

'Did he ever think of going into the mirror himself, to see if he could rescue them?'

The waitress shook her head again. 'He has five other children, and a wife to take care of.'

'So what did he do?'

'He broke the mirror, in the end. He couldn't bear to hear his little girls crying.'

When she had gone, Jack and Punipuni sat and drank their beers in silence. At last, though, Punipuni wiped his mouth with the back of his hand and said, 'You're thinking of trying it, aren't you?'

'What else can I do, Pu? I love her. I can't just leave her there.'

'Even supposing you manage to get into the mirror, what's going to happen if you can't get back out?'

'Then I'll just have to make my life *there*, instead of here.'

Punipuni took hold of Jack's hands and gripped them tight. 'If your loved one falls from a high tower, even the flamingos cannot save her, and they can fly.'

That night, Jack sat on the end of the bed staring at himself in the cheval-mirror, like a fortune-teller confronted by his own mischance. Outside, the city glittered on the ocean's edge, like Camelot.

'*Jacqueline*?' he said, as quietly as he could, as if he didn't really want to disturb her.

He thought of the day when he first met her. She was riding side-saddle on a white cow through a field of sunflowers, under a sky the colour of polished brass. She was wearing a broken wedding-cake on her head, and a white damask tablecloth, wound around and around her and trailing to the ground.

He stopped and shaded his eyes. He had been visiting his friend Osmond at the Mumm's Winery in Napa, and he had drunk two very cold bottles of Cuvée Napa *méthode champenoise*. He had taken the wrong turning while looking for the parking-lot, and he had lost his way.

'Excuse me!' he shouted, even though she was less than ten feet away from him. 'Can you direct me to Yountville?'

The cow replied first. 'I'm sorry,' she sighed, with a distinctive French accent. 'I've never been there.' She slowly rolled her shining black eyes from side to side, taking in the sunflower field. 'To tell you the truth, I've never been *anywhere*.'

But Jacqueline laughed and said, '*I* can show you, don't worry!' She slithered down from the cow and walked up to him, so that she was disturbingly close. The tablecloth had slipped and he could see that, underneath it, her breasts were bare.

'You're not really interested in going to Yountville, are you?' she asked him. She was wearing a very strong perfume, like a mixture of lilies and vertigo. 'Not anymore.'

'Have I drunk too much wine or is that a wedding-cake on your head?'

'Yes...I was supposed to get married today, but I decided against it.'

Jack swayed, and blinked, and looked around the sunflower field. Sunflowers, as far as the eye could see, nodding like busybodies.

'Hold this,' Jacqueline had told him.

Jacqueline had given him one end of the tablecloth, and then she had proceeded to turn around and around, both arms uplifted, unwinding herself. Soon she had been completely naked, except for the wedding-cake on her head and tiny white stiletto-heeled boots, with white laces. Jack was sure that he must be hallucinating. Too much heat, too much *méthode champenoise*.

Jacqueline had an extraordinary figure, almost distorted, like a fantasy. Wide shoulders, enormous breasts, the narrowest of waists, and narrow hips, too. Her skin had been tanned the colour of melted caramel and it was shiny with lotion. The warm breeze that made the sunflowers nod had made her nipples knurl and stiffen, too.

'I was supposed to consummate my marriage today,' she told him. 'But since I don't have a groom any longer...'

'Who were you supposed to be marrying?'

'A Frenchman. But I decided against it.'

Jack licked his lips. They were rough from sunburn and too much alcohol. Jacqueline rested one hand lightly on his shoulder and said, 'You don't mind doing the honours, though?'

'The honours?'

She turned around and bent over, reaching behind her with both hands and pulling apart the cheeks of her bottom. He found himself staring at her tightly-wrinkled anus and her bare, pouting vulva. Her labia were open so that he could see right inside her, pink and glistening and glutinous.

'Well?' she asked him, after a moment. 'What are you waiting for?'

'I, ah -- '

The cow stopped munching sunflowers for a moment. '*Si vous ne trouvez pas agréables, monsieur, vous trouverez de moins des choses nouvelles,*' she quoted, with yellow petals falling from her mottled lips. 'If you do not find anything you like, sir, at least you will find something new.'

Jack stripped off his shirt and unbuckled his belt, undressing as rapidly as he used to, when he was a boy, on the banks of his grandpa's swimming-hole. His penis was already hard, and when he tugged off his white boxer shorts it bobbed up eagerly.

He approached Jacqueline from behind, his penis in his hand, and moistened his glans against her shining labia.

'With this cock, you consummate our union,' Jacqueline recited.

He pushed himself into her, as slowly as he could. She was very wet inside, and hot, as if she were running a temperature. His penis disappeared into her vagina as far as it would go, and for a long, long moment he stood in the sunflower field, buried inside her, his eyes closed, feeling the sun and the wind on his naked body. He felt as if a moment as perfect as this was beyond sin, beyond morality, beyond all explanation.

With his eyes still closed, he heard a light buzzing noise. He felt something settle on his shoulder, and when he opened his eyes he saw that it was a small honey-bee. He tried to flick it off, but it stayed where it was, crawling toward his neck. He twitched his shoulder, and then he blew on it, but the honey-bee kept its footing.

He heard another buzzing noise, and then another. Two more honey-bees spiralled out of the breeze and settled on his back. Jacqueline groped between her legs until she found his scrotum, and she dug her fingernails into his tightly-wrinkled skin and pulled at it. 'Harder!' she demanded. 'Harder! I want this union to be thoroughly consummated! Harder!'

Jack withdrew his penis a little way and then pushed it into her deeper. She let out a high ululation of pleasure: *tirra-lirra-lirra*! He pushed his penis in again, and again, but each time he did so more and more honey-bees settled on his shoulders. They seemed to come from all directions, pattering out of the wind like hailstones. Soon his whole back was covered in a black glittering cape of honey-bees. They crawled into his hair, too, and onto his face. They even tried to crawl into his nostrils, and into his mouth.

'Harder, sir knight!' Jacqueline screamed at him. He gripped her hips in both hands and began to ram his penis into her so hard that he tugged her two or three inches into the air with every thrust. But now the honey-bees were gathering between his legs, covering his balls and crawling up the crack of his buttocks. One of them stung him, and then another. He felt a burning sensation in his scrotum, and all around the base of his penis. His balls began to swell up until he was sure that they were twice their normal size.

A honey-bee crept into his anus, and stung him two or three inches inside his rectum. This explorer was followed by another, and another, and then by dozens more, until he felt as if a blazing thorn-bush had been forced deep into his bottom. Yet Jacqueline kept screaming at him, her breasts jiggling like two huge Jell-Os with every thrust, and in spite of the pain he felt a rising ecstasy that made him feel that his penis was a volcano, and that his sperm was molten lava, and that he was right on the brink of eruption.

Jacqueline began to quake. 'Oh con-*sume*-AAAAAAAation!' she cried out, as if she were singing the last verse in a tragic opera. She dropped onto her knees on the dry-baked earth, between the sunflower stalks, and as she did so, Jack, in his suit of living bees, spurted semen onto her lower back, and her anus, and her gaping cunt.

He pitched sideways onto the earth beside her, stunned by his ejaculation, and as he did so, the bees rose up from him, almost as one, and buzzed away. Only a few remained, dazedly crawling out of his asshole, as if they were potholers who had survived a whole week underground. They preened their wings for a while, and then they flew away, too.

'You've been stung,' said Jacqueline, touching Jack's swollen lips. His body was covered all over with red lumps and his eyes were so puffy he was almost blind. His penis was gigantic, even now that his erection had died away.

Jack stroked the line of her finely-plucked cheekbones. He had never seen a girl with eyes this colour. They were so green that they shone like traffic-signals on a wet August night in Savannah.

'Who are you?' he asked her.

'Jacqueline Fronsart. I live in Yountville. I can show you the way.'

They lay amongst the sunflowers for almost a half-hour, naked. Jacqueline stretched out the skin of Jack's scrotum so that it glowed scarlet against the sunlight, like a medieval parchment, and then she licked it with her tongue to cool the swelling. In return he sucked her nipples against the roof of his mouth until she moaned at him in Mandarin to stop.

Eventually the cow coughed and said, 'They'll be wondering where I am. And anyway, my udder's beginning to feel full.'

'You shouldn't eat sunflowers,' Jacqueline admonished her.

'You shouldn't eat forbidden fruit,' the cow retorted.

But now Jacqueline was gone and the mirror showed nothing but his own reversed image, and the bed, and the dying sunlight inching down the bedroom wall. Dim jerky far away he heard a boat hooting in the Bay and it reminded him of the old dentist from Graham Greene's *The Power and the Glory*. Still there waiting last boat whistling in the last harbour.

'What's going to happen if you can't get back out?' Punipuni had asked him.

He didn't know. He couldn't see much of the world in the mirror. Only the bedroom, and part of the hallway, and it all looked the same as this world, except that it was horizontally transversed. Medieval painters invented a device with three mirrors which enabled you to see your face the way it really was. Frightening, in a way. Your own face, staring at you, as if your head had been cut off.

He stood up and pulled his dark blue cotton sweater over his head. He had never felt so alone. He unfastened his belt and stepped out of his stone-coloured chinos. He folded his chinos and laid them on the bed. At last he took off his shorts and stood naked in front of the mirror.

'Jacqueline?' he called. Even if he couldn't penetrate the mirror, he needed to see her, to know that she was still there. *Who hath seen her wave her hand? Or at the casement seen her stand? The Lady of Shalott.*

'Jacqueline?' he repeated. 'Jacqueline, I'll come join you. I don't care what it's like in the mirror-world. I just can't stand to live without you.'

The phone rang, beside the bed. He ignored it, to begin with, but it rang on and on and in the end he had to pick it up.

'Mr German-cellar? It is I Punipuni Puusuke.'

'What do you want, Pu?'

'I have decided that it is in the interests of both of us for me to open the restaurant this evening. I will be serving boiled pens in their own ink.'

Jack didn't take his eyes off the mirror. He was sure that he had seen the mirror-curtains stir, even though the windows were closed.

'Pu...if that's what you want to do.'

'We cannot afford to be closed, Mr German-cellar. The fierceness of the competition does not allow us.' He paused for a moment, and then he said, 'What are you contemplating, Mr German-cellar?'

'Nothing. Nothing at all.'

'You are not reconsidering a plunge into the mirror, sir? You know that it is better to rub margarine on your head than to run after a wig in a hurricane.'

'Pu -- '

'Mr German-cellar, I do not wish for throat-constricting goodbyes. I wish for you to remain on this side of the reflective divide.'

'Pu, I'll be fine. Just open the restaurant.'

'You must promise me, Mr German-cellar, that you will not do anything maniacal.'

Jack put the phone down. He couldn't make any promises to anyone. You can only make a promise if you understand how the world works, and after Jacqueleine's disappearance he had discovered that life is not arranged in any kind of pattern, but incomprehensible. Nothing follows. Nothing fits together.

He returned to the mirror and stood facing it. As he did so, the door in the reflection slowly swung open and Jacqueline slowly walked in. Her face was very pale, and her hair was elaborately curled and braided. She was wearing a royal-blue military jacket, with gold epaulets and frogging, and black riding-boots which came right up over her knees, but nothing else. Her heels rapped on the bedroom floor as she approached him.

Jack pressed the palms of his hands against the mirror. 'Jacqueline...what's going on? Why are you dressed like that?'

She pressed her palms against his, although all he could feel was cold glass. Her eyes looked unfocused, as if she were very tired, or drugged.

'It's a parade,' she told him, as if that explained everything.

'Parade? What parade? You're practically naked.'

She gave him a blurred and regretful smile. 'It's all different here, Jack.'

He felt a tear creeping down his left cheek. 'I've decided to join you. I've thought about it...and there isn't any other way.'

'You can't. Not unless the mirror wants you.'

'Then tell me how.'

'You *can't*, Jack. It doesn't work that way. It's all to do with vanity.'

'I don't understand. I just want us to be together, it doesn't matter where.'

Jacqueline said, 'I walked down to the Embarcadero yesterday afternoon. The band was playing. The bears were dancing. And there it was, waiting for me. A rowboat, with my name on it.'

'What?'

She looked at him dreamily. 'Jack...there's always a boat waiting for all of us. Still there last boat whistling in the last harbour. One day we all have to close the book and close the door behind us and walk down the hill.'

'*Tell me how I can get into the mirror*!'

'You can't, Jack.'

Jack took a step back. He was breathing so heavily that his heart was thumping and his head was swimming. Jacqueline was less than three feet away from him, with those salmon eyes and those enormous breasts and that vulva like a brimming peach. All of the days and nights they had spent together flickered through his head like pictures in a zoetrope.

Jacqueline said, 'Jack – you *have* to understand. It's not that everything changes. Don't you get it? *Everything was back-to-front to begin with.*'

He took another step back, and then another, and then another. When he reached the bed, he stepped to one side. Jacqueline stood with her hands pressed flat against the mirror, like a child staring into a toy-store window.

'Jack, whatever you're thinking, don't.'

He didn't hesitate. He ran toward the mirror, and on his last step he stretched out both of his hands ahead of him like a diver and plunged straight into the glass. It burst apart, with a crack like lightning, and he hurtled through the mahogany frame and onto the floor, with Jacqueline lying underneath him.

But this wasn't the soft, warm Jacqueline who had wriggled next to him in bed. This was a brilliant, sharp, shining Jacqueline – a woman made out of thousands of shards of dazzling glass. Her face was made of broken facets in which he could see his own face reflected again and again. Her breasts were nothing more than crushed and crackling heaps of splinters, and her legs were like scimitars.

But Jack was overwhelmed with grief and lust and he wanted her still, however broken she was. He pushed his stiffened penis into her shattered vagina, and he thrust, and thrust, and grunted, and thrust, even though the glass cut slices from his glans, and stripped his skin to bloody ribbons. With each thrust the glass sliced deeper and deeper, into the spongy blood-filled tissue of his penile shaft, into his veins, into his nerve-endings. Yet he could no longer distinguish between agony and pleasure, between need and self-mutilation.

He held Jacqueline as tightly as he could, and kissed her. The tip of his tongue was sliced off, and his face was criss-crossed with gaping cuts.

'We're together,' he panted, with blood bubbling out of his mouth. 'We're together!'

He squeezed her breasts with both hands and three of his fingers were cut down to the bone. His left index finger flapped loosely on a thread of skin, and nothing else. But he kept on pushing his hips against her, even though his penis was in tatters, and his scrotum was sliced open so that his bloodied testicles hung out on tubes.

'We're together...we're together. I don't mind where I live, so long as I have you.'

At last he had lost so much blood that he had to stop pushing, and lie on top of her, panting. He was beginning to feel cold, but he didn't mind, because he had Jacqueline. He tried to shift himself a little, to make himself more comfortable, but Jacqueline crackled underneath him, as if she were made of nothing but broken glass.

The afternoon seemed to pass like a dream, or a poem. The sun reached the floor and sparkled on the fragments of bloodied mirror. Jack could see his own reflection in a piece of Jacqueline's cheek, and he thought to himself, now I know what she means about the last boat whistling in the last harbour.

Eventually it began to grow dark, and the bedroom filled with shadows.

'For often thro' the silent nights
A funeral, with plumes and lights
And music, went to Camelot.

Or when the moon was overhead
Came two young lovers lately wed;
'I am half-sick of shadows,' said
The Lady of Shalott.'

Punipuni knocked on Jack's door at midnight. He made three paces through the room; then stopped.

'Oh, Mr German-cellar,' he said. He pressed his hand over his mouth to stop himself from sobbing out loud, although nobody would have heard him. 'Oh, Mr German-cellar.'

He wrapped Jack's body in the multi-coloured durry from the bed, and carried him down to the street. He stowed him into the trunk of his ageing brown Kamikaze, and drove him to the Embarcadero. The night was very clear, and the stars were so bright that it was difficult to tell which was city and which was sky.

He found a leaky abandoned rowboat beside one of the piers. He lifted Jack into it, and laid him on his back, so that his bloodied face was looking up at Cassiopeia. Then he untied the rope, and gave the rowboat a push, so that it slowly circled away. The reflected lights of Camelot glittered all around it, red and yellow and green.

Punipuni stood and watched it with his hands in his pockets. 'Men should never go looking for darkness, Mr German-cellar. You can only find darkness in a closed cupboard.'

During the night, as the tide ebbed, the rowboat drifted out toward the ocean, under the Golden Gate bridge.

As the tide began to turn, another rowboat appeared from the opposite direction, and in this rowboat lay a naked woman in sunglasses, lying on a bed of dried brown chrysanthemums. The two rowboats knocked against each other with a hollow sound, like coffins; and then they drifted away, their prows locked together as if there were only one rowboat, reflected in a mirror.